# A CALL
# FROM L.A.

Novels by Arthur Hansl

*Freeze-Frame*

*Sunstroke*

# A CALL FROM

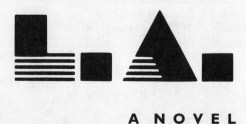

## A NOVEL

# Arthur Hansl

ST. MARTIN'S PRESS
*New York*

*Editor: Jared Kieling*
*Copyedited by Daniel Otis*
*Design by Claire Counihan*

Library of Congress Cataloging-in-Publication Data

Hansl, Arthur.
    A call from L.A.

    I. Title.
PS3558.A51363C35   1987     813'.54      87-28363
ISBN 0-312-01375-2

First Edition
10  9  8  7  6  5  4  3  2  1

This one is for
Captain John Duberg,
who made everything possible.

# ACKNOWLEDGMENTS

My gratitude to Jon Green, director of the Los Angeles Police Department TV Studios, for lending his time and expertise to this project. And thanks again to my friend and sometime collaborator, Ross White, for his patience and his help in filling the holes.

# A CALL
# FROM L.A.

# PROLOGUE

fine rain drifted down on West Los Angeles, not much more than a drizzle but enough to slick the roads after the long dry spell. Gil Buckler was driving State Assemblyman Willis Clewes back from his speech in Marina Del Rey to his home in Beverly Hills, using surface streets instead of freeways because he knew them so well it saved time. Sepulveda Boulevard south of Pico was a deserted stretch this late at night, a commercial district of lumberyards and warehouses long since closed and darkened. The street lights were set high and far apart, pale aureoles in the heavy mist. Bored, Gil listened to the tires of the four-year-old Plymouth sing against the wet asphalt.

Clewes had spoken eloquently enough about the ongoing pollution of Santa Monica Bay, scoring the perfidy of politicians and industrialists alike, but now he seemed tense and preoccupied. Gil found his mood understandable, given the fact he was well behind in the polls with only three weeks to go until election day. This, despite a glib, professionally run campaign and the unlimited wealth his wife had put at his disposal, along with her fame. Monica Loring, the undisputed queen of mellow rock for a decade and a controversial political firebrand for longer than that, had backed her husband with all her resources through two victorious and very costly assembly races, and now it seemed they would founder together after a contest as bitter and dirty as the state had ever seen. Gil didn't think Willis Clewes had a chance to be the next United States senator from California, but he didn't say as much because he was being paid to be a bodyguard, not a political analyst.

"Stop at the filling station up ahead," Clewes said to him. "We'll gas up."

"We don't need gas."

1

"Well, stop anyway. And drive up close to the office, I want to use the john."

The Arco station jumped out of the night at them, a patch of brightness in the gloom. Gil pulled into it and drove up between the self-service pumps and the office. Clewes opened the door and climbed out, hurrying away through the rain. Gil got out too, stood under the roofing that sheltered the pumps, and reached for a cigarette; Clewes didn't like anyone smoking in the car. He watched a Ford two-door that had been behind them pass the station and then suddenly turn in at the far end of the service area as though the driver had changed his mind. Headlights swept toward him as the car approached at an oblique angle and stopped short of the pumps, facing him. Gil squinted because the bastard had his brights on, then flung away his cigarette and reached under his jacket, understanding.

Rogelio Méndez, the sole attendant on duty, had a pretty clear view of what happened. He saw the Plymouth pull up and a man emerge on the passenger side. A taller man in a light suit got out of the driver's seat and went to stand near the pumps, pulling out a cigarette. Rogelio was trying to decide whether to go out in the rain and tell him not to smoke there when another car drove in from the opposite side and stopped a dozen feet from the tall man.

The first man out of the Plymouth opened the office door, but this did not distract Rogelio because now he saw a man in a black ski mask carrying some kind of weapon jump out of the second car. He couldn't move a muscle as he heard the rapping of a fully automatic weapon and saw the tall man flung away like a bag of laundry.

The man who had entered the office lunged forward and tackled him, pulled his legs out from under him anyway, and then flopped down next to him on the damp cement floor. After that he remembered the shards and splinters falling all around them as the plate glass window was shot away, and the hammering impact of bullets on the opposite wall. Then sirens coming.

2

Rogelio and the man who had saved him stayed down on the floor for what seemed a hell of a long time to make sure that crazy *hijo de la puta* had gone away. *Ay, mierda,* he'd never been through anything like that in El Salvador! No matter what he'd told the sanctuary people.

# ONE

didn't learn Gil was dead until after the funeral. Thinking back, that day didn't even begin well.

Without opening my eyes I reached over toward the far side of the bed to find it cool and uninviting. Chispa had not slept here then, a development which surprised me only until I started getting signals from the night before through the obstructive funk of my hangover.

I'd taken her to El Farolito, a rather grungy restaurant frequented by impecunious tourists and local characters ranging from artists to hookers and drug dealers. In fact, I've seen coke deals go down in there without even paying much attention. The mules are usually sailors off American cruise ships who dump the stuff into Los Angeles Harbor on the way in to be picked up by speedboats. It's not my country but I have to live here, so I don't interfere. Besides, I'm not a cop anymore.

It wasn't really Chispa's kind of place and I should have known better, but I can be perverse, as she likes to tell me. Why else would I provoke the only human being whose goodwill I currently seek to make a prim understatement? I had it once for a brief, magical time and then lost ground because of a simultaneous affair I was having with the bottle, at least according to her. Having been married to a drunk has left her with an understandable prejudice against alcohol, but I never stagger and seldom become surly, so I resent being compared to her ex. In El Farolito, I saw the anger building behind the obsidian eyes above her strong, high cheekbones, a harbinger of the storm to come, and I ignored it. Chispa means spark in Spanish, after all, and I was courting the explosion. Maybe I was making a point, if I can remember what it was.

Chispa Estrada is a stately, bilingual Aztec who makes a good living selling the time-share condominiums that are sprouting up along the coast. She has the kind of classic Mexican beauty even a young Katy Jurado might have envied. Her generous curves may someday translate into considerable heft, but standing five-ten will help her carry it well. I've tried to convince her she is a comfortable fit against my expanding six-two, but it's a question of coming to terms. I enjoy drinking and I enjoy El Farolito. I won't be tethered.

She was dressed in a peasant blouse with generous décolletage and a pleated skirt with a wide belt. Her gleaming black hair was pulled straight back and fastened behind her neck, accenting the slightly dangerous tilt of her eyes. She waved her hand to dispel the smoke that is a lingering part of El Farolito's atmosphere. "This is very nice, Jonny," she said. "I like to go to funky dives and have smoke blown in my face." She pointed at the appetizers on our table. "What are these little things floating around in the grease?"

I stubbed out my cigarette. She knew I hung out in El Farolito sometimes, but I'd never before been foolhardy enough to take her there. I thought of it as kind of a test. "Mushrooms," I replied. "Good for the libido."

"I don't need anything for my libido." Which was true.

I snapped my fingers for the waiter, a slovenly ex-convict known as El Alacrán, the Scorpion. "The señorita does not like the appetizers," I told him in my rough-and-ready Spanish.

He shrugged and stared down the front of her dress so intently his eyes crossed. "Perhaps something else."

"Bring the menu. And more drinks."

"I don't want any more. The glass isn't even clean." She was drinking beer, obviously the only thing she trusted, because she's not a beer drinker.

"Just bring her the bottle," I told El Alacrán, and he shuffled away.

She leaned back in her rickety chair and looked at me levelly. "You're doing this on purpose," she said. "I don't know why, but you're trying to enrage me. And you're succeeding."

"Doing what on purpose?" I asked, all innocence. "I'm only

trying to share a little corner of my life with you. The part of me that gets tired of Gringo Gulch and goes downtown once in a while." Gringo Gulch is the expatriate American colony, where the money is and where we socialize because Chispa's business contacts are there too.

El Alacrán came back with a couple of grimy menus and the drinks. He banged down Chispa's beer bottle and some of the liquid spilled out to pool on the table. "I go to Gringo Gulch with you," I pointed out. "And I go to the Solemar and hang around watching you charm tourists." The Solemar was the condo she sold units in and I knew our frequent dinners there were mandatory, but the leaden bores that dropped by our table and forgot to go away purely put me off my food.

"That's business, Jonny, and you don't support me, you know."

That stung me into a spontaneous remark. "I've been considering it," I said, surprising myself.

Her reaction to what amounted to a proposal was indifferent. "I'm not sure you can afford it." She looked around her with distaste. "Not if this is an example."

I thought that one over and decided to take offense. "Well, we'll only come here when you think you can climb down off the scaffolding and mingle."

At that point one of the regulars, a sultry little semipro named Alma, walked past our table and brushed against me in an elaborately casual way. She turned to give me a steamy look and a dirty grin. "*Hola*, Jonny, *mi guapo*," she purred.

I'd never said ten words to Alma, so I figured someone had put her up to it, but I didn't get to run that theory past Chispa. She was on her feet in a single, graceful lunge, scooping up her handbag on the rise. " 'Water seeks its own level,' " she quoted. "That's an Americanism. You're at low tide." She stalked out with chin high, back straight, and just a little sway below the waist, making me wonder if she'd developed that marvelous carriage balancing stuff on her head when she was a kid.

Now, lying alone in my bed, I missed her savagely. I like to make love in the morning, unbenumbed by alcohol, rested and revitalized. Sometimes I'll catch her in the shower, lather us up with that wonderful-smelling local soap made of coconut oil, and then we never make it back to bed. Kinky, she says, and the soap stings, but I've noticed no lack of enthusiasm. In a cold, bleak part of my mind, I wondered if it would ever happen again.

That thought coupled with the hangover made me want to go back to sleep. Down below, I could hear the surf sweep in and then recede with the sound of a thousand billiard balls clicking together as it raked the gravelly beach, soothing as rain on the roof. But then I heard a banging sound outside my door that announced the presence of another transient member of the household, Ernestina, the world's laziest maid. She lives with her parents in a *palapa* somewhere in the jungle and comes in to clean up when the spirit moves her. I call her "No Hay" (the "H" is silent), which means "There isn't any," her usual reply to any request I might make, but when supplies can be found she cooks a little, mostly goat and iguana, surprisingly good fare once you acquire the taste, as I have after nearly five years in Mexico.

With sleep banished, I got up and pulled on a pair of shorts, stuck my head into the living room, and yelled for a glass of orange juice.

*"Es que no hay, señor!"* came the cheerful response. It was a game we played.

That's the kind of trivia I remember about the day I learned Gil was dead and buried.

I live just south of Puerto Vallarta, Mexico, where I couldn't get a phone if I wanted one. The only available lines service the big condos springing up along the coast on either side of me. My place, on a spit of land jutting into the sea called Punta Negra, is still pretty isolated, but that can't last. In the nearly five years I've been here, developments have erupted along the face of the green mountains like a stucco plague. The once-sleepy seaside village is burgeoning haphazardly, spawning discos, restaurants, and condos overnight, and the tentacles are reaching for me.

I rent a four-room, red-brick cottage with a tile roof on the ocean side of the highway to Manzanillo for forty thousand pesos a month. Yesterday that was a little over a hundred bucks but I may be doing better today, given inflation. There's a path meandering down the face of the cliff to a patch of beach surrounded by great chunks of granite that trap clear tide pools along with their assorted marine inhabitants. Water is pumped from a nearby river into the tanks on the roof of the house, and I tap electricity from the poles running along the highway. Some days I go to town and some days I don't. I read voraciously to compensate for an aborted education, and I paint. For money, I'm happy to say.

So I didn't hear about my friend Gil Buckler until I went to the gallery that sells my stuff and, incidentally, accepts any phone messages or mail intended for me, rare phenomena indeed. Galeria Uno is owned and operated by an American named Jan, an elfin lady in her late forties with wide-set eyes and blond bangs, long on wit and sometimes short of temper. She features new, trendy Mexican artists, usually catching them on the way up, and sells mostly to tourists who know what they want, so I'm a maverick in good company. Nearly four years ago Galeria Uno became the answer to my problem, which was money. I've been a doodler and a dabbler for as long as I can remember, but I never thought I'd make a living at it. Now, depending on the size of the canvas, I get between five hundred and a thousand. Dollars. I don't pay attention to the throes of the peso or to taxes either. I'm self-taught, and I've heard my style called "primitive" and "naif," words that still bring to my mind the image of a simple-minded native slapping paint onto tree bark, but I'm unoffended at these prices. After all, Grandma Moses made a fair country living cranking out a not altogether dissimilar product.

When I came in late that afternoon, Jan handed me a piece of paper with a name and a phone number on it. "It sounded urgent," she said, and shrugged. "But hell, you didn't come in for three days and I can't be running around checking all the bars, friend."

The name on the paper was Terri and the Los Angeles number looked familiar. Terri Buckler, of course. I asked to use the phone and bullied my call past the local operator in under ten minutes. It was six-thirty in Puerto Vallarta, two hours earlier in L.A.

Terri answered the phone, but the connection was terrible. When I told her who I was, it got worse. "—been killed," was all I got.

"What? Say again!"

"—been murdered. Shot to pieces with a machine gun." I couldn't hear the name, but I knew it had to be Gil. She wouldn't call me about anyone else because we had no one else in common. I took a deep breath before I asked her.

"Yes, Gil." I could hear better now. Her voice was listless. "I've been trying to get you for days. The funeral was yesterday."

"How did it happen?"

"They were after that goddamn politician he was babysitting and they got Gil instead." She sounded indescribably bitter. "You missed a great funeral. Lots of cops and that fucking politico with his rich-bitch wife. You can bet he got plenty of mileage out of it."

The rich-bitch wife was Monica Loring and maybe some of Terri's bitterness was directed at me because we'd been kids together—Monica, Clewes, Gil, and I. Monica and I were Hollywood brats, the progeny of movie stars, Willis Clewes was the class wimp (we called him a "weege" in those days), and Gil was the resident prankster. We were split up after two years at Beverly Hills High when Monica and I were exiled to private schools back East. I lost track of Clewes, but Gil and I palled around whenever I was in California. And everyone knows what became of Monica.

About a year ago Gil wrote me he'd landed State Assemblyman Willis "Bill" Clewes as a client and wasn't that a bitch, considering how we used to ride his ass? He had run into Monica at some function, batted his long lashes at her, and given her his card, reminding her of old times. Later, when she and Clewes started getting some threats and felt they needed more than routine police protection, she called his agency and asked for him. Gil was delighted to handle such a prestigious assignment personally. Nor was the irony lost on him. At the end of his letter he asked me again if I wouldn't for Christ's sake put my act together, get out of that banana republic, and join the agency. Look at the laughs we'd have. Willie the Weege, can you believe it?

"I called because Gil would have wanted you to know," I heard Terri say.

"I'm sorry—" But she had hung up. Sorry. How inadequate.

Galeria Uno was settling into the social hour. Among expatriates and a few natives, the place is a little like a club. People help themselves to wine at a bar made of green tile and lounge around a furnished central patio. Browsers and prospective customers are intrigued by the easy acceptance they find and amazed that no one really tries very hard to sell them anything. But rooms filled with the wild, colorful folklorics of such Mexican masters as Tamayo, Zuñiga, and José Luis Cuevas beg attention. There's no lack of business.

Ordinarily, I hang around for the wine and the chat, but now I left without a word to anyone. My battered Chrysler ragtop was parked on Calle Madero, almost in front of Galeria Uno. It's an early seventies model, built when they used more steel than plastic and equipped with a big gas guzzler that's barely stroking along at ninety. The car was a jewel when I drove into town, but a few years of being nudged around in Puerto Vallarta traffic has left it looking like it was assembled in the dark and painted with a broom. The leather seats are slashed, the radio and stereo are distant memories, and I leave the top down when it isn't raining to prove there's nothing left to steal.

I drove home along the cobbled, crowded streets on automatic pilot, my mind back in California with Gil, thinking of things we'd said and done seemingly just yesterday. Now that he was gone—if I was ready to accept that—his ghost sat next to me vivid as life, dressed in one of those elegant outfits, white teeth clamped on a skinny cheroot, mocking eyes scanning the streets for action. Look at that, Jonny boy! Chicken hawk working at two o'clock. Let's hassle him a little. That might have been back in the early days, when we were working Vice together. They seemed funnier then.

My place is furnished in rough, native mahogany. The chairs, called *equipales*, are covered with pigskin. The living room gives onto a terrace overlooking the ocean. To the south I can see the mounds of three islands, called Los Arcos because of the tunnels running through them, rising out of the sea. I've painted them more than once, adding in the listing cruise ship that plies to and from Yelapa, a peninsula beyond the reach of roads and phones. The last rays of the setting sun reach out to me from the horizon, and I've painted that too. It's a special time of day.

From his perch on the dinner table Fred, the grizzled tomcat who lets me share the house, opened his eyes and raised a tattered ear in honor of my arrival. I scratched it absently and went into the bathroom for the nearest glass, where my mirror told me I didn't really need any more tequila. My ropy blond hair hung over my collar, but that could be fixed. The bags under slightly watery eyes and the puffiness beneath the chin and over the belt line were a tad premature at forty-three. I imagined Gil standing there in the corner, arms crossed above his lean waist, shaking his head sadly. I'd been almost as trim as he was when we'd seen each other last.

I took a bottle of Conmemorativo out onto the terrace, sat in one of the *equipales*, and poured the velvety smooth tequila into my glass. I drank and smoked the sweet little Mexican cigarettes I favor, sitting there until long after the sun had done its thing, wondering why I couldn't cry, though there was some sand under my eyelids. Gil was the brother I never had. Even though I hadn't seen him in almost five years, it was okay because he was out there somewhere, after all. Hell, I could pick up the phone at the gallery and call him any goddamn time I wanted to. He was going to take a vacation and come down as soon as the season started and the weather cooled off. (Or was that last year?) Much later, when I'd finished the tequila and gone to bed, I stared up at the ceiling and asked aloud, "How the fuck could they have foxed you, Gil? You were fast and smart and had all the right moves." This time I thought I saw him sitting on the sill of my open window dressed in a tailored white suit because that's the way he would handle the tropics. He tossed his cheroot out into the night and grinned at me. "Hell, chum, these things happen. I guess I just zigged when I should have zagged."

# T W O

Two days after Terri's call, I left for California. No Hay was delighted to look after the house and Fred until I got back because her parents' *palapa* leaked and it still rains in mid-October. On my way to town, I had to pass right by the tall twin towers of Solemar. Common sense told me to keep on going, so I pulled into the semicircular driveway and gave a kid defying the heat in a gold-braided green uniform some pesos to watch my car.

Chispa wasn't in the air-conditioned office she shared with another broker, but the young woman told me I could find her checking the carpeting in a unit on the twelfth floor. I rode the elevator up, wondering why anyone would want to live in a high-rise in the tropics. The building smelled dank and a uniform lack of charm overshadowed the conveniences.

I found Chispa standing in the middle of 1206, frowning at the floor. She wore a beige, tropical-weight linen suit and her hair was up in a French twist. She looked both remote and beautiful.

"A brand new carpet and it's already stained," she said when she noticed me. "The air-conditioning was off and it got moldy in a week."

"These places aren't designed for the climate."

"Jan told me about your friend. I'm sorry."

"That's why I came by. I'm driving up to California for a few days." Of course I could have called her, but I wanted to see her.

"Why don't you fly?"

"I've got to renew the car permit anyway. And it could use some work and spare parts."

"You ought to sell it and get something more practical." She walked out to stand on the cramped little balcony and I followed her. The view was good, I'll admit. At night you would see the crescent of lights limning the bay.

"I'm sorry about the other night," I said.

"No you're not. At least, not if you can get away with it. You were teaching me a lesson. Things are going to be done your way. Macho Man's way."

"I overreacted."

"To what? Dining in vermin-free restaurants? Being exposed to reasonably polite society?"

"Overexposed. I guess I needed some R and R."

"R and R?"

"That's a military expression. It stands for rest and recreation. Or rape and revenge, take your choice."

"That's charming." Another time she might have laughed. I sighed. "I'll be back in a week or ten days."

"You don't have to check in and out with me." She stared out to sea.

"Look, I'm trying to apologize and make things right between us."

"So I'll be waiting when you come back, like any other convenience."

"I think I offered more than that the other night." Again, it just slipped out.

"I'm surprised you remember. Was it a proposal or a proposition? And why? Because you feel winter coming on and you can't handle it alone?"

I'm only twelve years older than Chispa, hardly an eon, and the remark annoyed me. "Whatever it was, I retract it." I reached for a cigarette and lit it, a habit she deplores.

"Fine."

I couldn't just leave it there. "The trouble is, you're insecure. You hang around that rusty Gringo Gulch crowd looking for approval instead of being yourself. You don't need to do that."

She whirled on me, her dark eyes hoisted almost to the level of mine by her high heels. "Let me see if I read you." She spoke quietly, but I knew she wanted to shout. "You, being a movie star's son to the manor born or some such crap, can afford to be nonchalant about your social contacts, while a little Mexican girl like me, born on the border, can look forward to a continuing struggle for acceptance. Even in my own country! Is that it?"

That wasn't it at all and she knew I didn't like to be reminded whose son I was, but it was time to lighten up. "Well, I wouldn't say 'little.' "

It was too late; she had her teeth into it now. "Sure, that's right! Be glib." Her voice rose with her temper. "Let me tell you something. I hang around the Gringo Gulch crowd for a couple of reasons! They know other Americans who come down here and buy condominiums! And they're better company than your weird pals who stumble around drunk on the beach all day, pretending to be painters or writers!" She took a fresh breath and her voice rose a few more decibels. "And why do I need to explain myself to you, anyway? You're older than I am and you're not rich and you drink! You've got a very goddamn modest talent at best, and you're not as funny or handsome as you were a couple of years ago—"

"You okay out there, Chispa?" a voice growled behind us.

I glanced back into the apartment and saw Carlos Freebaker standing there, looking confrontational. Carlos is tall and lean. He wears his dark hair in a preppie brush cut and likes to stand with his hands in his pockets, shoulders hunched forward aggressively. His American father made a fortune in Mexico and Carlos was born here, making him a citizen. He went to all the right schools in America and then came back to join the looting.

I don't like Carlos. Not just because he lives in Gringo Gulch and likes to hit on Chispa, but because he's a crook. He's the developer of Solemar and he sells thirty-year leases on studio condos for twenty-five thousand dollars apiece. Every buyer gets one week a year for his money, so Carlos sells each unit fifty-two times, meaning he gets a hundred and thirty thousand dollars for a glorified hotel room. A one-bedroom apartment goes for twice as much and Solemar has two hundred and forty units altogether. In thirty years everything reverts back to his company, of course. It's a rip-off, but it's not against any law. What makes Carlos crooked is he uses shoddy building materials, a lot of sand in his concrete and cheap piping, so the walls crack and the pipes break, leaving damp streaks and rank smells. He doesn't bother with upkeep and when buyers complain and refuse to pay their maintenance fees, he takes his money and runs. Carlos has left a trail of crumbling condos behind him from Acapulco to the U.S. border.

Chispa's gone out with him a couple of times because he's her boss, but she can't stand him. So she says.

"We're just rehearsing for the local play," I told him. "So piss off, Carlie."

Chispa walked past me and said, "Jon is just leaving, Carlie. About dinner tonight, I've changed my mind. I'd be delighted."

I followed her off the terrace into the living room and looked at her, ignoring him. "You don't have to put yourself through something like that just to bug me."

Carlos said, "You know, you can be a real bore, Jonny boy." Very Ivy League.

"Did you hear that?" I asked her. "Coming from him?"

"At least he doesn't hang around El Farolito with hookers," Chispa said, a little wearily.

I turned to Carlos and nodded approval. "Glad to hear you don't do that anymore. Well, I don't blame you, old buddy. Isn't that where you told me you got herpes?"

My father would have called it a good exit line.

I put the Chrysler on the ferry that runs from Puerto Vallarta to Cabo San Lucas and then drove up the Baja California peninsula. North of La Paz the road to Mulege runs along the east coast with bald, stony mountains on one side, plunging to wide beaches and a sapphire sea dotted with offshore islands on the other. At Mulege I turned inland and followed the central valley nearly to the border before angling west to cross at Tijuana. I drove with a heavy foot and made the trip in two days.

The tourist sections of Tijuana had undergone a face lift in the form of broader avenues and a few new shopping centers, but beyond such cosmetic changes the same shanty towns festered on the stunted brown hills surrounding the city. Long lines of traffic backed up at the border while harried American customs officials made futile searches intended to impede the flow of wetbacks and drugs into the United States. Once past the country's most porous border, there's the transitional voyage through San Ysidro and Chula Vista to San Diego, where you finally decide you might be in America after all.

I hadn't seen it in nearly five years. The country had been on a roll when I left, with a new administration hosing the bitter residue of its inept predecessor out of the corners and a tentative mood of hope in the air. Unfortunately, this general rise in public expectation coincided with my personal downfall, a classic case of being in the wrong place at the wrong time. That sometimes happens to cops.

I had twelve years in the Los Angeles Police Department and was currently at the West L.A.P.D. station in Santa Monica as detective two, or sergeant, possessor of a clean record and a reasonably bright future. Cops don't use the word "secure." I shared a duplex on the beach at Marina del Rey with Gil, who had been my partner for a long time by then, ever since we'd worked Vice in Hollywood. We made a good team and personnel had let us stay together through three divisional transfers and nine years. Gil had talked me into joining the L.A.P.D. when I got out of the Marine Corps, and I hadn't regretted it.

We were having a good time. Sometimes our duplex reminded me of a way station for airline stewardesses, young divorcees, and assorted groupies in transit. We lived well without stealing. Oh, we accepted gastronomic and even electronic freebies and Gil played the horses with some success, but we were pretty good cops. Appearances were important and I remember some of Gil's sartorial elegance rubbed off on me. We both wore tailored clothes, had our hair razor cut, and drove sleek cars. Golden years, I'd have said then, but my perspective has changed since.

For me they ended during a plethora of pre-Christmas parties sandwiched in between a heavy workload. I was driving from the Marina to L.A. International Airport to pick up a lady and stopped at a bar on Lincoln Avenue. I'd had a few beers and needed to use the men's room, but I should have tied a string around it and driven right past this place. It was cramped and claustrophobic with a sour loser's smell, maybe half a dozen black men and one woman at the bar. I walked past their vaguely bitter eyes, inured to hostility in or out of uniform, and down a narrow corridor to the toilet.

When I came out, the scene had changed. Radically. A slight man was pointing a large, cocked revolver at the woman, vowing to blow her whoring ass into eternity or something like that. He seemed to mean it. I had options. "Why didn't you just turn around and tippy-toe out the back door or climb out a window if there wasn't a door?" Gil asked me later, exasperated. Why not indeed? Who needed this kind of shit, off duty? What I actually did was pull out my piece, take aim at the man, and yell, "Freeze! Police officer!"

He barely hesitated before turning the gun on me. I aimed at the widest part of him, the diaphragm just below his breastbone, and fired twice. He flew backward and slid along the floor, kicked his heels a time or two, and lay still. I could have gone over there to make sure, but there was no need. The gun had skidded under a table where I couldn't see it, but I watched the rest of the customers and they stared back at me, unmoving. What I needed was a police unit, so I backed into the narrow corridor where I'd seen a phone. Maybe I took my eyes off them for just a moment while I freed the receiver and dialed. Anyway, someone made good use of the time.

When the black-and-white arrived with two patrolmen there was no gun to be found and the crowd looked to be a man light, but I hadn't counted. Everybody, including the prospective victim, was ready to testify that this honky mother had pulled out a gun and blown the brother away after the brother told him to leave. The cops were sympathetic, but they took me in. One smelled beer and so they checked me out at the station and I blew a .8 on the breathalizer. That indicated some mild drinking.

Things got worse. A shooting team headed by a lieutenant from Robbery and Homicide investigated and of course found I'd used hollow-point ammo, which had just become a no-no for police, though hoods could buy it at any gun shop. The lieutenant sighed, "Nice shooting, though. Could've covered both those entry wounds with a quarter."

I was temporarily relieved of duty and the media had a field day. "Movie Star's Son Named in Possible Manslaughter." Then the ACLU jumped in with both feet on behalf of the deceased and the trial by headline was on. My father tried to be helpful, I'll say that. "I'm sticking with you, kid," he told me. "Christ, all you did was shoot a nigger." I hadn't seen him for some time, but people told me Pop was already getting a little out of touch with things. I told him thanks, but no thanks.

A TV crew with a jungle of equipment camped outside our place in the Marina but our groupies stayed loyal until a Molotov cocktail was tossed through the picture window one night. Gil was sore enough to shoot someone but he hung in there with me. The investigation went on for a long time with no final judgment. I called up the RHD lieutenant a dozen times and couldn't find out a thing. Except I was embarrassing everyone.

The bartender finally copped out and named the individual who had scooped up the gun and slipped out that night. The bartender was settling an old score before leaving town, I was told, and that should have been the end of it.

It wasn't, of course. The harassment went on with no end in sight. Our landlady evicted us and Gil moved in with Terri, who had been around for some time, standing in line with the others. I couldn't handle the hatred that followed me around or ambushed me, and I felt betrayed by the department. Nowadays, I could probably claim a stress pension and come out ahead of the game, but those were different times and I was a different person. I simply quit and went to Mexico to sulk.

The house on Mulholland Drive hadn't changed since I'd last seen it. It's a castle actually—a turreted, flamingo-pink confection my father built in the forties to overlook the San Fernando Valley back when you could still see it every day. Now the valley's usually covered with a blanket of brown smog you could land a plane on, but you can still get a panoramic view when the wind shifts. Last year, they like to say, that happened on a Wednesday.

The place used to be surrounded by a ten-foot brick wall topped with broken Coke bottles set in cement, but that's against some city ordinance, so now there's just a fence made of wrought-iron spears rising to about the same height. The gate is between two pillars of stone with carriage lanterns on top of them. A pair of Dobermans patrol the perimeter and I wouldn't be surprised to find a machine gun nest up in one of those brooding towers.

Martins, Pop's chauffeur, bodyguard, and general gofer since

I can remember, answered the chimes and opened the gate to me, flanked by the Dobies, a new brace since my time. He looked the same—short, wide, and very powerful, perhaps a bit more lined and grizzled now. He grinned all over his broad face to see me again and thank God he called me "Jonny," not "Master Jon" as he had when I was a kid.

"Your dad's in a screening," he told me as he took my duffel. "All your stuff's here though, just like you left it."

I got acquainted with the dogs and followed Martins through the high-ceilinged antechamber, our heels clacking against the tiles. A "screening" meant my father was watching one of his old pictures, a nightly habit that seemed to be starting earlier, since it was only late afternoon. He'd let me store the clothes I wouldn't need in Mexico and now seemed a good time to pick them up, since I was wearing only the shirt, jeans, and huaraches that comprise my Puerto Vallarta outfit. The weather was definitely nippier here in Los Angeles.

Martins showed me into the projection room unannounced and I found a seat in the dark. I could see three heads barely rising above their chairs when my eyes became accustomed to the dark, but no one spoke and I turned my attention to the screen.

Pop was in pantaloons, blond hair flying around, laying about him with a saber. A dastardly crew of pirates gave way before his blade or fell bleeding at his feet. Then he was in the cabin of a galleon with the leading lady, the oiled muscles of his arms writhing as he drew her close to him.

"Great tits," said someone out of the darkness.

"Nice ass, too," another commented. "Bet you got some of that, Stormy." No one ever called him Bob. Robert or Stormy was all right.

"Yeah," my father's gravelly voice replied. "But Jesus, was she dumb. Couldn't swim, ride—nothing. Needed a double to do everything but fuck."

General laughter.

My father could ride, I'll give him that. He could fight, too,

21

with fists, swords, guns, you name it. He grew up on a farm in Wyoming with six large brothers, the runt of the litter, and he had to fight just for a place at the table. Pop once had a reputation for being just as feisty off-screen as on.

Maybe that was because of his size. He's about five-seven and his elevators barely get him over five-nine. They used to cast him with tiny actresses like Veronica Lake or Wanda Hendrix, but when the lady was taller he had to stand on a box or, if they were shooting exteriors, they'd have to dig trenches all over the place for her to walk in. I guess I took after my uncles because I'd outgrown Pop when I was thirteen. Or maybe I favored my mother, who crashed taking flying lessons when I was four. Her pictures are still around and I'm told she was tall.

"Jesus, who's smoking shit?" my father asked, and I doused my harsh little Mexican cigarette in the ashtray on the arm of my seat.

I watched the screen again. I've seen all of Pop's pictures and whether he played a cowboy, a private eye, a pirate, or a pilot, he walked through them all exactly the same way. Hard eyes, a flat voice, and a slightly sulky expression were his trademarks. Critics loved to take him apart, but he topped the box office for five years running in the fifties. He could still be working at sixty-five if he'd accept anything but young leads.

When the lights came on, he saw me right away. "Jonny boy!" He bounced up and came over to grab my hand in his hard little paw, slipping around me to take the high ground, the famous quick smile narrowing his gray eyes. He still had to look up. "You look like shit, kid. That bean food's making you fat. *Gordo.*"

I couldn't argue with that. "You look good, Pop," I told him.

It was true, more or less. He had jowls and a hard little drinker's gut, but he was still wiry and light on his feet. He kept his hair blond and the famous widow's peak was still mostly intact.

"Meet Cruiser Barnes and Billy Rivas." I shook hands with

the other two. One turned out to be an ex-jockey, the other a former bantamweight boxer, so they were little men, which figured. My father's cronies all had to be shorter than he was.

We had drinks on the terrace, watching the valley lights come on and try to fight their way through the smog. "Sorry about Gil," my father said. "He was a good kid. Shit. Getting himself killed for that fucking pinko."

Gil had been around a lot when I was growing up here and at the horse ranch Pop used to have on the way to Ventura, tucked into a small valley between the mountains like a little bit of Kentucky, white fences, lush grass and all. Gil had liked to ride the horses, among other things.

My father must have read my mind. "I remember when you and that bastard put that scrub quarterhorse in with Stormy Weather just to watch them fuck." His face darkened, thinking about it. Gil and I got the beating of our lives for that little experiment in horse breeding. Stormy Weather was Pop's prize brood mare, but she sure threw an ugly foal that year. "Boys will be boys," I murmured.

My father shook his head. "You couldn't stay mad at that kid. All that Mick temper and Guinea charm. He looked like Ty Power, you know?"

It was true. Gil had inherited his father's short Irish nose and his Italian mother's smooth olive complexion. He was outrageously handsome and used his God-given advantage to the maximum.

The Chinese cook announced dinner at eight, another ritual. "Hey Wun, you plick," my father called. "Come see who's here!"

When he saw me Wun giggled and capered around, the most scrutable Oriental I've ever known. I had to pick the little man up to hug him and, yes, he called me Master Jon, to my embarrassment. His name is Wun Hung (you can imagine the mileage my old man gets out of that) and he owns property in Long Beach, which he calls "Wrong Bitch." He always said he'd retire there once he put his two sons through law school, but he's done that and he's still here. Probably because he gets as many laughs out of being around Robert Storm as my father gets out of him. ("How do you get to that property you bought anyway, One Hung Low?" "Take Wrong Bitch Fleeway!" And everyone roars.)

Cruiser and Billy stayed for dinner and we had teriyaki steaks, a sad waste of Wun's culinary talents, but Pop's a meat-and-potatoes man so the little chef's delicacies go largely unappreciated. Listening to the banter between Pop, his pals, and Wun, I had a brief but eloquent impression of being eighteen again, just before I'd quit UCLA and left home. There were fewer people around now, but nothing else had changed at all. Which was exactly the way Robert Storm wanted to keep it.

# THREE

woke in the morning with the same sense of disorientation I'd felt listening to Pop and his friends. The familiar room with the framed pictures, the ULCA pennant, and the trophies that represented my modest athletic achievements peeled away a quarter of a century of time. I wondered if Pop had left it that way out of sentimentality or because of his obsession about change in any form.

The clothes I'd stored before leaving for Mexico didn't fit anymore. The jackets were wearable, left unbuttoned, but the trousers were as tight as tourniquets. After breakfast, I drove down to Sunset Boulevard and over into Westwood, where I remembered a tailor who did alterations. Then I phoned Terri, who told me to come over right away because later she had to go out and look for a job. She didn't sound particularly surprised or happy to hear from me. The phone call cost two dimes instead of one.

More changes became apparent after I passed through Beverly Hills on Santa Monica Boulevard. Above the gas station at the corner of Doheny and Santa Monica, a large billboard featured two young men embracing and the message IMPORTANT NEWS FOR TWENTY-TWO MILLION AMERICANS over the name of a gay publication. Tank tops and short shorts seemed to be standard dress for the fellows mincing along the boulevard, and there was a lot of loitering. Five years ago they had loitered on Sunset, east of Laurel Canyon. And they were girls.

Terri lived in an apartment tower on Holloway Drive near LaCienega. It was a security building gone slightly to seed with a guard and a receptionist in the lobby. Still, you had to dial the apartment you wanted from outside and the tenant would call down and tell the receptionist to have the guard let you in. Terri came to the door in a robe, but her makeup was on and she smelled fresh from the shower. She peered at me and said, "You look awful, Jon. What did you do down there, go native?"

"Can I come in anyway?"

Her apartment was on the fifteenth floor, a modern affair as sleek and impersonal as a hotel suite. There was a picture of Gil on the mantel above the fake fireplace, but nothing else to indicate he had lived there. Terri brought coffee and then sat in the corner of a low sofa covered with throw pillows. "Why did you come up, Jon? There's no cemetery to visit, you know. Gil hated the idea of Forest Lawn so I had him cremated and scattered his ashes at sea. I couldn't afford to rent a yacht so I took that tourist fishing boat that goes along the coast in Santa Monica but never gets more than about a hundred yards offshore. I guess you could go out there and stand on the pier." She leaned forward to set down her coffee cup and her robe parted, offering me a casual view of tanned breasts with small, dark nipples.

I'd never known Terri well in the old days; she was just one of the girls. Gil married her after I left for Mexico, about the same time he quit the department to go into the security business. She was clever, pretty, and very sexy then. She hadn't lost her looks, but now the luster was gone. She seemed slack, without the bright edge I remembered, but that was understandable. Maybe she'd get it back.

"I came up to find out what happened. I'm kind of out of touch down there."

"Don't you know? It's had plenty of publicity. The son of the guy Clewes is running against just went crazy and tried to do daddy a favor. Some think that. Others think his father gave him the idea. Sounds ridiculous but you know the media rumor mill, and they say old Rydell is quite a cowboy. I don't give a damn either way. It won't bring Gil back."

I had heard most of that on the radio driving up from San Diego. About the politics involved, I knew only that Clewes and Rydell were both running for the United States Senate and Rydell was already a California senator. Before I left, Willie had been a controversial first-term assemblyman, a populist hero to his supporters and a crass opportunist to his enemies, who accused him of buying the election with his wife's money. Back then I wasn't much interested in local politics or in Willie, for that matter. "The kid denies everything, I hear."

Terri crossed her arms over her breasts, pushing them up and together. "They found the gun he used in his garage along with I don't know what all. No, he'll go to some country club for a few years with the kind of courts we have here. But the old man might as well fold his tent with the election two weeks away." She rocked gently back and forth as though her pain were physical. "Why couldn't that bastard shoot straight, anyway?"

"You said you're going to look for work."

She stopped rocking and pulled the front of her robe together. "That's right. You don't get a pension if you quit the department before twenty years and Gil never saved anything. I mean, you've got to know that, being his best friend! There's a little insurance and his damn Mercedes, but he owed on that. The agency barely broke even and he probably owes the three men he had working for him and maybe his secretary. I haven't found out yet how much he owes."

Her bitterness ran deep, the words dropping out of her mouth like cold stones. I began to sense a self-pity deeper than her grief, and it depressed me. Terri was young, they'd had no children and she could begin again. For Gil, it was over.

I stood up. "I'm keeping you from your job-hunting." I didn't think there was much she could help me with, and I wasn't comfortable in Gil's home. The feeling was all wrong. It was just a courtesy call after all, a gesture that needed to be made.

She rose with me. "Maybe you'd like something of his," she said, waving a hand around. "I don't know what. Clothes? He had more clothes than the Duke of Windsor."

I guess I didn't look very dapper in my tight jacket and blue jeans. "They wouldn't fit," I smiled.

Her eyes agreed with me. "Well then, how about his guns? I don't want his damn guns. Or maybe I'll just keep one to shoot myself with."

Gil had loved his guns. I followed her back into a master bedroom as undefined as the rest of the place and she brought a square leatherette case out of the closet. I opened it and found four handguns racked inside, along with a telescope and ear guards to use at the shooting range. There was a .380 Beretta with a fourteen-shot clip, a 9mm Luger, an accurized Colt .45 I knew Gil had a thousand dollars in, and a long-barreled .357 Smith and Wesson Magnum. There were two drawers in the case filled with boxes of shells.

I hesitated and then took out the Luger and handed it to her.

She was outraged. "Surely you don't really think I'm going to shoot myself!"

I shook my head. "You can sell it. It's worth a lot of money." Which was true. The Luger was an early World War II model in perfect condition.

"Oh."

I snapped the case shut and picked it up, feeling slightly

guilty. The other guns were worth a lot, too. Earlier on I would have pointed that out to her, but I'd decided Gil would want me to have them after all.

"What do you do down there?" Terri asked me at the front door.

"I paint."

"I mean, for a living."

"That's it. I sell the paintings."

She looked at me for a long moment and I saw speculation in her eyes. "I've always wondered about Mexico," she said.

I waited to see if she had anything to add.

"Will I see you again?" she asked finally.

I started to give her the answer and then changed my mind. "Sure you will, Terri."

Down on the street a traffic cop was writing me a ticket, his foot perched on my mangled back bumper. "That's not an abandoned vehicle, officer," I said, coming up behind him, and he jumped.

"You frightened me, sneaking up like that." He put a hand over his heart. His uniform trousers were tightly tailored over buttocks and thighs and he wore a well-trimmed little mustache.

I looked at the parking meter. "My time's not expired," I pointed out.

The cop arched his brows. "Your license plate *is*."

He had me there. I locked my case in the trunk and said to him, "You really need air traffic controllers around here, not cops."

I let that sink in, watching his lips form a thin, indignant line. He tore out the ticket and handed it to me with a flourish. "Better watch that kind of talk, big fella," he snapped.

Driving out of West Hollywood, on Olympic Boulevard this time, I looked up at another billboard and saw a huge likeness of Assemblyman Bill Clewes over the admonition IF YOU CARE staring down benevolently. I had to smile because I remembered the pale, studious kid in junior high and then, over a decade later, pictures of him long-haired and wild-eyed, pouring blood (not his own) on draft cards. Now he was up there neat and trim as an Arrow shirt ad. The multiple faces of Willie the Weege.

The West Los Angeles Police Station was on Butler Avenue in Santa Monica. I went through the bright red-tiled entrance and asked a corporal at the desk for Lieutenant Kling, hoping he hadn't been transferred.

"Captain Kling," the corporal corrected. "And your name?"

I told him and he looked at me for a moment as if he were trying to remember something. Finally he spoke into an interphone and listened in turn. "Go on up those stairs," he told me. "First office on your left."

I knew the way well enough. Fletcher Strickland had been commanding officer in my time and I assumed he'd been kicked upstairs after he solved the murder of Marla Monday, the movie star. Trouble was, one of his own men killed her. It had been a strange case.

Norman Kling got up to shake hands when I came in. He had the kind of baby face that ages badly once it begins to go. The deep lines bracketing his mouth and the network of creases at the corners of rather tired blue eyes were incongruous with his snub nose and blond brush cut. He looked like a wrinkled child. Maybe it was the weight of new responsibilities.

"Captain Kling. It's got a good sound," I said. "Congratulations."

He pumped my hand. "Well, Jon. I'll be damned!"

"Won't we all?"

It was hard to tell whether he was embarrassed to see me. Five years ago he was the lieutenant in charge of Robbery and Homicide investigating my case. He'd done his work dispassionately and kept his distance throughout. When I was vindicated, too late to save my job, it was because the bartender copped out and no thanks to him. Norman Kling was a cautious man. "Hell of a thing about Gil." He shook his head and his face folded in on itself. "Right here in our jurisdiction. Isn't that a bitch?"

"I know. That's why I came by, Captain. I thought you might not mind filling me in."

"Hell, call me Norman."

"Okay . . . Norman."

He walked over to take some folders out of the current file in his metal cabinet and went back behind his desk. I took the chair in front of it. At least everything seemed to be at his fingertips.

"We're all heated up over this," Norman Kling said, "Gil being one of our own once. I tried to talk him out of quitting, you know? But he went for the glamour. Bodyguarding the rich and famous. Movie stars, politicos, goddamn rock-and-rollers. Be alive today if he'd stayed in the department. Well, maybe."

"Any doubts about this Rydell kid?"

"Not a one. We got a tip right after the murder made the news. Next morning, in fact. The owner of a bar called the Pit Stop in Venice phoned and said Rydell had been in his place mouthing off about killing Clewes early the night before. Three other witnesses that hang out there'll confirm it. We found out where Rydell lived, got a warrant, and shook the place down. Found the Uzi submachine gun with his prints on it, a typewriter he'd been using to send Clewes threatening letters, even the poison he'd used on their dog. The stuff was in his garage."

"He poisoned their dog?"

"Yeah. That's when Monica Loring brought Gil in, maybe a year ago. There was a lot of publicity about the hate mail and the dog. This Chick Rydell is a surf bum with a record of misdemeanors. He's made threats against Clewes before. Senator Rydell disowns his son but also claims he's innocent, of course. The kid says he was drinking with some bikers at the Pit Stop and passed out in his car. Doesn't even remember how he got home."

"Someone told me this could blow the election for Rydell. I'd think with a kid like that he might get a sympathy vote."

Kling shook his head. "In another election maybe, not this one. This is the dirtiest campaign in California history. These guys hate each other personally and ideologically. Rydell's called Clewes a traitor and a Communist and said he should have been hanged fifteen years ago for supporting the Vietcong. Clewes calls Rydell a Nazi and a racist. At one point Rydell wanted to fight a duel, only it's illegal. Hell, they've both got the public believing they'd kill each other. Or have it done."

"I've been away. What do you think of these guys?"

"I think they're both off the wall, but they got nominated when the incumbent decided not to run again. There was nobody with enough recognition taking the middle ground in either party. Rydell's colorful and Clewes has all that money behind him."

"He has that." I smiled, thinking about Monica. Her story was common knowledge. Everything she touched turned to gold, or platinum. If she started a restaurant, it turned into a chain. If she brought out a record, it went to the top of the charts. She could get a couple of million to act in a movie, but that was just a hobby now. Add the headlines she made marching and demonstrating and you had a very colorful lady.

Kling lit a cigarette and I used that as an excuse to pull out my Mexican lung-busters. "Can you give me the details of the killing? Unexpurgated?"

"Sure. Clewes and Gil stopped at a gas station on Sepulveda near Pico at ten-fifteen on a Thursday night two weeks back. Gil got out and headed for the self-service pump to get gas. Clewes went toward the office to use the toilet. One man was on duty, a Latino named Rogelio Méndez.

"A car, later found to have been stolen for the occasion, pulls up over the curb and this guy in a ski mask with an Uzi jumps out and opens fire. He cuts Gil down first, point-blank. A burst right through the middle. Then he turns and fires into the office just as Clewes hits the deck, pulling this Méndez down with him. The suspect shoots the office to pieces but doesn't aim low enough to get them. Then he jumps in the car and takes

31

off. A classic hit gone wrong, but then Chick Rydell's an amateur."

"So he took Gil out first."

"Makes sense to hit the bodyguard first. He's presumed armed. Even an amateur can figure that."

Kling handed me some photos. One showed Gil sprawled there, an incredible amount of blood splattering him and pooling on the asphalt around him. I felt sickness and rage but forced myself to look at it closely. There were shots showing the entire area taped off, with different angles relating the position of the body to the automobile, the gas pumps, and the shattered office. In these Gil had been removed, his silhouette represented by a chalk outline.

"He just split, without taking out his target?" I asked.

Kling shrugged. "Maybe he thought he had. He'd been drinking, according to the bartender, and might not have been too steady. Or maybe he ran out of ammo. We figured he fired a whole clip into that place. An amateur, like I said."

"An amateur with an Uzi?"

Kling leaned toward me, putting his elbows on his desk. "Look, how long have you been gone? Five years? Well, things have changed. We've got stranglers, stalkers, slashers, rippers . . ."

"We always did."

"Only now we're outgunned. Punks use high-tech weapons. Mac-tens, Uzis, Mini-fourteens. Nowadays they just pull out a fully automatic piece and grease you! They don't have to be pros."

Kling took a deep breath, his face getting red. "We've got a state supreme court headed by a turkey who runs multiple felons and even serial killers through a revolving door so they're back on the street before we get the paperwork done. We've got a police commission made up of civilians who won't let cops use a choke-hold, for Christ's sake . . ."

"Norman, I just got back. I thought the country was going law and order."

"I talk about what I know, and I know L.A.! The police commission has decreed, in its wisdom, that we must accept a quota of women and so-called minorities and that they must be on the firing line. So now a cop can be five feet tall, of any or a variety of sexual persuasions . . ."

"Could I see the police report, Norman? And the kid's sheet?"

Kling hesitated. "I can't let you take anything out of here, not even copies."

"Can I look at them here?"

He let me use an empty office and I spent an hour and a half going over the report of the investigating team and the rap sheet on Charles "Chick" Rydell. The young man had been in trouble since his early teens. Nothing serious, but the potential was there. Drunk and disorderly, possession of narcotics and firearms, driving violations. Not the first California politician's heir to give his father a cross to bear, but this one might have done a terminal job. There were photocopies of the letters he had allegedly sent to Clewes. Fairly routine hate mail, scatological trash and death threats. They were laced with right-wing political slogans and were fairly literate, as though the writer had at least a modicum of education.

At two o'clock in the afternoon I thanked Captain Norman Kling, turned down an invitation to lunch at his favorite Mexican restaurant, and drove down to Chez Jay's, a place near the Santa Monica pier where Gil and I had hoisted many a glass. It's a drinkers' bar that serves good food, a dim, cozy place that has retained a unique personality since I can remember. It was good to find something that hadn't changed. Or maybe I was beginning to think like Pop.

Jay was there in person, a husky man with a little more gray in his beard than I remembered, who likes to fly hot-air balloons when he's not being an innkeeper. He said welcome back and told me he was sorry about Gil. I ordered a tequila backed by a bottle of beer and a seafood salad. "You know a place called the Pit Stop?" I asked him, because it was in the neighborhood.

Jay nodded. "A sleaze joint in Venice. Bikers and assorted bad-asses. A guy they call A-Frame runs it."

"I don't remember the place."

"It's new since your time. Been there maybe three years. Over on Washington. Not your kind of place." He poked a finger at my beltline. "Getting a little porky there, amigo."

After lunch I crossed Ocean Avenue to the Santa Monica pier and got a shock, even though I'd read about the storm. Half the structure was missing, swept away by an angry sea a couple of years back. The harbor master's station and a restaurant that had been at the end of the pier were gone, and Sinbad's, a landmark hash house, was boarded up. The garish old amusement park with its merry-go-round was still there, along with a shooting gallery, an arcade, and a seafood bar, and there was still a colorful succotash of humanity on the boardwalk—bums and bag ladies, cyclists, hucksters, and tourists. A couple of kids on roller skates skimmed by in baggy pants and tank tops. The sides of their heads were shaved and they wore mohawks of spikey pink and curly purple, respectively. I think they were girls.

It was a brisk autumn day with an offshore breeze and I could see Catalina Island across the water. I leaned against the railing and looked north toward State Beach, where Gil and I had surfed before a sand bar had built up and diminished the waves. The boards were lighter now—you could run around with them under your arm—and there were a lot more kids in the water. They all wore wet suits and looked serious about what they were doing, but we'd given equal time to chasing girls. By our early teens we were enjoying some success but we were scared to death of getting someone pregnant and young enough to balk at buying condoms. That was when Gil discovered Saran Wrap. I smiled, remembering how we'd try to lure girls under the pier. Gil perfected a number of approaches and ran up the biggest score.

Now he was washing around down there among the pilings.

• • •

Back at the castle, I put the case of handguns in my bedroom closet, relieved to get them out of the car trunk, where anyone could jimmy the lock in about five seconds. I went downstairs and found my father in the den, his small fist wrapped around a glass of vodka. All the furniture in the room was miniaturized. The mahogany bar was low, with short stools, and even the sofas were abbreviated and close to the ground. A pair of matched Winchester carbines were crossed on one wall and a branding iron stood upright by the fireplace. It was the room Pop once used for photo interviews.

"Plan to stick around for a while, son," he said. "You know you're welcome."

I didn't, but I was glad to hear it. There was a time when he was always shipping me off somewhere, or else I was leaving on my own. I think he was uncomfortable about my height and I know I was god-awful tired of being "Robert Storm's kid," of lacking an identity of my own. Well, we were both older now. "Thanks," I said. "I want to see this Rydell kid before I go."

"I can understand that," Pop said grimly, not understanding at all. "Remember when Buck Rydell had that spread down the road from ours in Hidden Valley?" he asked. "You and Gil were maybe fourteen and that boy of his wasn't born yet."

I nodded and went behind the bar to pour some Jack Daniel's over ice. "You two did a lot of shooting."

They'd get drunk together and work on their fast draws, shooting bottles and cans off the fences, bullets flying everywhere. The neighbors would call the sheriff, but he'd end up drinking with them and maybe taking a few shots himself. Storm and Rydell were very big names out in Hidden Valley.

"Ol' Buck was almost as good as I was," Pop remarked. "Almost. But close only counts with horseshoes and hand grenades, so he lost his money. He always figured 'next time.' Now his kid's in jail for shooting Gil. Small world."

"Very small. When I think you made pictures with Monica's mother." Kitty Mars had been a queen of B pictures, a flashy redhead with little of her daughter's talent. Pop had passed her on his way up, and maybe again on the way down.

"Since before you were born, when I was just starting. Jesus, she was a lousy actress. Walked into every scene looking around on the floor for her marks. But she had plenty of Irish temper." He looked down into his empty glass. "And heart. Yeah, she had lots of heart. Enough for everybody."

I recalled hearing her husband had finally committed suicide. Loring had been a gentle soul who hated Hollywood glitz. Maybe his misfortune was to be in love with Kitty Mars.

My father lit a cigarette and reached for the vodka bottle. "She's at the Motion Picture Home now, broke and living in one room."

That jarred me. "Why? Monica could buy her the place." I remembered Kitty Mars from when I was a kid invited to Monica's birthday parties. She was a brittle, chattery person, but vivid and striking as well. And she'd liked kids.

Pop laughed. "Kitty won't take a dime from her. She'll never forgive her for marrying Clewes."

"Why?"

He hesitated. "Maybe she couldn't forget he used to live over the garage."

Willie's widowed father had been a chauffeur for Kitty Mars and her husband, Oliver Loring. He and his boy lived in an apartment above the garage, but Willie got to go to the birthday parties, probably because Monica insisted. I remember him there, wan and clumsy at games, an easy target for the casual cruelties of children. That was long before junior high. "What happened to all her money?" I asked.

"She pissed it away." Pop drank from his glass and changed the subject, perhaps reminded of how much he'd gone through himself. "Wun's going to cook some of that gook food of his for dinner. In your honor."

I couldn't turn that down. "What are we watching tonight?"

*"Shawnessy's Castle.* You loved it when you were a kid. Shit, I nearly got nominated for that one."

We made fresh drinks to get us through the evening news on TV. Toward the end there was a shot of Chick Rydell, ducking his head away from the cameras as he was rushed through a crowd outside the county courthouse by about a dozen cops. He had just been formally indicted for murder.

It was after ten o'clock when I got to the Arco station on Sepulveda near Pico Boulevard. Fog was moving in from the coast, picking up a petrochemical taint as it rolled inland. The gas station occupied a lonely spot between a wholesale lumberyard and an empty lot. The street was dark but fluorescent tubes bathed the island in a cold light, emphasizing its isolation. I couldn't think of a better place for an urban hit.

I didn't really expect the place to be back in business, never mind to find Rogelio Méndez on duty, but there was a young Latino standing behind the cash register in the office. From outside I could still see signs of damage, in spite of a crude paint and putty job and new glass all around. I opened the door and walked in. "Rogelio Méndez?" I asked.

The young man gave me a flat, wary glance and barely nodded. I could understand his reticence. "I just want to ask a few questions," I told him. "I'm not a cop."

"Then why are you asking questions?"

I smiled and offered my Mexican cigarettes. He looked down at them and shook his head. "How can you smoke that shit, man?" He fished a Winston out of a pack on his counter.

I lit us up and said, "These are friendly questions, but I used to be a cop."

"That don't mean anything."

"I know the man in charge of the investigation. Captain Norman Kling."

His eyes said, So what? but I think he registered the name.

"My name is Jon Storm. The man who was killed was my friend. Have you ever had anything bad happen to a friend?"

"Not that bad."

"I don't want something for nothing, Rogelio."

"I'm not going to give you something for nothing, Juan." He used the Spanish version of my surname. Yes, this one was ballsy. Mexicans would say he had *huevos*. He was scrawny and cocky, like one of those roosters they fight down there.

"I want you to tell me what happened," I said, putting a twenty on the cash register. "It doesn't matter if you tell me the same things you told the police. I'm trying to get a *feeling* of what happened. I want to *see* it, you understand?"

I thought he would and he did. "You want to act this out or something?"

"Why not?"

He had a flair for drama. We walked through it, Rogelio variously playing the parts of Gil, the killer, Clewes, and finally himself. Picking himself off the floor he said, "That Senator Clewes, he's got my vote, you know?"

I nodded, wondering if Rogelio was registered. "Quick thinking. Pulling you down like that."

We were interrupted by two customers, the only ones who had showed up since I arrived. When Rogelio had serviced their cars, I got a bottle of Conmemorativo out of the Chrysler; there was a chill in the air. We passed the tequila back and forth. "Could it have been a woman?" I asked.

Rogelio chuckled and shook his head. "Didn't move like a woman."

"Nowadays there are women who move like men."

"And men who move like women!"

We both laughed.

"Why do you think Gil never got his gun out?" I asked Rogelio. "He was fast."

"The guy had the lights right in his eyes, man. He couldn't see no mask or anything."

I closed my eyes to picture it. They had pulled up to the self-service section, putting the car between the pumps and the office. Gil went to pump gas while Willie peeled off for the head. But I remembered from the photos that the car was parked with access to the gas tank on the side away from the pump. Gil had been driving Clewes around long enough to know that. Unless they used different cars and he got confused.

I was confused myself. It felt strange, standing here where Gil had been murdered, getting drunk with the primary witness. Well, Gil would see the humor in that. But I kept hearing him say, "Come on, Jonny. Would I pull up where the hose wouldn't reach the goddamn tank?"

# F O U R

The next day a Santa Ana wind was gusting in from the desert, turning the weather from cool and damp to hot and dry overnight, in the best California tradition. I put on a light windbreaker, which went better with jeans than the wool blazer anyway, and finished breakfast before Pop got up. In the driveway, Martins was holding a hose in his hand and looking glumly at my ravaged Chrysler, trying to decide whether it was worth washing. I got behind the wheel, sparing him a decision, but he wouldn't let me go until he'd fetched a little electronic genie I could use to let myself through the gate unaided. "So I don't have to get up in the middle of the night again," he explained.

I took the Ventura Freeway north and drove past Thousand Oaks before turning off on a secondary road, heading west. After a few miles of winding through rolling brown hills it dropped down into a green valley studded with horse ranches. Miles of white fencing, irrigated pasture, and low rambling homes built away from the narrow road. Los Angeles could have been in another world. I passed my father's old spread, Storm Haven, and slowed to look for names. Thoroughbreds hung their long, graceful necks over the fences and watched me go by without

39

interest. Charles Rydell's ranch had been about a mile beyond Storm Haven, if memory served me.

It had to be the only place with an armed guard in the form of a cowboy packing a six-gun. He was in a jeep with a long radio antenna, parked by the gate. I swear he said, "Whoa, there," as I pulled up even with him. The jeep had a bumper sticker that read NUKE THE SNAIL DARTER.

"Howdy," I called. "I'd like a word with Senator Rydell."

The cowboy jumped out of his jeep without opening the door and ambled over. He wore a blue-jeans outfit, a Stetson, cracked boots, and a .44 revolver in a holster strapped to his thigh with a thong. "What makes you think he's here?" His eyes were suspicious pebbles set in a weathered hide.

Rydell could have been in Sacramento, Washington, or anywhere. I was just taking a chance since I didn't know how else to reach him. "Because you're here."

"You got an appointment?"

"No."

The cowboy just shook his head. "So long," he said.

I nodded toward his jeep. "Why don't you call and ask? My name's Jon Storm. I'm not a reporter."

"What are you, a cop?"

"I used to be."

"That don't mean shit."

I was losing patience. "Listen, old hoss, you get on the horn and let him make the decision, hear? You might be sorry if he finds you sent me away."

We stared at each other for a while. Finally he turned away from me without a word and sauntered back to the jeep. He mumbled something into his radio, listened for a moment, and then leaned back in his seat and let his hat drop over his forehead.

In about ten minutes a rider came cantering down from the main house on a big roan gelding. He was dressed just like the other cowboy, and when he got close enough I saw he looked like the Marlboro man with a touch of Clint Eastwood, except he was broad rather than lanky. There was a sweaty kerchief around his thick neck, his thighs bulged with saddle muscles, and his pale eyes had stared at their fair share of far horizons. I had no trouble recognizing the senator himself.

"Stormy's boy," he said. "Goddamn! I haven't seen you since you were knee-high to a grasshopper."

Stormy's boy. I kept my smile in place and got out of the car to reach up and shake hands. "A pleasure, Senator."

"How is old Stormy, anyway? Still the fastest gun north of the Rio?"

I laughed. "Still hanging in there."

"You look like him." His keen eyes made decisions at a glance. "A whole lot bigger, though. Favor your mother that way." He changed the subject abruptly. "What can I do for you?"

"Gil Buckler was my best friend."

The senator's wide trap of a mouth tightened. "My son didn't kill that man!" The gelding bridled and snorted, pawing the ground. Man and beast seemed to agree on that one.

"I hope he didn't, Senator."

"The boy's wild, and maybe that's part my fault. I was once, too. Difference is, he's got no sense and never had. Been a trial to me his whole life and never worked a day of it I know of. But he didn't try to kill that commie bastard or he'd have done it. He's no coward to cut and run like that." Clewes's survival seemed to gall Rydell.

"They've got a hell of a lot of evidence, Senator."

Rydell leaned forward in his saddle. "Now you didn't come out here to call my son a murderer, did you?" Even the cowboy in the jeep shoved back his hat and sat up at the suggestion.

"No, sir. I'm trying to learn what happened. To my own satisfaction. For my own peace of mind."

"I remember something about you," the senator said. "You were framed for shooting some nigger and you had to quit the police force. Well then, you know what a frame feels like. Someone planted that machine gun and the typewriter and the poison in my boy's garage. Now, they did it to get at *me*. Do you understand that?"

"Your son was heard to threaten Clewes the night of the killing and on other occasions, Senator."

The gelding stomped around in a full circle this time before the senator got him under control. "Charlie doesn't give a rat's ass about politics! He doesn't care about anything except waves. Waves! He goes to the beach and rides *waves!*"

"He seems to have made the threats."

The senator calmed his horse and sat still in the saddle. "Maybe he did," he admitted. "Talk is cheap. Circumstantially, the evidence puts my son in a very serious position. It also deals a severe blow to me and to my campaign. I'm not going to fog your mind with political detail, but let it suffice to say the disaster inherent in this situation lies less in the fact that I could be defeated running for high office than that my defeat would ensure Clewes's victory. I have no doubt about my qualifications and I would run hard against any man. I would rejoice in victory or I would congratulate my opponent if I were defeated, according to time-honored American custom." The horse began to get restless again. "But the possibility of Clewes gaining a seat in the United States Senate would set a precedent the nation can ill afford. That a man who gave aid and comfort to an enemy of this country in time of war and evidences no remorse could sit in the highest councils of our government is unacceptable!" This was Senator Charles Rydell speaking. Good ol' Buck was out to lunch.

"I can't even think about politics now, Senator."

He looked at me for a long beat, very soberly. "You want to get to the bottom of it."

"Yes."

"So do I. Why did you come here?"

"I want to talk to your son. He doesn't know me and he doesn't have to talk to anyone. Maybe you could persuade him."

The senator kept his shrewd, pale eyes on me.

"I think you know I'm not going to go in there and try to gun him down," I added.

He nodded. "I know that. When do you want to see him?"

"Today."

He rode his horse away from me as if they were going into private conference, and then came trotting back. "I'm putting investigators on this, as you might figure. You were a cop and you're Stormy's boy. I trust you. I'll pay you well if you can get Charlie clear. I need all the help I can get."

I shook my head. "I'm not a licensed investigator and I can't take your money. But I'll talk to your son and listen to what he says."

Another nod. "He'll see you." He looked off at those far horizons and Buck Rydell was back. "He gets out of this, I'll send the sumbitch to Hawaii with a one-way ticket. He can ride that forty-foot wave he's always talking about. Get wiped out, for all I care."

I didn't say anything.

"Come up to the house for a bourbon and branch water?"

I knew myself too well. "I want to get on with it, Senator."

"Anything I can do, you let me know." He pointed his jaw at the cowboy in the jeep. "Lew there, he'll write you down a phone number where you can get me or leave a message." He wheeled the gelding around and went galloping back across the pasture toward his big house in the distance. It struck me that he had never gotten off his horse throughout our meeting.

The drive back through the San Fernando Valley took me right past Woodland Hills, and because Pop had mentioned the place often enough, I remembered that Calabasas Road led to the Motion Picture Home. On impulse, I cut across three lanes of freeway traffic through an angry blare of horns to catch the off ramp. That kind of maneuver becomes automatic after a few years in Mexico, but I was lucky there weren't any CHPs around. Murder is treated more leniently than reckless driving in California.

Anyone with a good arm could throw a rock from the freeway to the Home. I turned off Calabasas into the guest parking area, drove past the hospital, and found a slot in front of the main office. There was plenty of room because residents aren't allowed to have cars. Pop told me once their average age is eighty-two, so that seems reasonable enough. In his cups he shudders at the idea of ending up in what he calls a purgatory for the outcasts of his industry, but it's just a fantasy. He's too rich to qualify.

Two old-timers lounged at the top of the steps shouting into each other's hearing aids, but they were more likely to be grips or technicians than ex-movie stars. Only a minority here could claim celluloid immortality, and even they would be no more immune to decline than any other aging flesh.

In the office, a white-haired woman with the sweet, seamless face of a young grandmother asked if she could help me. I told her I'd like to see Kitty Mars, and she wanted to know if I was expected. I shook my head no.

"Are you a member of the family?"

"No, but I used to call her Aunt Kitty." I gave her my name. She smiled and said, "Let's find out if she'd like company."

She went into an inner office to make her call and then came back and said, "Miss Mars would love to see you, but she wants you to give her ten minutes. You understand."

"Of course." I killed the time looking at the framed photos covering the walls. Gable, Bogart, Colbert, Cagney, and a host of others. All caught and preserved for posterity at their peak, and when the light was just right. You couldn't imagine any of them having blemishes, bad breath, or even natural bodily functions. A few of them were probably here now, unrecognizable except to their peers.

After the white-haired lady gave me directions, I followed a walkway under a giant oak propped up by iron rods and past the John Ford Chapel and the Louis B. Mayer Memorial Theater.

Great, bushy squirrels chased each other across the manicured grounds and through the stunted trees. A few illegals were trimming hedges and I passed half a dozen staff personnel in white, but the residents evidently stayed indoors a lot.

The "cottages," which might have been called modern when they were built in the forties, sprouted TV antennas and were a uniform neutral beige. They weren't detached but stood in ranks, with three or four tiny garden apartments to a building. The whole place had the aspect of a very quiet college campus, neither lively nor cheerless.

A few crows squatted in the branches of the antenna over Kitty Mars's bungalow and there was a little square of concrete bordered by flower pots in front of her door. She opened to my knock and stood back blinking up at me. "Is it really you, Jonny? Come in, come in!"

She was a short woman and I had to lean down to kiss her cheek. She took my hand and drew me with her, peering up at me. "Well, it looks like you've got your full growth!" she said, and we both laughed. It was hard to believe I hadn't seen her since I was about seventeen.

Kitty Mars had changed, of course. Only her hair was the same, gathered in a riot of red curls on top of her head. Her cheeks sagged, there were wattles under her chin, and her mouth was a crimson smear, the decay accentuated by brazen eyelashes, layers of face powder, and electric-blue eyeshadow. Frills at the neck and wrists of her embroidered housecoat just drew attention to the savaging of time.

"Don't stare, Jonny. I know I look like hell." She turned and I followed her into the minuscule apartment.

Every inch of wall space was covered by old movie stills, just like in the office lobby, but here they were all of Kitty Mars in her glory days. Actually, she had been a queen of B pictures who got occasional second leads in A's, but she'd been prolific. Huge pale eyes and a dazzling smile stared back at me from a hundred places on the wall, reminders of Saturday afternoons long ago and movies that cost a quarter.

"Not much, but I call it home." She gestured at the single overstuffed chair and chose an abbreviated sofa for herself. The rest of the space was taken up by a single bed crammed into an alcove and a large TV. There was no kitchen.

"You look fine, Aunt Kitty," I told her.

"Liar. I had a lift years ago, when it was something new. They pulled everything so tight I looked like a goddamn dead teenager for about two years. Then everything fell back into my lap and I said to hell with it. Some of my friends wear their bellybuttons between their eyebrows now."

I had to laugh. She'd never talked that way around us kids. She'd been a movie mom, plying us with ice cream and cookies. I decided I liked both versions.

"I'm older than your father, you know? It didn't show when we worked together in the forties. God, he was a beautiful man! How is he?"

"Fine. Hanging tough."

"We got along." She looked wistfully through me at some distant point in the past. "We had everything going for us in those days. Youth, money, you name it. We did what we wanted and to hell with the rest of the world. And then ..." Her expression lapsed into infinite sadness. "Well, then it was over."

"Pop told me you were here. I've been living in Mexico."

"I've been here six years. For a long time after Oliver died, I tried to keep everything together. It was too much, too much. . . . Anyway, I don't need more than this."

I cleared my throat. "Pop said you wouldn't let Monica help you."

A hard light came into her faded blue eyes. "That's right," she said quietly and changed the subject. "Did you come back because of Gil?"

"Yes."

Her face crumbled. "I loved that boy. And you too, Jonny." Then an utterly baleful look came into her eyes. "If only they'd got the bastard they were shooting at!"

I was jarred in spite of myself. I knew she disliked Willie, but I couldn't have guessed how much. "Pop told me you didn't approve of Monica marrying the chauffeur's son," I ventured.

Her eyes locked on mine, suddenly bulging with fury. "The damn fool knows better! I'm no more a snob than he is! I came from nothing. Went from a shack in the desert to a chorus line in Vegas when it was a one-horse town and chorus girls did double duty, if you get what I mean!"

I looked away embarrassed, wishing I'd kept my mouth shut.

She bent forward from the waist, aiming those eyes at me, anger cutting through the layer of years, and I could see why the tabloids used to call her the Fireball. "I don't get many handsome young men come to call anymore, but I'd throw you out if you weren't Stormy's kid."

She seemed unaware of any contradiction. I sighed and stood up. "Those were his words, not mine."

The fire left her eyes and she nodded almost absently. "Ah, yes. Now I remember why he'd tell you that." She pulled herself up off the couch and I had the impression she'd grown heavy under the voluminous housecoat. The wiry energy I remembered was gone. "Sit down, Jonny. Have a drink with me. I try not to drink alone."

"Okay." I sat down. She was harder to refuse than Buck Rydell.

She brought a bottle of Scotch with a supermarket brand name out of a cupboard and rummaged around for glasses. "Neat or with water?" she asked.

"I'll have some water."

She poured Scotch and added water from the tap in the tiny bathroom. Then she came back and handed me a glass. "Health," she muttered without much conviction, and drank.

I echoed the toast and took a sip.

When she was back on the couch she said, "I've been feeling poorly. They found something wrong and I'm going to have some surgery Monday. Exploratory surgery, they call it."

I couldn't think of anything to say to that.

She coughed and lit a pink cigarette with a gold filter. "You're

**47**

a lot like him, you know. Come in a bigger package, but you've got the same look. Like you don't give a damn."

I refused a cigarette and took a swig of the Scotch. She couldn't guess I wasn't that fond of the comparison.

"I was crazy about him, did you know that?" She leaned forward and squinted at me. "Cat got your tongue?"

"I guess I'm just surprised, Aunt Kitty."

"I loved Oliver Loring too in a different way, but I never felt good enough for him. He was a gentleman, you see. I was a hellion out of a chorus line. I liked them with hair on their chest, like Stormy." She studied me with crafty old eyes. "I'm not trying to shock you, Jonny. Nowadays, I say what I like."

I smiled at her. "Didn't you always?"

She shook her head, slumped back on the sofa, and polished off her drink. "Ah God, if it had only been Gil or you my Monica wanted to marry!"

I made a frail attempt to lighten things up. "Well anyway, it looks like you might be the mother-in-law of a senator pretty soon."

"God help the country!" She reached to pour herself another drink, without water this time.

I wondered what Willie had done to earn her hatred. Kitty Mars had had an affinity for children we'd all felt. It was almost as if she'd been one of us.

As if she read my mind, she said, "I always loved kids. Willis was a strange boy, and I tried to be kind to him. But he despised us all, you see. Oliver saw through him from the beginning. 'That's a rotten apple,' he'd say . . ."

"We were hard on Willie. Maybe it turned him bitter," I suggested.

"No," she said definitely. "He's a monster, that's all."

"Someone tried to kill him, maybe Buck Rydell's son. I want to be sure because of Gil, Aunt Kitty." I finished my drink and put the empty glass on top of the TV.

She gave a wry laugh that became a cackle. "And for Gil's

sake I wish you luck. But I'll bet whoever it was had to stand in line to get a shot at that son of a bitch."

She didn't object when I stood up this time. She struggled off the couch, ignoring a helping hand. "I'm not that old yet, Jonny. Why, around here I'm a spring chicken!"

At the door curiosity got the best of me. I turned and asked her, "What did Willie do, Aunt Kitty?"

She stared up at me for a moment, her red slash of a mouth working. "Ah, never mind," she said at last. "There's no remedy anyway. Ask your father, if you're curious. But after I'm gone, understand? Not until then." She put her hand on my arm. "Come see me again, Jonny. Give my love to your dad. The old horse pistol."

"I will, Aunt Kitty."

She leaned against the doorjamb, smiled, and gave a great bawdy wink. For just an instant the years and the encumbering flesh slipped away and I glimpsed the Kitty Mars of long-gone Saturday matinees, lounging at the entrance of her boudoir or watching the hero canter his horse up to the saloon.

Well, sometimes we see what we want to see.

I drove down the ramp to Highway 101 and merged with the thickening traffic. It was Friday and everyone was trying to get out of town before the freeways turned into parking lots. Hollywood depresses me so I went over the pass on the 405 and then took the Santa Monica Freeway east. It was a clear day thanks to the desert wind and I could see downtown L.A. long before I got there, a cluster of high-rises against the distant crescent of snow-capped mountains.

The downtown area was still polishing its image and I counted a number of glassy new towers crowding the skyline, reflecting the bright sunshine from myriad windows, but there were also constants like the Central Plaza and Olivera Street, a bit of Mexico hemmed in by Chinatown, Little Tokyo, and the perennial blight of Skid Row. Union Station, all stucco arches and Spanish tile, had been around since the twenties to welcome the hustlers, starlets, and assorted expatriates who gave the town its color.

The county jail was behind Union Station, a dun-colored building that looked the part. As I went in, prisoners were being loaded into a paddy wagon called the Gray Goose for the short ride to the county courthouse a couple of blocks away. The place brought back memories. Everything was still painted a monotonous poison green and designed for maximal efficiency and minimal comfort. I identified myself, stated my mission, and proceeded through several grillwork doors, passing the booking area where handcuffs dangled from a long bench that was now prudently fastened to the wall so manacled prisoners couldn't simply get up and walk out with it, as had been done. Some fairly rough trade was being processed in, all blacks and Latinos, like the personnel admitting them. Around the corner was a cubicle for the bail bondsmen, who would be springing most of them when the process of arraignment was barely complete. There was an aura of acceptance and casual despair, the smells of antiseptic and decay.

Sordid as it was, I felt a tug of nostalgia. There's something exciting about the mean streets I can't easily explain. Maybe just the feeling of accomplishment when something goes down right against all those odds. Yet, right at the beginning, I'd been ready to quit. Working Vice had been almost more than I could handle, which is one reason no one is kept on that assignment much more than a year. The other reason is that some get to like it. Gil told me about his first partner, long before my time, a monster named Conrad who combed his eyebrows back over his forehead and claimed he had three rows of teeth. Gil believed him.

They were on what was referred to as "faggot patrol," staking out restrooms in Huntington Park, spying on the denizens through a peephole. Conrad would go down into the cubicles and entice them, which was illegal. When the subject put his penis through one of the holes bored in the wall between stalls for that purpose, Conrad burned it with his cigar. "One time," Gil swore, "he put a knitting needle right through a guy's joint and walked out leaving him trapped like that. Screaming."

Gil refused to continue working with Conrad, citing a personality clash because it was against the code to rat on a fellow officer in those days. I never met a cop remotely as bad as Conrad, but working Vice could be corrupting. I had to get past that.

They let me talk to Rydell in a room with a sheet of shatterproof glass between us. We used interphones and there was a monitoring device on the wall. I caught him looking up at it. "That's just to watch us," I told him. "No one can listen. This is a privileged conversation."

"My old man said you were a cop before." Young Rydell was as tall as I am and rawboned like his father with the same shelf of jaw, but there was no steel in his eyes, and instead of peering at far horizons they stared at something behind my head. He had long, sun-streaked brown hair, which he wore clubbed behind his neck. He wasn't a kid, at least twenty-five, but he seemed unformed to me, as if he hadn't set into any mold yet.

"I was, but I'm also a friend of the family." I kept my tone civil, even courteous, and tried to forget there was every chance this man had killed Gil.

"So that's why you're here. Not because the guy who got offed was your pal." He sounded detached, almost smug. I wanted to bring him down a little.

I smiled at him. "Let's get it straight from the beginning. Gil Buckler was my closest pal, almost a brother. I'm here to figure out for myself if you killed him. If I decide you did, I'll be around when you get out. That'll be in four years, seven max these days. You're fairly safe 'til then." I propped the phone against my shoulder and lit a cigarette, to hell with the NO SMOKING sign. My hands shook slightly.

Rydell didn't seem alarmed, but at least his eyes focused on me. He shook his head. "Wrong approach. I'm not scared of you, man. I'm talking to you because my old man asked me to, and he's paying for the lawyers. I don't have to listen to threats."

Maybe there was some steel in him after all. "What do I call you, Charles? Charlie? Chick?"

He shrugged. "I don't give a damn."

"Okay, Charlie, I've stated my purpose and my intention. Now I'd like you to tell me what happened the night Gil was murdered."

"You know how many times I've told it?"

"Once more, please?"

He thought it over and then gave me a recitation. "I went to the Pit Stop early, maybe seven, after surfing near the Venice Pier. I changed in my van and went in for some drinks, okay? I didn't have that many, but they really hit me. Maybe because I didn't eat anything all day, or since breakfast anyway. When I left it was dark, I remember that, but not what time it was. I got to my van and maybe I flaked out and maybe I drove home. I must've driven home because that's where I woke up. Feeling like a buzzard's lunch."

"You go in this Pit Stop a lot?"

"A lot. It's near where I live and near where I surf. The price is right."

"It's a dump though, isn't it? Who hangs out there?"

"Bikers. A few surfers, like me."

"Everybody gets along?"

"The bikers are heavies, but A-Frame doesn't like trouble, and he's big. He runs the place and lives there. I don't worry much because I'm big, too."

"And rough. Drunk and disorderly. Resisting arrest. Possession of narcotics and firearms. Et cetera."

Young Rydell shook his head as if I just didn't understand anything. "That was yesterday, man, in another life. I don't do that anymore. No violence. No guns."

"How about drugs?"

He hesitated and shrugged again. "I get high now and then."

"Okay, Charlie, what about the threats?"

He looked at me blankly. "Threats against Clewes," I reminded him. "Verbal and written on the typewriter they found."

Rydell looked as if he were disappointed in me. "I thought Dad told you all that stuff was planted."

"Let's talk about the threats you made that Thursday night in the Pit Stop. And others you made before."

"Listen, man, I said things maybe a year ago. Back when it still mattered to me what the old man thought. It got around because I'm his kid and because he was already in a big fight with Clewes." He paused for a moment and leaned back in his little plastic chair, perhaps organizing his material. "See, I grew up thinking Buck Rydell was God and I wanted to shine in his eyes," he said at last. "He taught me to ride, hunt, all that shit. I was never quite good enough to make him smile, but I kept trying. It made me a loud, angry bastard, trying to be just like him. Even a year ago I was trying, mouthing off about Clewes, still trying to make the old man smile." His free hand made a dismissive gesture in the air. "I don't give a shit anymore, you can believe that or not. I just want to be free to catch those big ones, maybe in the islands. There's something clean about the sea. If my old man wants to pay my way out of here hiring big-time lawyers or guys like you, hey, that's fine with me. He's just doing it for Buck Rydell, anyway."

That touched a nerve and I felt a moment of kinship. Buck Rydell's kid talking to Robert Storm's kid. "What about the other night, Charlie? You were still at it. This A-Frame says you threatened to kill Clewes then. He's got witnesses."

He seemed genuinely puzzled. "I can't figure it. I remember what I did and said, most of it, until I left. Why would I say anything like that anyway? I don't care about Clewes. They made it up, man."

"To frame you for the kill?"

"What else?"

"Why, Charlie?"

He couldn't answer that one.

"Did anyone even know you were going to the Pit Stop? Or when you'd be there?"

He still didn't say anything, but there was something furtive about his silence.

"Charlie," I said softly, "if no one knew you were going to be at the Pit Stop, then how could anyone set up the kill and lay it on you? You could have an alibi and then it wouldn't work. I mean, they *had* to know where you were, didn't they?"

He was slumping now, holding the interphone to his ear and gazing through me again.

"Your story won't play, Charlie," I told him, and stood up, cradling my phone. As I began to turn away I saw his lips move, so I sat down again to listen.

"A-Frame knew I was going to be there."

"Go on."

"He told me to be there, and he told me when."

"Why?"

"He had some stuff for me." The words dragged themselves out of him.

"Oh? What kind of stuff?"

"Coke."

"Let me guess, Charlie. You hustle shit for him. That's why you hang around the place."

"No. It was just for me." But there was no real denial in his voice.

"Horseshit. If it was just for you, you would have told the cops. It's not that bad a rap. What do you do for money? Your father doesn't give you any. You don't work. What keeps you in vans and surfboards?" I leaned back and stared at him. "You deal, Charlie."

His eyes flashed and he leaned forward, pressing the interphone to his ear with white knuckles. "I didn't kill your friend and that's all you need to know! You don't like the way I make a buck, then fuck you!"

I eased up a little, not wanting to lose him now. "You're

54

right about one thing. I don't give a goddamn how you make a buck. But I need to know anyway, because it's your only possible alibi. You can think of it as a threat or anything you like, but you're better off with me on your side, chum."

He relaxed, very slowly, and looked up at the monitor again. "Privileged conversation, you said."

"That's right."

"The bikers bring the shit up from Baja, okay? Wrapped in plastic and shoved in their gas tanks, or maybe up their ass. Three guys, very heavy. They deal with A-Frame and he puts it out on the street. Sometimes he lays a dime bag on me and I lay it out around the beach. Nothing like riding the waves with a little nose candy, you know? I do it myself, no big deal."

For a minute back there he had me thinking he was straight and that made me sore. I stood up and said to him, "There might be something clean about the sea, Charlie, but there's something dirty about you."

I hung up the phone and walked out. Another good exit line, but I didn't feel that righteous either. I remembered that Gil and I had snorted a time or two. Just for giggles, you understand.

# FIVE

ittle Tokyo still had the best sushi bars outside of Japan. I had a late lunch in one of them, tender slices of raw fish washed down with sake and Japanese beer. Then I drove out to Westwood and picked up the clothes that had been altered to my current dimensions. We were back on standard time, so the light was failing by five o'clock. Still, it was much too early for what I had in mind and I didn't want to go back to the castle. I changed a couple of bills and found a phone booth. Things to do to keep from drinking.

First, I called Capt. Norman Kling and persuaded him to give me Bill Clewes's unlisted phone number. He didn't want me to say where he got it. A woman with an undefinable foreign accent answered at Clewes's residence and when I gave her my name and asked for Monica Loring she said, "I will see if she is here," in a tone that implied the chances were pretty slim.

But Monica came on the phone almost immediately. "Jonny," she said. "Jonny Storm."

"Hello there, Monkey." I'll bet she hadn't heard that one in a long time. That's what we called her when we were kids, not because of any simian resemblance but because she could climb a tree or run around bases with the best of us.

She asked, "How long has it been? I'm almost afraid to hear."

"Oh, maybe a quarter of a century." I didn't remember her voice, or maybe it had changed. Well, it had been a long time.

"We feel terrible about Gil," she told me.

"At least they didn't get Willie, too."

"Bill. No, and I think he feels almost guilty about that. He doesn't say so but it's there. I know I feel guilty."

"Gil wanted the job, didn't he?"

"Yes."

"Then don't feel guilty." I wanted more from her than a chat on the phone. "I'm up from Mexico for a few days and I wonder if I could see you before I go back."

"Gil told me you live in Mexico. He said you went there after that awful mess with the police department."

I hoped she wasn't avoiding my suggestion. "I'll be going back in a few days. Any chance we can get together? I want to talk about Gil."

She hesitated, and I could feel her reluctance. It couldn't be her favorite subject. "Of course we can, Jonny. Look, everything's in turmoil with what happened and the campaign coming down to the line. Bill's on the road almost all the time and I'm right there with him, front and center. There's a lot of heat . . ." she paused, probably realizing I didn't much give a damn about her campaign under the circumstances, then went on after a beat. "Here's what we can do. Tomorrow we're having kind of a late brunch thing at the beach house. A few friends and supporters. A little pep talk to keep everyone on their toes, that kind of crap. Around one. It'll be nice to see you, Jonny. All those years. My God!"

I took down the directions to their house at Point Dume, listening for something to remind me of the girl I remembered, but it was the voice of a stranger. I sensed a lot of brisk, no-nonsense drive, an impatience with formalities.

After we hung up I drove to Santa Monica, parked on Ocean Avenue, and walked along the bluff overlooking the sea. The wind had shifted again and a fog bank hovered off the coast, ready to roll in. Older Santa Monicans had always used the park as a picnic ground and joggers had worn trails in the grass. Closer to the pier I began to see a new element, street-smart prowlers with calculating eyes. The predators were moving in.

I sat on a bench and smoked, watching them all go by—the old folks holding on to each other, joggers lean or suety, many wearing earphones to dispel boredom, grifters slinking along casing targets. Twilight turned to darkness while I thought about things that had happened long ago, and I couldn't really blame Monica for hesitating to invite me over.

Willie Clewes must have hated Gil and me. Thinking back, I wasn't proud of the way we treated him. At best we were casually arrogant, at worst downright cruel. Gil, who had the desk behind Willie's one semester, used a magnifying glass and a ray of sunshine to burn holes in Willie's shirt. The trick was to make your hole without burning the skin so you could go on to the next one undetected. It didn't occur to us that maybe Willie couldn't afford a new shirt. After that, Gil got an anonymous note saying, "I'll get you if it's the last thing I do," and we laughed, figuring it had to be from Willie.

Nature had conspired against Willie, too. He was pale in a tanned world, myopic, and possessed of too little chin. His complexion was bad, his teeth irregular. He had no athletic ability, shunned social events, and never went to the beach.

Even more unforgivable, he was smarter than we were. I remember he was captain of the junior high debating team, and when he was behind a rostrum, people listened. I won't say he was transformed or became a mesmerizer. Rather, he scored points with relentless logic and mild disdain. We didn't like him for it.

After we passed puberty and our relationships were altered by a new awareness of sex, the games we played underwent a not altogether subtle change. Monica was still a tomboy, a player even if she wasn't on a team. She went to the beach and surfed with us, one of the few girls who did, and now we were suddenly competing, showing off for her. She still had a spray of freckles across her nose, avoided makeup, and cut her own hair, but there were those new nubbins of breasts and the ripening heart-shaped butt. Gil liked to get her out in the water and play grab-ass, and I experienced my first searing pang of jealousy watching them out there.

Willie was never part of it. He lived on the grounds and Monica was civil to him, but that was all. The electricity was between the three of us—Monica, Gil, and myself. Once I kissed her in the surf, too, and when she responded I lived on it for a week. She played us off against each other with an instinct dating back to Eve, but Gil always had the edge. I thought then that it was his looks or his easy grace on a surfboard, but now I realize it was a matter of attitude. At his most effective, Gil didn't *seem* to try at all, and no one could leave indifference unchallenged. But he never did get Monica under the pier. I would have known.

Trying to relate all that to the present suggested there were no easy equations in life. Monica marries Willie, whom she scorns, who hires Gil, whom he hates, who loses his life protecting Willie, whom he despises. Of course, people change and many years had passed, but I couldn't wait to see what evolution of personality had led to this string of ironies.

The fog rolled in, turning the evening cool. I ate at a seafood restaurant just in front of the Santa Monica pier and then walked back to my car. Despite the weather, I left the top down as I drove along Ocean Avenue toward Venice; I'd be back in the tropics soon enough. South of the pier the city grew seedy. The streets were littered and derelicts roamed the shadows. Gangland graffiti defaced crumbling walls and businesses lowered heavy iron grilles to protect their wares at night. The Pit Stop was at the end of Washington Street near the beach, a sprawling saloon that looked as if it were assembled from odds and ends of driftwood. I cruised around until I found a place to park half a block away and walked back. Three bikes were parked in a cluster out front, Harley-Davidson choppers, of course. They were hardtails with Springer front forks, mean bikes, and only one had chrome trim and a helmet affixed to it. A black helmet with white Maltese crosses on the side.

Inside, the place was mayhem waiting to happen. Sawdust on the floor, bits and pieces of motorcycles racked on the wall, bar stools chained together. A rock-a-billy quartet was warming up, testing their electronics for later, when the Saturday-night clientele came out from under their rocks. Meanwhile, at ten o'clock, there were a few early drinkers hunched over glasses at the bar or sitting at small wooden tables along the wall. They were mostly rednecks with bellies and beards, a few hard-looking women in jeans.

The bikers were easy to make. They sat at a table together drinking shots and beers, an oddly assorted trio. Two of them must have been around my age, a thin one in a sleeveless Levi's jacket with long, lank hair fringing a bald crown and a burly, mustachioed type wearing a leather vest and studded leather thongs on his wrists. Nothing unusual there, but the third one caught my attention. He was younger, maybe thirty, and his blond hair was spiky on top and slicked back along the sides. He wore leather too, all leather, but it was soft, expensive, and tailored. The jacket emphasized broad shoulders tapering to a tiny waist; the trousers molded muscular thighs and were tucked into shiny boots. He was clean-shaven and looked clean-cut, though his eyes were hidden behind mirrored, wrap-around shades. He would be the one with the fancy bike and the helmet. Color him Roger Ramjet. They all had one thing in common, though. Heavy shit-kicking boots with steel rims. Stompers.

You couldn't miss A-Frame either, looming behind the long bar. He was a pinhead. His huge body had the shape of a pyramid, beginning with the tiny head, swelling into a thick neck that widened somewhat to massive, sloping shoulders, much broader hips, and legs like tree trunks. The face was an evil child's with little, close-set eyes, a button nose, and pouty, rose-petal lips. The hair looked like rat's fur, colorless and cropped. His physiognomy was clearly the result of some disease but I didn't feel any sympathy for him. I chose a bar stool away from everyone and when he came over I ordered a beer, just in the bottle, thanks. When he brought it, I said, "You must be A-Frame."

The little eyes, devoid of brows or lashes, peered at me sullenly. "No one calls me that." He had a high, reedy voice. "My name is Chester Herlinger. My friends call me C. H. You can call me Mr. Herlinger."

"Whatever's right," I replied equably. "I'd like to talk to you before you get too busy. Got a moment?"

"Gimme one reason I want to talk to you."

"Chick Rydell."

That got to him. He blinked and the little lips puckered. "So?"

"I just paid him a visit. He told me things he didn't tell the cops, probably because I'm not a cop. I mean, he told me about your biker pals bringing shit up from Mexico for you to spread around and how he got it out on the beach for you. He wouldn't tell the cops because it's a bad rap, almost as bad as murder these days. But I put him in a bind and I think he'll change his mind."

"You're not a cop, who are you?"

"An interested party. A friend of the deceased, meaning the guy who was killed."

"So what's that to me?"

"Chick says you set him up."

"Fuckin' Chick Rydell's crazy! He was in here yelling he was going to kill that Clewes. When he went and did it and I heard about it, I reported it like a good fuckin' citizen. I got witnesses he said that!"

"Those guys?" I inclined my head in the direction of the bikers.

"Yeah."

"That's great. I'll bet they're all real clean."

"Shakedown artist." He made it a statement.

I shook my head and drank beer out of the neck of the bottle. "No, it's worse than that. I don't want money. I want names, two names. The name of the individual who put out a contract on the assemblyman and the name of the punk who hit Gil. You don't fit the description."

The malign baby face screwed itself up in rage and the little mouth popped open. "You're not gonna bum-rap anyone, asshole!"

I went on. "Here's how it looks to me. You put Chick to sleep while one of the punks went out to hit Clewes and got Gil instead. Afterward someone planted all the stuff at Chick's place, while he was still out. Now, you wouldn't want to kill a politician, what for? But you and the fellas over there would do anything for money, right?" I looked steadily into the tiny, furious eyes. "Your punk blew the job and you're probably in deep shit right now, so I may be doing you a favor. I don't give a damn about you or the coke trade. Give me names that check out and you can stay in business," I lied. "Hang tough and I'll take your act apart, with Chick naming names, times, and places. The narcs will be all over you like a wet dream even if you don't take a fall for murder one."

Someone hollered at him, one of the bikers. A-Frame turned away from me without a word and drew three draft beers, which he put on a tray along with three shots of whiskey. He waved away a slatternly waitress and carried the tray to the table himself. I watched the bikers turn to look at me as he passed the drinks around, three blank, passionless faces examining a foreign object that might require removal. The young one took off his shades for a better look. He wore fine black gloves. It wouldn't have bothered me at all back when I had a badge and a gun.

All I had now was conjecture. I could beat the bushes and see what came slithering out, but if they stood pat I didn't have any fresh moves. A-Frame came back carrying the empty tray. "You got nothin'," he said. "Maybe a little nuisance value."

I finished my beer and stood up, putting the bottle down. I sighed and looked around the Pit Stop. "You can say good-bye to this joint, A-Frame. *Sayonara.* I'm going to change your lifestyle. There are a whole different kind of bars in your future."

His skin went pale and greasy as he held himself in. "Nuisance is all," he repeated. "Worth maybe a couple of bills not to get hassled."

I put down a bill of my own, a five. "I don't need money, just names. Keep the change."

He leaned on the bar. "You got a name? Someplace you live if I want to get in touch?"

"To talk?"

He shrugged.

I picked a pack of house matches off the bar and looked at the phone number. "I'll call you." But it was all wrong. I didn't get the idea he wanted to talk, just stall me.

When I turned to leave the bikers were gone and I thought, Oh shit. I went out into fog as thick as cotton batting, walking fast. The street lights were far apart, dim halos in the night, and the fog drifted by in patches, allowing glimpses in between, but I didn't see the goddamn Harley-Davidsons anywhere. I ducked between parked cars and crossed Washington Street toward the Chrysler. Two shadows slouched by arguing in Spanish and someone started a car with a porous muffler, making me jump. It didn't really sound like a bike, but the flatulent roar would drown out other engine noises. I found the Chrysler, jumped in and fired it up, then got the hell away from there.

Traffic was light on Washington, but by the time I reached Lincoln and turned north toward the freeway there were lights oncoming and behind me. I couldn't pick out any singles that looked like motorcycles and decided I was just getting antsy in my maturing years.

A-Frame hadn't given me much beyond a feeling; I believed Charlie Rydell now, or wanted to. I could talk to Kling and tell him about the coke dealing, but it wasn't much to act on and it probably wouldn't help Charlie. Cops don't like to open a fresh can of worms when they think they've got a case all wrapped up, and I rated Kling a cautious man from experience. But there wasn't much else I could do. Tomorrow's reunion with Monica and Willie wouldn't be much more than a formality, a polite exchange of consolations. After that I could give my information to Kling and drive back to Mexico telling myself I'd given it my best shot.

The hell I could.

I turned off the San Diego Freeway at the Mulholland off ramp, heading for the castle. Just above the bridge over the freeway I broke out of the fog into a clear, bright night. Warm, dry desert air had fought the ocean-borne cold front to a standstill just below the ridges of the Santa Monica mountains, and the lights of the San Fernando Valley looked like a carpet of stars.

Mulholland curves sharply along the ridge and I was too intent on driving to see the bikes until I was through the dogleg beyond Roscomare Road. The three of them came snarling up behind me and one gunned on by to pull in well ahead, like an outrider. The other two stayed back and rode side by side, just as they must have back in the fog, to look like any ordinary car in case I checked my mirror.

Instinctively I hit the gas, but they'd picked their spot well. Mulholland winds for miles along the summit, a narrow, treacherous road with hairpin turns and sheer drops into steep ravines already littered with the twisted, burned-out shells of nocturnal drag racers. On a straight course I could have run away from them, or over them if they got in my way, but the big Chrysler was mushy even on gentle turns and I didn't want to end up airborne over the valley.

One of the pair behind me cut out to pull alongside and they had me bracketed. It was the skinny guy in the sleeveless Levi's jacket, long ratty hair blowing back from his bald head. He turned to grin at me and then I saw him pull a sawed-off shotgun from a canvas scabbard chained to the sissy bar. The stock was chopped down too, so he could fire it single-handed like a pistol.

As the twin barrels came up, I yanked the wheel hard left, ramming the Chrysler into him, herding him completely off the road, over the shoulder, through a fringe of brush, and into space above the canyon. He howled into the void, firing his shotgun in final, bitter defiance, and I glimpsed the orange muzzle blast and the red gleam of a falling taillight as I wrestled the convertible back onto the road, rear end fishtailing and wheels churning to find purchase in the loose dirt.

The road dropped into a draw and I used all of it getting the car back under control. Another rider was still behind me and my headlights picked up the one in front, looking back now, his face a pale blur beneath the black helmet. I didn't know if they were familiar with the road, but I was. Pop's place was less than a mile away, just west of Beverly Glen. Beyond the next turn lay about a hundred yards of straightaway, so I came out of the curve fast with the biker right on my tail and when I hit the brake he had nowhere else at all to go. The Harley smashed into my rear with an impact that jolted the big car and the rider flew over his machine into the Chrysler's front seat. He hit the windshield with enough force to kill him, I suppose, but that probably wasn't what did it. His head wedged into the angle between the raked-back windshield and the dashboard while the body slumped down below the level of the seat. They must have heard his neck break down in the valley. From this grotesque position he faced me in the moonlight, with dead, unfocused eyes, black blood leaking through his mustache below the smashed nose. I reached around him to open the passenger door and then leaned back and braced a foot against his shoulder. Finally it took both feet and three hard kicks to dislodge him and roll him out of the car.

When I turned my attention back to the road, the last rider was straddling his bike just within range of my beams. He was peering back, probably trying to make out what was happening, but I doubted he could see much looking right into the lights. Maybe I could suck him in. I kicked the dimmer switch, blinking the lights up and down in a signal I hoped he'd interpret as friendly. He'd heard the shotgun and if he hadn't seen his pal go over the cliff, he might just think they'd taken me out.

But he was cautious. He came tooling back slowly, my lights glinting off the chrome on his bike and the Maltese crosses on his helmet. I dropped the gear shift into low, waiting for him to come closer, trying to see if he had both gloves on the handlebars or if he was holding a gun.

He stopped half a dozen yards away, a trim, sinister figure astride the rumbling machine. "Chucho?" he called. "Noodle?"

I decided he wasn't coming closer and stepped down on the gas pedal, but the wheels spun on the pavement before they grabbed hold, giving him a moment he shouldn't have had. The big car jumped at him but he was very fast, leaning away from the left fender as it brushed him and then roaring past me back in the direction of the freeway. I didn't even try to turn the Chrysler around and go after him. It would have been a waste of time. At least I'd memorized the license number on his Harley.

No one at all had come by during the encounter, but Mulholland was a lonely road at that time of night. I left Noodle or Chucho where he was and drove the short way to Pop's, letting myself through the gate with the little genie gizmo. The Dobies came ghosting out of the shadows, sleek, silent and dangerous, but they recognized me and let me pass after a sniff or two.

Everyone had gone to bed. I poured myself a beaker of Jack Daniel's at the bar and took it up to my room. I sipped bourbon and tried to watch TV but couldn't track with it even though the tube was something of a novelty again after five years. Time crawled by like a snail on Valium while I stared blankly at the on-screen violence and planned some of my own. At one-forty-five I took out the Beretta and shoved fourteen shells in the staggered clip. I didn't take along any extra rounds. If you can't do it with fourteen, forget it.

# SIX

The Pit Stop was closed and darkened, just as I'd hoped to find it. I parked well away and reconnoitered the street. Nothing leaped at me out of the fog but I heard stirrings in the dim passageways between decrepit buildings. A cough, a murmur, the clink of a bottle. Venice night sounds.

Charlie Rydell had said A-Frame lived on the premises and the Pit Stop was a single-story structure, so his quarters shouldn't be hard to locate. The building fronted on Washington Street and sided on a bike path bordering the beach. That part would be the bar and no light was showing, suggesting A-Frame lived in back. A high, weathered wooden fence enclosed the space between the saloon and the adjacent property and I circled past the front to the far side, looking for an easier way.

A low chain-link fence guarded the alley. I climbed it easily, hoping there was no junkyard dog back there. The alley was narrow and half a dozen foul-smelling plastic garbage containers nearly blocked the way. I squeezed by, breathing through my mouth and hearing the scurry of disturbed rats, and went around to the rear.

There was a back door and next to it a grimy window with peeling sashes that looked painted shut. I peered cautiously through glass so dirty it was nearly opaque. A-Frame was in there, though, facing the door, his shapeless bulk crammed behind a metal desk.

I drew back and examined the door. It looked flimsy enough to kick in, but I tried the knob anyway. Locked. I pulled the Beretta from my waistband and booted the panel just under the lock as hard as I could. Wood splintered and the door flew open with me right behind it, the Beretta raised at arm's length. "Get your hands on the desk!" I yelled. The room smelled as sour as an animal's cave.

A-Frame didn't hesitate at all. He put his hands behind the desk and shoved. The desk, on casters, came rolling across the hardwood floor at me and I had to jump aside. A-Frame came right after it, ignoring my gun, a fast fat man. When they do that, they're either on something or plain crazy. Everyone thinks when you've got a gun people are going to obey you, but cops should know better. I hesitated because I didn't want to kill him, compounding my error. I lowered the Beretta and tried to blow off his kneecap but the bullet took him higher, in the meat of his massive thigh, with no visible effect. He clubbed me across the head with an arm like a log and I flew backward into a wall, dropping my pistol. He crowded in and rammed the same massive forearm against my throat, pinning me against the wall and leaning against me. He weighed well over three hundred pounds and the room began to go dim, blackness edging in around the corners.

I reached down to grope for his genitals, got a grip on scrotum and testes, and twisted hard. He screamed like a woman and the arm fell away from my throat as he leaned forward in an awkward bow, clutching at himself. I picked the Beretta off the floor and brought the barrel down on his head, peeling away scalp to the bone. Blood welled up and poured from the wound, but he didn't go down. I stepped forward, bringing my knee up into his face, and he finally toppled onto his side and then rolled over on his back. I put the same knee, sore as hell now, into his huge belly and jammed the pistol into his mouth through whatever might be left of his teeth. He gagged and blew bloody bubbles through his nose and mouth.

"When I take the gun out, you're going to give me some names," I told him. "Nod if you agree. If you don't, you're dead. You've got maybe three seconds."

The monster beneath me convulsed and heaved, throwing my two hundred and fifteen pounds off of him like a dog sheds water. I rolled away toward the wall, saw him looming above me on his knees, and tried to bring the gun around for a head shot, finish this nightmare once and for all.

Someone else opened fire before I could lift the Beretta. A red blossom appeared on A-Frame's forehead, bits of hair, bone, and brain tissue splattering the wall behind me. The small room echoed with gunfire, making it hard to judge the number of shots. A-Frame collapsed beside me, his body jerking as more bullets found him. I sheltered in back of him like a cowboy behind his downed horse and swung up the Beretta.

Roger Ramjet crouched in the doorway holding a snub-nosed revolver in both hands, a surreal figure in black leather with the spiky hair and wrap-around shades, fog coiling around him like chemical smoke on some futuristic movie set. I snapped off two shots that went wild, splintering the door frame beside him, and he sprang back into the night. I rolled away from A-Frame, got my legs under me, and ran to the door, but he was out of sight in the fog, boots clicking far down the alley.

The office smelled of gunsmoke and feces, for A-Frame had voided in death, as though the corruption had seeped out of him to find another host. His walls were covered with photographs, all kiddy porn. Children of both sexes exhibiting their immature genitalia, innocently or under duress. Children servicing adults or being abused by them. Children naked and in bondage. I looked down at A-Frame and wished he were alive so I could kill him myself.

It occurred to me to search the place, but even in Venice someone might report that much gunfire and I didn't want to risk a confrontation with the cops. I killed the lights and slipped out, going around to scale the fence on the beach side. It was a high son of a bitch and I fell heavily onto the cement bike path, but I didn't want to go down the alley where Roger might be waiting with a reloaded gun.

A few dogs barked but no lights came on; no police sirens wailed in the night. The fog covered everything with a cold, clean blanket—littered, pitted streets, bindle stiffs huddled in alleys and doorways, the living and the dead. No one cared what happened at the Pit Stop because it hadn't happened to them. Venice was inured to violence.

For the second time that night I found my car in the fog and drove away from there, this time making very, very sure there was no one behind me, weaving an intricate pattern through the deserted streets before picking up the freeway. After that, the car seemed to find its own way home, like a horse with an exhausted rider. It had been a long day.

Point Dume is a northern outpost of Malibu on the ocean side of the Coast Highway, perched on a stretch of high bluffs overlooking the sea. Once it was too far from Los Angeles to be geographically desirable, but the city has reached out to change that. Now the elaborate homes of celebrities stand cheek by jowl with the little cottages and cement slab houses of earlier arrivals. High-walled estates coexist beside hardscrabble *ranchos* that seem to raise little more than tall grass and domestic animals.

To reach what Monica called their beach house I turned off the highway at Zumirez Road and followed it down to the bluffs above the sea. The house was at the end of the street, surrounded by a stone wall as high as Pop's and guarded by a gate of green sheet metal. Maybe that was because the property next door had a couple of rusted-out Chevys up on blocks in the front yard and a dozen chickens pecking around an unkempt lawn. The common touch is just fine, my hosts seemed to be saying, but within (or outside of) boundaries.

It was twelve-thirty, making me early, but I wanted a chance to talk to Monica before things became hectic. I'd slept late and dressed in a blazer, tan cavalry twill slacks, and reasonably comfortable loafers, ready for anything. Over coffee, the radio informed me of current events. On the local front, two motorcyclists had died on Mulholland Drive in accidents that may or may not have been related. One had plunged over a cliff, starting a brush fire in the canyon below that was swiftly extinguished. Identification was being withheld pending notification of next of kin. More surprising to me was the news that an explosion and fire had totally gutted the Pit Stop at approximately 5:00 A.M. The charred remains of a body believed to be that of the proprietor who lived on the premises were found, but positive identification would depend on dental records. There was no report of any earlier disturbance or of gunshots. Mulling that over, I stopped off in Santa Monica, broke down the Beretta, and walked out on the pier to dispose of the pieces in the sea. I'd left too many bullets around the Pit Stop, including one in A-Frame.

Two gentlemen in an unmarked car stepped out of their vehicle to check my name against a list before passing me through the gate, and I guessed Gil's successors were from the Malibu sheriff's office, even in civvies. They had the look and anyway I doubted security was still in the hands of private enterprise after what had happened. Beyond the gate lay a long semicircular gravel driveway with half a dozen cars parked along its perimeter and room for more. The front door was informally open and I walked through high-ceilinged rooms with paneled walls and hardwood floors, throw rugs and casual, overstuffed sofas. A solid home for just plain folks but pretty big for a beach house.

The party was out in back on a half-acre or so of manicured lawn leading to a bluff with a view of the Pacific. Looking around for Monica, I took a quick reading on other early arrivals. They were a diverse and colorful group that could have been sent over by central casting. There was a Jesse Jackson look-alike, flamboyantly tailored in a dove-gray suit with spread-collared shirt and wide tie. Listening to him was a stereotypical aging radical with facial hair and balding crown, rumpled tweed jacket, blue jeans, and sneakers without socks. Maybe an old Berkeley alumnus, nodding and dreaming of Mario Savio. A clutch of Latinos in neat suits stood together self-consciously, speaking in Spanish. I saw a youngish woman dressed like a bag lady with a trio of kids who looked like they'd been sired by three different fathers clinging to her soiled skirts.

Monica came out of the house carrying a tray of hamburger patties and hot dogs, followed by Willie with the buns. They put the food down near an outdoor barbecue and people seemed unconsciously to edge over in their direction. I'm not an avid rock fan but I've always liked Monica's laid-back California style and there's no way to miss her media coverage, even in Mexico. Now she was wearing tight jeans, an oversized man's shirt—which failed to hide the firm, unhaltered thrust of her breasts—and not a trace of makeup. She had a quick, positive stride, both sexy and athletic, and from where I stood she looked not unlike the teenager I knew long ago. Beside her, Willie was no surprise either. He was still a stranger to the sun and he hadn't grown any more chin. He wore baggy flannel trousers, a cardigan sweater, and had a five-dollar haircut. He didn't look like a politician, but then he no longer looked like a dangerous revolutionary either.

I worked my way over to them and said, "Hi, Monkey. Willie. Jon Storm, in case I've changed."

"Well, Jonny!" She flashed me a quick smile and gave me a firm hand to shake. Her hair fell across her forehead in bangs and she still had a trace of freckles around her nose that made her look younger than any amount of makeup could. "Of course I recognize you!"

I shook Willie's hand in turn. He looked up at me with a thin smile. "You've filled out," he told me, and we all chuckled at that. I'd been lanky as a boy.

We said things like "It's been a long time" and of course

Willie told me how sorry he was about Gil, but we quickly ran out of small talk. The Berkeley type came to my rescue, putting a hand on Willie's arm and murmuring in his ear. I grabbed the opportunity and said to Monica, "Can we talk alone for a moment? I came early because I knew you'd be busy later."

She hesitated, then made up her mind. "Sure. Come along with me."

I followed her to the edge of the bluff and down a long flight of wooden stairs to a private beach not unlike the one below my place in Puerto Vallarta, only larger. The water would be colder, too. I glanced around and said, "Very nice."

"I used to come here with Fang." She suddenly looked sad. "He loved to go swimming."

"Your dog?"

She nodded. "A beautiful German shepherd. He was poisoned soon after we started getting the letters. They didn't bother us that much, just a lot of threats and obscenities. Everyone in politics gets hate mail, but after someone poisoned Fang I was really shaken and I called Gil."

I remembered the photocopies I'd seen at the police station. They'd been graphic and they'd mentioned the dog. "The letters got in the papers, didn't they?"

"Excerpts from them. There was some publicity after Fang was killed." Abruptly she changed the subject, shaking off her gloom, and pointed at the stairs. "A hundred and ninety steps," she said. "Every other day I run them two at a time, twenty times. Very aerobic."

I looked at the face of the cliff, high above us. "I'm just wondering how I'll get back up."

She laughed then, crinkling her eyes in a remembered way, and I experienced an instant of *déjà vu* that transported me to another beach and a time long ago. "You look like Bob Mitchum," she said, breaking the spell. "Only younger."

"So I've been told."

"It's in the eyebrows. A skeptical look."

"Maybe because I was a cop." I took out a cigarette and lit up.

Monica wrinkled her nose. "God! You still use those things? They'll kill you."

"How about Willie? Does he run up and down the stairs, too?"

"Bill. No, I can't get him to exercise but I'm not giving up yet."

"Looks like you've changed everything else about him."

She wasn't sure she liked that remark. "If you mean what I think, he changed himself. Not in substance or principle, just his style and tactics. He's the first person now to condemn violence. We can accomplish change through the avenues open to us and we're proving it."

"Which implies we're a democracy after all. Not a Fascist state as he's been quoted to say. And you, too."

The laugh crinkles disappeared. "Are you trying to provoke me?"

"No, Monkey. Just trying to understand how you got to be the fire-eating darling of the left. It seems the system intact has worked wonders for you."

She was angry now, and I could see that where the years had slackened Terri Buckler they had hardened and sharpened Monica Loring. The ridge of her jaw stood out sharply and two harsh little brackets formed at the corners of her mouth. "Do you remember when we were kids?" she asked me. "Those silly parties. Children being driven to them in chauffeured limousines like that horror of your father's with the silver antlers on the hood? My mother half drunk and bullying the servants, like Bill's father? I guess that's when it began. And later, being married to Ernesto brought everything into sharp focus."

"You seem to have made the most of it while knocking it, is what I'm saying. They're even opening a Moniquita in Puerto Vallarta."

"I've done well, Jonny, because I have a knack. I started the

73

first Moniquita to serve Mexican fast food because I saw a need for it. A marketing type came along and talked me into franchising. Moniquitas proliferated and a conglomerate bought me out. I still have a percentage worth a vulgar amount of money. I won't even bore you with how much the last album I produced made. I have half a dozen golds and as many platinums, do you know that? You're right, Jonny, I'm a huge success. Measured in dollars."

"And this flair for capitalism makes you feel guilty."

"Wrong!" Another line appeared between her brows and I couldn't honestly say she was beautiful when she got angry. She just looked hard. "The money I make will benefit the people one way or another. Most of it goes out as fast as it comes in. I invest it in the future of this country with the eventual goal of throwing out this elitist, warmongering government of ours and evolving a system that guarantees justice to all women and men!"

"By backing Willie's political campaigns," I suggested.

"Call him Bill, dammit! Yes, that's exactly right. Bill Clewes, a servant's son, will soon sit in the United States Senate. I'm proud to say I'll have helped put him there, just as I helped put him in the state assembly three times. After that, if you haven't guessed, I'm going to dedicate all my time and all my money to see him elected president of the United States! That's the only goddamn thing money's good for!"

She started to say more and then stopped abruptly. I was sorry, because she'd caught my interest. "But that's not what we're here to talk about, is it, Jonny?" she asked.

"No, it's not. I guess I'm just curious. Listen, you don't have to answer but how in hell did you get together with Willie . . . Bill, anyhow? I just know what I read."

For a second I thought she'd tell me it was none of my damn business, but then she relaxed and shrugged. "I was just another kid who could sing. Maybe a little better than my mother could act, which isn't saying much. I had a sugary style I copied from

Dinah Shore because girls couldn't sell rock in those days, you see. You may have read my first husband was that distinguished Colombian playboy, Ernesto Rojas, king of coffee and, it turned out, cocaine. Life with Ernesto was an education. I was twenty, he was forty-seven. Handsome, cultured, suave. And kinky. My mother loved him. There was the old family manse in Bogotá, the holiday house at Cartagena, some retreats in southern France, Switzerland, and New York. On the plantation he'd dress up in a Panama hat and jodhpurs and ride around with a whip. For sport he liked to shoot Indians out of the trees for stealing bananas . . ."

Maybe there are banana trees on coffee plantations, I don't know. I cut her off. "About . . . Bill," I prompted.

"Bill . . ." She paused as if to remember. She kicked off her loafers and snuggled her feet in the sand, standing hip-shot. I found it sexy. "I divested myself of Señor Rojas or he of me, I barely recall. I got serious about my career and won a Grammy for that saccharine I used to sing. But I found it didn't mean anything. Vietnam was going on and I learned about the enormity of the crime. Our crime. I changed my style and sang protest music. Mellow rock with a message. Joan Baez without the guitar. I was involved but I wasn't organized, and people laughed. Rich little Hollywood star, they figured. Female, on top of that." She shook her head and bit her lip, thinking about it. "Then I met Bill again. He'd been going to school in Mexico City at the University of the Americas. He came back when he didn't have to and became active. Stood trial for inciting a riot at the national convention that year. Went through hell but was vindicated finally. There's nothing on his record. Christ, he could have claimed a legitimate military deferment for a heart murmur, but he wouldn't do that." She snatched the cigarette out of my hand and took a deep drag, giving me back little more than an ember. "We talked. It was all wrong what we were doing. Not wrong, but we were going about it in the wrong way. The country wasn't ready for revolution . . ." She cut herself off right there and her eyes focused on me again—suspicious hazel eyes. "What is this, Jonny? You wanted to talk about Gil."

I lit another cigarette, just to buy a moment. I wanted to talk about Gil, true, but I thought I should clear the air first. I held up my left hand, calling attention to it for the first time I could recall. "Count 'em, Monkey. Four and a half, right?" I'm without the first joint of my little finger. I don't really miss it and nobody ever notices. It's just a reminder. "I'm pretty apolitical, Monkey, but while Willie was in Mexico and you were developing your social conscience wherever, I spent a year in Vietnam. It was a short tour and I was lucky. Eight months in combat without a scratch. Scared shitless, mind you. Not of little Charlie, you hardly ever saw him. Of the tiger traps full of bamboo spears he covered with human shit for you to fall into and the grenades he rigged to bounce up and explode at knee level, blowing your balls off. Charlie was a sneaky little runt who wore no uniform and never heard of the Geneva Convention . . ."

"You were in his country!"

I managed to speak softly. "No. He was in his neighbor's country." I kept my hand up to ward off rebuttal. "I'm almost finished. After eight months, I took R and R to Saigon. I got all dressed up, found the best-looking hooker all that saved-up pay could buy, and took her to the fanciest restaurant in town, which happened to be on a barge in the river. In the middle of the main course, some little birds baked in clay if I remember, a bomb went off and blew about forty people away. Almost all Vietnamese." I lowered my hand, feeling mildly ridiculous. "I was lucky again, just got nicked by some passing debris. The little darling with me wasn't, and I won't go into—"

"Don't you lay that on us, you bastard!" Monica shouted. "You Nazis and your concubines! We tried to keep America out of it, and when that didn't fly, we tried to stop the whole bloody mess."

"What you did," my voice rose with hers, "was bully the

politicians who ran this country out of giving us the kind of air support that would have saved the lives of about thirty thousand American infantrymen! And even then, I can testify that we lost a war without ever losing a battle! Not to mention what the South Vietnamese lost, beginning with their freedom."

A vein was pulsing on her forehead now and her face was a mask of rage. "Get out of here, Jonny! Swim out! Don't even come back to the house!" She whirled and started for the stairs.

"Hold it!" I shouted at her back. "Rydell's kid didn't try to kill Willie. That guy is still out there. Believe me, I know this!"

She paused, one bare foot on the first step, loafers forgotten back in the sand. I walked over to her. "Hell, Monkey, I probably can't even climb out of here." I lit two cigarettes and handed her one, just like they used to do in old movies. She puffed on it furiously, which I took to indicate a truce. "I said I wanted to talk about Gil, and I do. Willie—excuse me, Bill —didn't like me very much, but he really hated Gil. Why would he hire him?"

"We were kids, for God's sake! You're just like all the other righteous idiots. No one can change, according to you. Well, they got along fine! Gil was professional and Bill was correct. They didn't have to love each other!" She flung away her cigarette. "Now you just said something that requires an explanation. What makes you think Buck Rydell's son isn't guilty as hell?"

I wondered how much I could tell her and decided on a very edited version. "I talked to him and he told me he was set up," I said. "Then I talked to the man who fingered him, the owner of a dump called the Pit Stop, as you must have read, and provoked a violent reaction." A fair bit of understatement, that. "This morning I heard on the news that the Pit Stop is no more. Blown up along with its owner and most of the block, it seems. I'm enough of a cop to question coincidence. There's a strong stench of cover-up emanating from this whole matter. I'm suggesting Charlie Rydell was framed, C. H. Herlinger of the Pit

Stop was murdered, and the perpetrator of both killings is very much at large. Unfortunately, it may not be enough to reopen the case, being circumstantial evidence."

She looked at me soberly, her anger on the wane. "I agree that it's not. The Rydells have a motive. And they're Fascists." But she was listening.

I was getting tired of politics, Monica Loring's or Buck Rydell's. Gil's murder was becoming obscured in the mire of contending hatreds. "Willie might just have a few other enemies, don't you think?"

"Yes." She shivered, as though she felt a chill despite the sunshine, and her face softened. I had a fleeting impression of vulnerability and her beauty returned with it. Then she had herself in hand again. "I've got to get back, Jonny. There'll be a lot of guests by now. Thanks for the warning. We'll be very careful." She turned and started up the long flight of stairs.

Not much reaction to what I'd thought was rather startling news. But then it would be a pretty inconvenient time for Charlie Rydell to be released for lack of evidence and presumed innocent. His arrest had turned the odds on the election right around, from what I could gather. I followed Monica slowly up the stairs, watching the clench and roll of firm buttocks beneath tight denim, feeling the visceral tug of an old desire. I wondered how she could still burrow under my skin after all these years. I could almost hear Gil saying, "Go ahead, Jonny. You know she's too much woman for Willie the Weege. Take a swing at it! *I* would."

I wondered if he had.

The party on the lawn had grown, as Monica predicted, but I had the impression the people I'd seen earlier had simply cloned themselves in my absence. There were more blacks and Latinos, self-consciously well-dressed in contrast to the whites, who wore deliberately mismatched clothes and shaggy hair, as though they needed to defend their radical credentials. Most of the women were intense and unlovely, with the look of militants about to organize a march or a riot. They'd have made good parade marshals. A smattering of yuppies seemed uncomfortable but determined to fit in. I recognized a character actor known to be at the forefront of liberal causes and a former California governor, each presiding over his own circle. Willie's coalition had some stretch to it.

I rooted around in a plastic cooler full of melting ice and located a beer among the soft drinks. People were scattered around munching hot dogs and hamburgers in a picnic atmosphere, but there was that air of anticipation you see just before a show goes on. When Willie ambled out of a group to the center of the lawn, it was the signal for everyone to gather round. Someone rolled out a barrel, presumably for him to stand on, and that got a laugh. But there was more expectancy than humor in the crowd.

Willie stood with his hands in the pockets of his cardigan, blinking around mildly at his audience. He put one foot on the barrel, acknowledging the joke, and another little ripple passed through the spectators.

"It's going to be close," were his first words, "but we're going to win. Oligarchs and oil barons beware!"

There was immediate, enthusiastic applause. Someone yelled "We care!" and the cry was taken up, so I guessed it was a campaign catchphrase. Willie looked around with the slight, crooked smile I remembered and held up a hand.

"You will have made it possible," he continued. "You, the people—freethinkers, independents, Democrats ... Republicans."

The last word produced muffled sounds of scoffing, but Willie overrode them. "I said Republicans, yes, because we are all the people and we welcome the allegiance of individuals from every party, race, religion, or sexual persuasion." He raised his voice just a little. "And this is very important. In these final days every one of you, each in his or her capacity, will have hundreds of contacts with voters, as individuals and in groups. Many will be hostile. For our message to have the widest appeal finally, it must initially be concentrated as narrowly as a laser—on the simplest, strongest concerns affecting the audience before you at the time." He paused and looked around. "Any reporters here today?"

That got a laugh and I could safely assume the press had been screened out of this gathering of the faithful.

"I've said it before, I'll say it again," Willie continued. "And again, and again. The rich breathe the same air. They own the coastal areas that will overlook oil derricks and drilling platforms. From Malibu to Beverly Hills to the enclaves of privilege in the north of the state, we're going to talk about pollution and pollutors, about oil companies and oil spills, about manufacturers, smog, and toxic waste dumpers, and we will tuck them all between the sheets with Buck Rydell."

There was applause interspersed with shouts of "We care!" but I noticed the black and Latino politicos were more reserved, almost condescending. Willie's eyes turned to them. "Our brothers and sisters in the inner cities know their people and they don't need my advice. Older people on fixed incomes know we are the party of rent control and justice for seniors. The poor and needy will turn to us." He took another pause and then said, very soberly, "But we have problems."

I believe he had most of them holding their breath, rapt, though what he was saying could hardly have been new to them. Standing there, not tall, and somewhat rumpled, his slightest signal produced a Pavlovian response. Then I remembered him on the debating team, all those years ago. He had the gift; it was as simple as that.

"In recent years we have seen a return of jingoism, of false patriotism and the kind of false pride that goes before a fall," he said quietly.

A rumble of agreement.

"There exists an element all across the social spectrum of this nation that rejoiced in the rape of Grenada and would welcome a similar solution to the turmoil in Central America. I don't have to tell you how our present administration welcomes and encourages this." He had to hold up a hand for silence. His listeners hissed and spat like a sackful of angry cats.

"You will confront this attitude with a single word," Willie told them, and then paused for effect. "Vietnam . . . Vietnam . . . Vietnam!" With each "Vietnam," he struck his thigh with his fist. It was the emotional part of his delivery, and his flock went wild. Throughout the ovation he looked at the grass near his feet, frowning, disturbed.

Someone standing next to me clapped resoundingly, exactly three times, and murmured, "That's my boy!" perhaps to himself. I turned and saw a man near my own age with a round, ruddy face and fine, flaxen hair that stirred in the slightest breeze. He was watching me, little eyes twinkling like cold, blue sapphires, dimples bracketing his smile. He looked like the good guy on a police interrogation team, or maybe a friendly Gestapo man.

"Monica told me you were one of the family," he said, sticking out his hand. "I asked about you because you looked kind of like a square peg in this bunch. Not one of the troops, I mean."

"Thanks." I took his hand, which was stronger than it looked. "We were kids together. The three of us and Gil Buckler."

The man shook his head sorrowfully. "Gil. We had a lot of laughs, Gil and I." He bowed his head for a moment of silence, then looked up and said, "I'm Jim Quest. I call myself a public relations counselor."

"And you knew Gil."

He nodded. "We were a tight little group, each with his or her own function, part of a team. Gil talked a lot about you. I feel as if I know you myself."

"Did he tell you how we used to treat Willie?"

Quest threw back his head and laughed. "Oh, yes! And that's one thing Bill doesn't like to be called. Gil found it a hard habit to break."

"I've kind of wondered why Willie ever hired him."

"Well, Monica had a lot to do with it and I think Bill kind of enjoyed the idea, you know? He never treated Gil like a servant but he gave the orders and there must have been some satisfaction in that."

"In getting even?"

"Hell, no! But maybe just as a little reminder of how far he'd come. That's only human. And Gil, well, he was being paid and he found the situation amusing. Gil found everything funny, didn't he?"

"Just about."

We looked back at Willie, who was fielding questions now, the little smile back on his face. A hefty creature with a butch haircut wearing camouflage fatigues and combat boots raised her hand and shouted something I didn't catch about the death penalty.

"I'm with you, Selma." Willie nodded agreeably. "But we're going to walk right around that one. You see, first we've got to win."

His remark met with general approval, but I heard the big woman mutter, "Shit, that's a cop-out," as she shook her massive shoulders.

Gil, who put women into categories, would have called her a Beef Trust, his tag for the fat ones. Girls with big breasts were Guernseys and little ones were Spinners. This one looked like the bouncer in a lesbian disco.

"One of the troops?" I asked Quest.

He shrugged. "We've been trying to lose that dirtbag for months, but she keeps coming back like herpes. Some of the others may look pretty loosely wrapped too, but they're good foot soldiers. Work their little hearts out for the cause." We were on the outer fringe of the crowd around Willie. Quest nodded toward the dapper Jesse Jackson look-alike standing slightly aloof at the opposite side of the circle. "But there's muscle here, too. The black guy with the fag tailor's Lester Prime—real close to the mayor. One of the Latinos is on the city council and I guess you've seen our ex-governor and a former president of the Screen Actors' Guild.

"See, our problem is running for the United States Senate isn't like running for the state assembly. Bill's district was full of welfare bums and old folks concerned about rent control. That's all he had to talk about to win. Maybe throw in the environment and recycling bottles and cans, shit like that. Now he's got to appeal to a wide constituency and face a lot more issues. Trying to win this year in California if you're against the death penalty and for gun control is like pissing against the wind, and Rydell's pushing hard. So we've got to back-pedal on those things, hit hard on others. We've got to form alliances."

Willie had taken his foot off the barrel, indicating his address was coming to a close. "Something always to remember," he cautioned, serious now, his voice cutting through the commentary. "We're out to win an election, not an argument. Never let yourselves be baited. Never talk down to anyone, no matter how ignorant you find them. And never, never show contempt."

"At least not until after November fourth!" shrieked the Beef Trust, probably stealing his exit line. November fourth was election day, and the big woman got a hand. Even Willie smiled his thin little smile and waved good-naturedly, but I don't think he liked it.

Quest nodded approvingly. "I taught him that. Bill used to like to stick it in people and break it off. That doesn't win votes."

I asked him, "If Willie's on the wrong end of the big issues, what's he got going for him?"

"If I were immodest, I'd say me." Quest smiled. "Seriously, then. The environment. Nuclear disarmament among the young and everyone else who's scared shitless of the bomb. Most of the unions, especially the teachers and farm workers. Everyone on welfare who votes. And the liberal press. Bill gets good press and we work at it. Think that doesn't count? Remember when people wanted to hang him for going to Hanoi?"

"Yeah."

"Well, there are still some of those out there, but we turned it around. He apologized for *how* he acted, never for *why*. In World War II, he'd have been strung up, but the media hated Vietnam, so they bought it and Bill's a concerned liberal today. Nixon covered up a second-rate burglary he never even authorized and got run out of the most powerful office in the world." Quest held up his finger like a schoolteacher. "Power of the press!"

"Is it going to be enough?"

"No."

I stared at him. "Then you're saying Willie's not going to win."

"Oh, he'll win."

I was confused. "Why?"

Quest's merry little eyes twinkled at me. "Because Buck Rydell's kid tried to kill him."

We sauntered across the lawn together in the direction of the house. Apart from the nucleus competing for Willie's attention, the crowd had separated into clusters. Some of them were fishing in the cooler for soft drinks or lining up for burgers and hot dogs. It looked like a carefree neighborhood picnic. From a distance.

Jim Quest was explaining himself. "I'm more like Henry Higgins than Rasputin," he confided. "I alter the image without converting the subject. You should have seen Bill when I found him. Both of them, for that matter. They weren't in the political fast lane or even on the track—they were out in left field. And she had all that money . . ." He shook his head in recollection. "I took Bill on as a client, got that long hair cut off and took him out of his dirty Ho Chi Minh T-shirt. Dressed him up like Everyman in those baggy flannels and shit-kicking shoes and that skinny tie with the little bitty knot. Know how hard he has to pull to get the knot that small? We even fray his shirts as soon as we buy 'em and throw away the collar stays." Quest laughed and bummed one of my cigarettes, but when I lit it for him he choked on the smoke. "Jesus, what are those?"

"Mexican. I started them when I was trying to quit and got to like them. At least there's no nicotine in horseshit."

He pitched away my cigarette and pulled out a pack of Winstons. "Anyway, I restructured Bill Clewes to make him a palatable candidate for the common man. That's my business. Winning. I package winning products."

"You just do the cosmetics, then."

"A little more than that. I also put my expertise and my staff at his disposal. We have early access to most polls and we're equipped to make our own surveys on issues that concern us particularly. Then we combine information with experience and prep the candidate. We're the cutting edge of his campaign. It's an expensive service, but I'm the best and they can afford me."

"So you've been with Willie since he went into . . . conventional politics?"

"Since day one, and I'm staying for the whole trip."

"And you believe in him."

"Once he gets past this one, he'll be in position and he could go all the way. He's bucking a conservative tide right now, but the political climate can change overnight once this president's out. Some international crisis, a return to inflation or unemployment, you name it. The public's a conglomerate whore, legs in the air, waiting to get raped."

I took a closer look at Jim Quest. He was bouncing along beside me with his hands in his pockets, a little shorter than I am and light on his feet. His face was round as a baby's but I had a feeling he wasn't soft. "You've been pretty frank with me," I remarked.

He gave me his dimpled grin. "Why not? You were a friend of Gil's." He winked at me. "And Monica likes you."

Well, well, I was being stroked. "Willie's lucky to have you working for him with all that dedication," I stroked back.

Quest laughed out loud. "I'm dedicated to winning, not people or causes. Hell, I cut my teeth working for Buck Rydell under old Sam Poole, the best there was at the time."

That surprised me and I guess I showed it.

"Now, that was easy," he looked pleased at my reaction. "Buck was almost prepackaged. He looks good on a horse and has a voice like an actor. All you got to do is keep him galloping at camera and not saying nigger, spic, or hebe every other word. Bill's more of a challenge, not only because he's no Robert Storm, but I've had to talk him out of locking into some positions that would make a lot more than half the population of this country run screaming in the opposite direction."

I had to smile at his reference to my father. "Then why didn't you stay with Rydell?"

"He can't afford me. And there's something else." He stopped walking and peered up at the sky, hands still in his pockets. "Bill has a quality that's hard to explain. People listen to him. Hate him or love him, they listen. I can work with that."

I couldn't disagree with him, remembering Willie behind the rostrum in junior high. "No matter what the political angle?"

He laughed again. "Hell, I don't give a shit about politics. I've never even registered to vote."

# SEVEN

hen I got back to the castle, Pop and Martins were playing gin rummy at the bar in the den, a Saturday-afternoon ritual I remembered from childhood. It gave Pop an opportunity to bitch and Martins a chance to double his monthly salary. Pop had started on the vodka and Martins was drinking beer. They grunted at me as I went behind the bar to build myself a rich bourbon and water.

I carried the drink to the far side of the room and sat down in the little leather chair behind Pop's low desk, squirming sideways because my knees wouldn't fit under it. I fondled the telephone, trying to make up my mind to call Norman Kling.

The leather freak I thought of as Roger Ramjet had killed Gil, I was sure of that. It was the same M.O. he'd used on me—the wild attack, spraying bullets until his weapon was empty. I didn't for a minute think he—or A-Frame for that matter—had originated the hit, but he was the only one I'd seen who was still alive. He'd be easy enough for the cops to pick up, given a description and the fact that he was a "witness" against Chick Rydell. They could sweat him or plea bargain with him, I didn't give a damn. Just so he talked. As for myself, I was in for a serious amount of grief for my part in the shoot-out at the Pit Stop, not to mention details like withholding information. It wasn't easy to pick up the phone, but I finally did.

It took a few minutes to get through to Kling down at the station, and when he came on he snapped, "Yes?" sounding cranky.

"Norman. Uh ... I heard about the Pit Stop on the radio ..."

"I still can't fucking believe it, Storm! All of them dead! *All* of them! Four witnesses against Rydell and now they're all dead!"

"All?" I didn't have to feign astonishment. Four dead would include Roger Ramjet.

"One drives over a cliff on Mulholland and his buddy seems to have crashed up on the road. An accident, maybe. They could have been stoned and screwing around on their bikes. But then C. H. Herlinger's place blows sky high in the middle of the night and all they find is a lump of roast fat the coroner says is full of bullets wearing his I.D. bracelet—" He broke off to yell at someone about a report missing from a file.

I held tight to the phone, waiting to hear about Roger.

Kling came back on. "Then—about two hours ago—one Felix Hubner strolls out of his beach shack down below Topanga and becomes the victim of a hit-and-run. We found the pickup that nailed him a mile away and I haven't got a make on it yet. Four out of four, in twenty-four hours!"

"Who were they?"

"Punks known as Noodle, Chucho, and Felix the Cat. C. H. Herlinger was called A-Frame. He and Felix were convicted felons, the others collected misdemeanors."

"Some witnesses."

There was a shrug in his voice. "Some parts of town you can't find anyone without a record. They can still bear witness."

"What about Charlie Rydell? Does he get to walk now there're no witnesses?"

"His lawyer's going to be down here asking that one soon. Answer's 'no way.' We got the gun, the typewriter, and the poison. They speak for themselves."

I hesitated. There didn't seem to be much point in baring my soul now that there was no one alive to go after. At least, no one I knew. A tide of relief washed over me, accompanied by just a twinge of guilt. But what was to be gained by putting my neck in a noose? Kling would be facing the same dead end, even provided with my information.

"Can you get a trace on that stuff?"

"I doubt it. No label on the poison, no serial number on the Uzi. The typewriter's about twenty years old."

"Doesn't sound like an amateur's M.O."

"Any punk can file the number off a gun or buy one that way. Want to know what I'm trying on?" he asked grimly. "Someone who has access to muscle wiped out four witnesses against that kid. Or maybe only two, if you believe in coincidence. Old Rydell has always played hardball and I'll bet I can find some mob connections. I read he spends time in Vegas."

I didn't bother to tell him I knew better, about three of them anyway. Roger was up for grabs, and the senator could have had him taken out for revenge, though I doubted it. "Where's the car Gil and Clewes were riding in that night?"

"Down here at our impound lot. Held as evidence."

"Anyone notice how much gas was in the tank when they stopped?"

"Why?"

"Didn't Clewes tell you they stopped for gas?"

There was a long pause. "I'd have to go to the file. Look, I'm kind of busy now, Storm."

Maybe I was nit-picking. Anyone can pull up to the wrong side of a gas pump.

After we hung up, I wandered over to the bar and looked over my father's shoulder at his hand. It was his turn to discard. I tapped a seven of spades with my finger and he hesitated, then tossed it out.

Martins picked up the card. "Gin," he said.

"Aw, goddamnit!" Pop threw his hand down.

I freshened my drink. "How well do you figure you know Buck Rydell, Pop?"

"Known him since he bought the spread next to Storm Haven. Must be almost forty years now," he said, watching Martins shuffle the deck.

"And you were good buddies?"

He shrugged. "He knew a little about guns and horses and he'd take a drink. We got along."

"Make his own money?"

"Yeah. He went through college on a football scholarship, but he played with his helmet on. He was already pretty well set up when he went into politics. Real estate, I think."

"Everyone says he plays down and dirty, or is that just his reputation?" I could tell by Martins's pained look that I was interrupting. Gin rummy was a paying proposition for him.

"Don't know as I'd want to cross him. I've seen him turn ugly a time or two." Pop picked up the hand Martins had dealt him.

I finished my drink and asked a final question. "Do you think he'd hire a killing done?"

My father looked up from his hand and stared at me for a long moment. "Not any more than I would," he replied.

"Your play," Martins said impatiently.

• • •

They were still at it when I left, just before six o'clock. I drove along Mulholland as another short day ended, watching the lights come on in the valley and filtering fragments of the evidence surrounding Gil's murder through my mind. Police work is labyrinthine. Run into a dead end and you backtrack until you find a fresh opening or angle and then start over. What I did was return to square one and begin with the alternate assumption that Gil himself was the target. As an ex-cop who had his share of enemies, it wasn't altogether unthinkable. The trouble was I hadn't seen him for five years and I was out of touch with his life. It didn't help that I no longer had the resources of the department behind me.

Terri was my last close link to Gil, and there was something in her attitude the day before that didn't ring true. I'd put it down to the bitterness of being suddenly left widowed and insolvent. And to the shallow if understandable resentment of someone who was self-centered to begin with. But that didn't mesh with what I remembered about Terri. She'd radiated optimism, in love with Gil and her plans for their future. The woman I'd seen yesterday had been hurting for a lot more than two weeks.

Then I remembered Monica's reluctance to see me and her evasions when I brought up the subject of Gil down on her private beach. In retrospect, I could see she'd manipulated the conversation into channels of her own choosing, then escaped back to her guests before I could steer it back on course. I'd been outmaneuvered like a rookie.

Another clue might lie in Gil's character. He was a chaser and Monica was still a beauty, as well as a star. He didn't have anything against celebrities and she'd eluded him when we were young, which would provide an element of challenge, knowing Gil. I couldn't see her running away screaming either. She'd always looked a little humid around him, and Willie, for all his political ardor, might be so much soggy pasta in the feathers.

I drove to Terri's apartment building in West Hollywood and parked on a side street opposite the gates of the subterranean garage. I walked around to the front and dialed her apartment number on the squawk box, watching the receptionist and the guard trying to stay awake in the lobby.

"Yes?" Her voice was husky and inviting.

"Jon Storm."

A pause. "I'm busy tonight, Jonny." The invitation was withdrawn.

"It won't take long."

"Another time, Jonny. Really, I can't tonight."

"This won't keep, Terri. I'll pitch a tent out here until you let me in."

She didn't say anything more and I thought that was it until the uniformed security guard came over and opened up.

Terri was waiting for me in the doorway to her place. Once again she wore only makeup and a gown, but this time the gown was silk that clung to her breasts and the slight mound of belly below her sash. If her outfit was blatantly seductive, her attitude toward me was not. "You've got about five minutes, Jonny. I'm expecting someone."

I walked through the heady cloud of her perfume into the living room and rested an elbow on the mantel over the fireplace. Terri stalked over to an end table and recovered a tall highball. She didn't sit down and she didn't offer me a drink.

"I'm not here to interrupt your social life, Terri," was as close as I could come to an apology.

She just shrugged. "Please get on with it."

"Did Gil have any enemies you know of?" I asked her. "I've been away a long time and I need your help."

She didn't answer right away, and I thought she grew a little sallow under her tan. "What has that got to do with anything? What are you trying to prove?" she asked finally, her voice definitely unsteady.

I watched her carefully while I said, "I'm turning everything around and assuming someone was after Gil. When you can't make sense of something one way, you opt for another. That's what I'm doing."

She tried ridicule next. "Enemies? Charming Gil? Why, I thought everyone loved him, just like you and I."

"I guess I loved him. I know you did once." I lit a cigarette, buying a moment to feel my way along. "But we don't want to kid ourselves, do we? Gil was dashing, handsome from any angle, charming, and funny. But he chased tail like a hound dog tracking possum and a lifelong habit like that isn't easily broken, even by the marital condition."

She swallowed some of her drink and then put it down to fumble with a cigarette of her own.

I went on. "When I saw you yesterday I knew something was eating on you besides Gil's murder. You're not just a bereaved widow, you're carrying a full load of anger. Knowing Gil, I'll take a swing at it and guess he was getting it on with Monica Loring."

I thought she'd throw her drink at me, but she just picked up the glass and drained it instead. "Good old Jonny," she said at last. "It takes one to know one, doesn't it? You boys must have had lots of fun cheating around in the old days. I'm surprised you didn't try me before you left."

I didn't comment on that.

"Yes, he was doing his number with Monica Loring," she told me dully.

"You knew for sure?"

"Gil was clever, but he was reckless and I don't think he really cared about anything or anyone." The words bubbled from her like acid, perhaps relieving some of the pain. "He had three men working for him, all ex-cops, and of course he drew up the security schedules, which included protecting . . . that bitch. Sometimes he sent one of the others with Clewes to Sacramento or wherever and stayed with her himself. Providing security, you see." Terri came over and stood closer to me, her chin up, looking at my eyes. "Being careless, Gil did things like leaving keys around, and being suspicious, I made copies of them. During one of Clewes's trips to Sacramento, I went to that beach house and tried all the keys until I found the right one. I walked in and found Gil providing a degree of security that was way above and beyond the call of duty."

" 'Flagrante delicto.' "

"I think it's called that, among other things. Anyway, Gil bounded up and said a lot of funny things while he danced around gathering up his clothes. She just strolled across the room naked and got a robe out of her closet. I remember what she said before she walked out. She looked at him and said, 'Let me know when you have things tidied up.' "

I sighed. "Gil could be kind of a shit, I guess."

"And still, I loved him. Loved him and hated him. At least, I couldn't leave him. He came back with one of the most imaginative excuses I've ever heard or read about for his grubby little affair with Monica. Why, according to Gil, he was acting in the line of duty. He was up to all kinds of things, it seems."

"Some kind of joke?"

"No joke."

She'd caught my interest. "What kind of duty?" I asked her. She shook her head. "Oh, no. No more freebees. I'm not giving anything away anymore."

I took a step away from the mantel. "Terri, this isn't a game—"

The buzzer on the intercom sounded and she crossed the room quickly. She listened to a metallic voice and then told them to let someone in before she turned back to me. "You've got to leave, Jonny. Right now."

"I need some answers."

"Not now." She opened the door.

"This won't keep, I told you. When can I come back?"

"Call me tomorrow." She practically shoved me into the corridor. I didn't think she'd want to talk to me tomorrow either, but I'd keep at her until she did.

I followed the long, carpeted hallway to the elevators. The doors to one of them slid back as I reached for the button and a man stepped out. He wore a tan gabardine suit and a Panama hat and he had wide-set pale eyes that looked directly into

93

mine for an instant before he went past me. Terri's date. Or maybe a john, I thought sourly, remembering her outfit and her remark about freebees.

Outside I realized I hadn't eaten since breakfast, so I walked to where Holloway intersects with Santa Monica Boulevard and went into Barney's Beanery, a Hollywood landmark for about half a century. Gil and I had gone there when we worked out of the Hollywood division. The bar still looked the same, though they'd expanded the dining area.

I sat at a corner of the long bar where I had elbow room, ordered a Jack Daniel's on the rocks, and looked down the line of drinkers. Barney's prices were right and his customers took their booze seriously. I lit a cigarette with the house matches and saw the inside of the folder no longer bore their famous admonition: FAGS STAY OUT.

Stomach rumbling, I took my second drink over to a table and ordered a large bowl of chili, a house specialty. Not without a pang, though, because it had been a favorite of Gil's. I could almost see him sitting across from me, wolfing it down cheerfully. Nothing bothered his digestion or put an ounce of weight on him. I tried to imagine what I might say if I could call him back for a minute.

"Why did you have to screw Monica, dummy?"

"Because she was there."

"You said you only liked young girls. 'No saggy-titted, stretch-marked nineteen-year-olds for me,' you used to say."

"Without exceptions there would be no rules."

"Never occurred to you it might be dangerous?"

"I laugh at danger."

"But getting caught by Terri. Jesus!"

"You should have been there."

"I wonder if Willie knew about it."

"I wonder, too."

"How the hell could it have been in the line of duty? What kind of crap is that?"

He merely winked, not helping me with that one at all.

The waitress brought my check, unfazed to hear me addressing thin air. Barney's was full of people like that.

To reach my car on Alta Loma, I had to walk back past the brightly lit entrance of the apartment building. The man in the tan suit and the Panama hat I'd seen in the elevator was just coming out the door. He paused to light a smoke, stepped down to the sidewalk, and headed for the street where I'd left the Chrysler.

I followed along half a block behind him, almost ready to believe he was a john. Terri had sure as hell been dressed like a hooker, and he hadn't been up there quite an hour. Assuming he was the one she'd been waiting for. There were plenty of apartments on the fifteenth floor he could have visited.

As I started by the garage, the iron gate began to swing slowly outward in answer to an electronic signal, and a black Caddy convertible with its lights on eased through and drove up the ramp to the street. I ran past it and under the gate in plenty of time, found the elevator, and pushed the button for fifteen. Terri might even let me in if she found me standing outside her door instead of locked out on the street below. I was ready to take a little heat if I was wrong about the man in the hat and she still had company.

She wouldn't answer the doorbell or my persistent knocking. There was a peephole and I could assume she saw who it was and decided not to open up, but I tried the knob anyway before turning to leave. Cop habit, I suppose.

The door swung open and I stepped tentatively into the empty alcove. "Terri?" I called.

She could be taking a shower, anything, but somehow I knew she was not. The little alarms fed by adrenaline went off, triggered by years of instinct and training that time hadn't erased. I crossed the living room and glanced into the empty kitchen. Beyond the bedroom, everything neat and impersonal as I remembered it, the door to the bathroom was open and the light was on.

Terri was in the bathtub. Only her drawn-up knees and the

points of her breasts broke the opaque surface of a fluid made up in large part of her own blood. Even her head was underneath, invisible. I turned away, fighting nausea, my legs gone suddenly weak. I'd seen death just last night, and many times before that. Messy, revolting death, but never quite like this. Maybe because it was Terri, whom I had known a little. Maybe because of what I was going to have to do.

I left the bathroom and sat down on the bed with its white nubby spread. When I could, I got up and went into the living room. There was some Scotch on the sideboard and I took a long drink from the neck of the bottle, remembering to close the front door before I went back to the bedroom. I stripped to the waist, laying my shirt and jacket neatly on the bed, then smoked a cigarette, which I flushed down the toilet. When I couldn't put it off any longer, I turned back to Terri.

First I pulled her head up out of the gore and water, by the hair. Rivulets ran out of her nose and the corners of her mouth, but there was no wound on her face, neck, or skull. Her eyes were closed and her features drained of color, waxy. I reached back under the surface and brought up her arm, saw the deep slash in her wrist that had severed arteries and veins. Her other wrist was similarly cut and still leaking blood.

There was no knife or razor, either on the floor or along the edge of the tub. I had to reach down again and search the bottom with my fingers before I found it. He'd used one of those all-purpose blades with a razor-sharp cutting edge sheathed in plastic you can buy in hardware stores. Because of course the son of a bitch I'd seen had killed her. Probably rendered her unconscious first with a little pressure on the carotid artery, then filled up the tub and done his work at leisure, no strain or struggle. "Widow, Despondent, Commits Suicide" would be the obvious verdict.

Suicide. Pretty much the last thing on Terri's mind.

I fought back a hatred I knew was counterproductive and fierce enough to hinder judgment, make me behave like a fool. The man in the hat was long gone and I didn't even know what he was driving. Useless to race out of here and range the streets, because he almost surely wouldn't be on foot. I put Terri's arms gently back where I'd found them and let her head slip down under the surface of the bloody water. The knife sank back to the bottom, too.

Meticulously I washed my hands and forearms, using no towels, waiting until the tap water drained out clean. I dressed and used a handkerchief from Gil's linen drawer to wipe all the surfaces I had touched, took another drink, and rewiped the bottle. The killer didn't seem to have made a search, so I didn't disturb anything either. There wasn't the slightest temptation to pick up the phone and call Kling this time. Things had gone way beyond that.

Making sure the corridor was empty, I went past the elevator and took the fire stairs down to the basement parking area. There was no traffic to raise the gate for me but I found a door that opened from the inside only and let myself out of the building. I got into my car and drove away from there, up to Sunset Boulevard and then west past Beverly Hills and Bel-Air. I needed to find someone to talk to.

# EIGHT

**T**he Jolly Green Giant still lived two houses away from the duplex I once shared with Gil in Marina Del Rey. It was an apartment above a garage, just across the bike path from the beach. The garage was large but there was barely room for one car because the Jolly Green Giant had equipped it as a gym, where he pumped iron with his girlfriends.

Gil and I had met Tom Grayson—his real name—when we'd busted him for running an LSD lab in Venice. He'd been interested in controlled substances of a hallucinatory nature for years, even traveled to Mexico to gain firsthand knowledge under the tutelage of Timothy Leary at a commune north of Acapulco. The Jolly Green Giant had found acid trips personally stimulating and decided to share his experience in the most profitable way possible. He manufactured the stuff by the caseload.

The bust we laid on him didn't stick, so he forgave us for it and we became good neighbors. Just as well, because Grayson stood about six-five and weighed around a hundred pounds more than I did then. He liked to pick Gil or me up and kiss us on the ear if he hadn't seen us for a couple of days. He'd also hold a car up off the ground by the bumper while someone stole the wheels. His women, who he changed as regularly as his socks, had one thing in common. Big or small, they had to be body builders. The last one I remembered was Frieda, a towering German Valkyrie with a dominant nature who I once saw hit him between the eyes with her fist hard enough to stun him.

The occasion was a New Year's Eve party at the Jolly Green Giant's Gil and I had been foolish enough to attend. The other guests were as motley a collection of felons and drug abusers as I've ever seen under a single roof.

"Listen, assholes," the Jolly Green Giant announced early in the evening. "These two fuckers are cops but they're also my pals, meaning they're righteous. They like to party so everything's cool and anything goes. Except don't do no capital crimes, *comprende?*"

This had the effect of making us pariahs until the grass, booze, and whatever else was being snorted, mainlined, or freebased had loosened everyone up a little. Then they got downright hostile. I was watching Frieda dance with one of the other girls, both of them naked. Maybe I should have known better —they were in a tight clinch with Frieda leading—but I decided to cut in. They both snarled until I retreated, but then a weasel of a man with a concave chest and long, dirty yellow hair shuffled over. "You wearing off-duty iron?" he wanted to know.

I opened my jacket amiably. "I'm clean. Just partying to-night." No hassles for me.

"Cops suck," he confided.

Maybe it was a plan, because two of his friends sidled up next to him. One was a black man wearing a leopard-skin jockstrap, my height but much broader, his massive, oiled muscles leaping and twitching. His chum, a Latino in a tank top, came in a smaller package, but he was visibly saturated with chemicals and had that psycho stare.

"This pig was hitting on my old lady," the weasel told them.

Despite myself I looked back to where Frieda had stopped dancing to kiss her partner's left breast. The girl buried her hands in Frieda's hair.

"That the one with the Three-in-One Flea Collar and the bone between her teeth?" asked Gil, who had ambled over to stare at the girls. He turned to the weasel. "She your old lady? No shit?"

I guess they hesitated because they couldn't believe he'd said that, but I could see things were about to turn sinister. Sometimes Gil really pissed me off.

The Jolly Green Giant unwittingly broke the tension. Maybe because it was midnight or just because he was feeling playful, he bent over and grabbed the girl with Frieda by the ankles, held her upside down, and bit her in the crotch. The girl screamed and cursed him so he carried her out onto his rickety balcony and held her over the railing above the cement bike path. Everyone trailed along to see what would happen, including Gil and me.

"Hey, what's going on out here, champ?" I asked lightly, just to cool him down. Standard police procedure when a subject is aggravated.

"I'm lookin' at life from a different angle," he answered, staring down between her legs, and guffawed.

The girl screamed and screamed.

"Happy New Year!" cried a drunk, staggering along the bike path below.

"You could hurt her," I pointed out. "Letting her fall from this height."

He nodded happily. "Break her fuckin' neck for sure."

"Don't do this, old buddy," I pleaded with him. "No capital crimes, remember?"

"Be a public service, cunt with a mouth like that. You hear what she called me, man?"

The weasel and his friends were watching the whole thing, but they never made a move. Gil gave it a try. "They won't see it that way down at the station," he put in. "They're blind down there."

"Fuck 'em. You can fix it. You're my pals."

It was Frieda who finally intervened effectively. She pushed through the crowd around the Jolly Green Giant and stood with her hands on her hips, a naked blond Amazon. "Bring her back or drop her," she commanded. "You are spoiling ziss party."

The Giant turned to look at her. "Aw, this party's lame anyhow." But he hauled the sobbing girl back over the railing and handed her to Frieda, still by the ankles. Frieda took the burden without visible effort and passed it on to the black man standing next to the weasel. Then she drew back her fist and belted the Giant between the eyes, a blow you could hear over the punk rock. "You are an idiot!" she pronounced.

The huge man blinked and shook his head. When his vision cleared, he looked around him. "You assholes see that?" he asked, his voice full of pride.

Gil and I took advantage of the diversion to leave without saying good night.

Now Tom Grayson stood filling the doorway in front of me, grinning. His thick hair was rumpled and he was stripped to the waist. "Hey, Fuzz!" he shouted to someone behind him. "Look who we got here!"

A tiny brunette in a leotard that showed off her awesome musculature padded over next to him, standing a little higher than his waist. They were a pair out of a circus.

He reached out and hauled me in with one hand, patting my cheek with the other. But he didn't pick me up and kiss me, so maybe I'd outgrown that. "Come in, baby. Don't just stand there." He turned to the small, dark woman. "Go get some beer and a bottle of tequila. Maybe some chips and shit like that."

When she walked away, the muscles of her trim buttocks coiling and bunching under the tight material, he said, "I call her Fuzz. She's some kinda Ay-rab. You ever think you'd find me groovin' behind a fuckin' Dune Coon? She's weird, like unpredictable. I'll prolly wake up some morning with my dick in my ear, but what the fuck, man?"

We sat down on rump-sprung furniture with a low table between us. I told him I needed to talk to him alone and he sent the girl out of the house as soon as she'd brought us food and drink. Looking at her chiselled, immobile features and into the black unfathomable eyes, I decided the Jolly Green Giant might have some cause for concern.

But he was worried about me. "You all right, kid?" he asked, peering at me closely once we were alone.

"I've had a couple of rough days."

"Well, tell your Uncle Tom."

I drank some tequila and chased it with beer before I got into my story. He listened, grunting and shaking his head but never interrupting until I'd given him the whole thing, omitting only the murder of Terri. Then he nodded and said, "I known them four assholes."

It didn't surprise me. Venice was his turf and that was why I was here. Without the police apparatus behind me, I had nowhere else to turn.

"So that's how it went down," he remarked. "Shee-it! I thought it was some rumble over chemicals, you know?"

I shook my head. "They were all in on the hit."

"Wasn't anything they wouldn't do."

"How did you know them?"

He shrugged his big shoulders.

101

"I'm not a cop anymore," I reminded him. "My ass is in a sling."

"That's right, isn't it, pal?" I think he took some pleasure in it because he grinned. "You're righteous now."

"What about those punks?"

"We did some business in cars. After the acid bust I had to go lame in chemicals. Everybody was on my case." He dragged on a cigarette, taking about half of it down. "But I needed bread to groove on, so I went into cars for a while."

"Chop shop?"

"Naw. I always been connected in Mexico. I know people in Tijuana and further down Baja who like nice cars. Police chiefs, politicos—people who can get papers for imported iron. They put out the word they want a Porsche or a Mercedes or a Jag. Give me the model, color, everything. Them bikers filled the orders for me."

I nodded. "Okay, then tell me about them. Nobody lives in a vacuum. They had to have friends, family, women. People they told things to. Punks like that build their image. They could have talked to someone."

The Jolly Green Giant shook his head. "I don't know. That Noodle and Chucho were from out of state. Real scumbags. I had to drop both of 'em one time when they tried to brace me. Wasn't a fair fight though, 'cause I used both hands. I had the red-ass so bad I woulda rat-fucked the Pit Stop too, only. . . ." He paused and gazed off into space reflectively.

"Only A-Frame was there," I finished for him, just guessing.

He nodded, abashed. "He wasn't human, so don't even look for a mother. They sewed him together in some lab, outta spare parts."

"That leaves Felix the Cat."

"Maybe." The Jolly Green Giant thought about it, scrubbing his unruly hair with a big hand, wrinkling his brow. "I known him better than the others. Wasn't anything on wheels he couldn't rip off in under five minutes. But he was badder'n them, too. He was an enforcer, an iceman."

"I figure he's the one who took Gil out." I leaned across the table. "Look, he lived down below Topanga near the beach. A cop gave me that much, but cops won't score with his peer group and neither will I. You might get in close. Shake something loose."

He just looked at me, and I knew he was waiting to find out what was in it for him.

"The senator would pay a lot to see his kid out of the slammer." I told him.

"I'd be workin' on spec. Jackin' around some real heavy dudes. That can get hazardous to your health."

Trying to think of something that might sway him, I poured tequila into my glass and raised it. "To Gil."

We drank to that and didn't talk for a while.

"All right, all right," he said at last. "This one time. For Gil." The Jolly Green Giant worked hard to disguise a dependable soft spot in his nature.

I was writing down my phone number at the castle for him when the dark girl came back with the liquor and cigarettes he's sent her out for. She paused to look at us on her way to the kitchen, her black eyes giving no inkling of what she might be thinking. I guess it irritated the Jolly Green Giant because he yelled at her, "Go stick pins in a doll or somethin', for chrissake!"

I got up to leave, feeling suddenly drained. As we shook hands he said, "You look like you need to get away. I got some real righteous stuff called ecstasy. I lay a tab on you, you'll trip in Panasonic and wide screen. State of the art, baby." He winked at me.

The Jolly Green Giant just couldn't stay away from chemicals.

Gil was standing on one hill and I was on another one, across from him. The gap between us was so deep I could see clouds below me. When I looked up again, the three bikers and A-Frame were surrounding Gil, everyone laughing over some joke at my expense. Gil was wearing his golfing outfit, a bell-sleeved alpaca sweater over a turtleneck, and Felix the Cat had an arm draped casually over his shoulder. Their attitude really bugged me.

"How can you hang around those turds?" I shouted over at Gil. "They're the ones that canceled your ticket!"

That got them laughing even harder. I saw Terri was with them now, one of the gang. Gil shook his head, still grinning. "Hey, I'm sorry, buddy." He held up a hand in apology. "It's hard to explain, but you'll know when you get over here. You'll know everything then."

I looked down at the clouds again. "How the hell do I do that?"

"Not now," Gil told me. "You'll have to wait. There aren't any flights."

They turned away from me and started to leave, Felix the Cat mounted on his chromed Harley-Davidson. Terri had to pull Gil away as if to keep him from saying something more, but A-Frame and the bikers gave me the finger. The clouds from the chasm between us rose to swallow them up, and I'd never felt so lonely. I tried to call them back, all of them, but they kept receding from me.

I woke reluctantly, trying to hold on to the shreds of the dream. In the gray moments between my return to the real world and the one I'd conjured, the notion of staying behind seemed logical. You didn't leave a pal alone with that bunch.

Martins had left a copy of the *Los Angeles Times* on the dining room table (my father calls it *Pravda West* but subscribes to it anyway). There was freshly squeezed orange juice in the refrigerator and coffee on the stove. Martins and Wun took Sunday off, and Pop would be sleeping late. Saturday night he usually had a few pals over and they stayed longer than other nights, drinking and watching movies into the morning hours. When he finally woke up he'd go over and spend the rest of the day and the night with his current girlfriend. That's the way it had always been. Pop didn't like empty houses.

The *Times* gave the deaths of all four witnesses in the murder case against Charles Rydell, Jr., front-page treatment. Without making specific prejudgments it neatly linked the fate of the four to Charlie's indictment for Gil's murder and the attempt on Assemblyman Bill Clewes. If that wasn't enough, a staff writer had managed to collect his thoughts in time to editorialize about the kinky nature of California politics, using as his primary example the Rydell case and stressing a relationship between the senator and his son that virtually cast the boy as an extension of his father. I remembered Jim Quest's remark about the power of the press. With nine days to go before the election, Buck Rydell already looked like history.

I heard a groan and looked around. At first I thought it was Pop weaving in from the living room holding his head on. The man was the same size and his hair was the same color. It took me a minute to recognize Rusty Naylor, the stunt man who had doubled Pop for about thirty years. He did an elaborate double take before he stuck out his hand. "Geez, kid, I wouldn't have known you. Stormy told me you were staying here for a while."

We shook hands. I hadn't seen Rusty since I'd left home. Pop took me on location with him once to Colorado and I'd been fascinated watching Rusty doing some of the stuff the studio wouldn't let my father do. He was a hell of an athlete and he looked so much like Pop the camera could get in really tight. It was a resemblance he was proud of and still seemed to cultivate.

"I've gotta quit trying to keep up with Stormy," the stunt man said, opening the refrigerator and taking out the jug of orange juice. He poured some into a glass and then went to the bar and added vodka. "Hair of the dog," he mumbled and drank it down.

I got up and spiked my own juice from the vodka bottle. Why not? These old bastards seemed to thrive on it. I'd heard them singing and stumbling around when I got back from the Jolly Green Giant's, but I hadn't felt like joining the party. "You still get paid for falling off horses?" I asked Rusty.

"Hell no," he snorted. "I quit when Stormy did. All the kicks went out of it and anyway I'd busted everything twice by then." He peered off into the past and shook his head. "But geez, the laughs we had. We made forty-three pictures together. The big honchos were always tellin' me to keep Stormy out of trouble. Shit, we'd go out lookin' for it together. Stood back to back punchin' out Joads in bars all over the country. They'd've liked to fire me, but where were they gonna get anyone else looked that much like Stormy?"

"You're still the spitting image," I told him.

"You too," Rusty said generously. "Only bigger. I never could figure out why you didn't go into pictures."

"I can't act."

"That never stopped your old man. Hell, you coulda gone all the way. You had the name to begin with."

"Maybe that's why."

He looked at me with something akin to pity. To people like Rusty and Pop there's nothing out there beyond the world of movies. They've effectively transposed myth and reality, living comfortably within the cocoon of the former. "Well, I guess we need some cops around, too," he said kindly. Maybe he'd forgotten I wasn't doing that anymore.

The same two men were on duty in front of the house on Zumirez Road, their unmarked car parked exactly where it was the day before. They both wore short-sleeved shirts outside of their trousers to hide the guns and cuffs. After I gave my name, the older one, who was tall and skinny, kept an eye on me while his partner fumbled under his shirt for a little two-way radio called a Rover and contacted the house. Then we stood around and waited.

"I was Gil Buckler's partner for twelve years when I was with the department," I volunteered, just to break the silence.

"Hell yes," said the younger cop, as though he should have known all along. He was a florid man with earnest blue eyes. "At least they got the son of a bitch who did it."

"Sure," grunted the tall cop. "He could do a couple of years, maybe."

Jim Quest appeared at the gate. He watched me walk over with his little blue chips of eyes. "Was this trip necessary, sport?" he asked, not quite as friendly as yesterday. "We're having a busy day."

"Absolutely, Jimbo. I need to see the lady of the house."

Quest sighed and drew open the gate. As we walked up the driveway I recognized the vehicles parked near the open front door. There was a truck that would hold a generator bleeding cables into the house and a van full of sound equipment. We followed the cables through the rooms and out to the backyard, where the action was.

A section of lawn had been peeled away to create a garden, the squares of turf carefully laid aside for convenient replacement. Rows of leafy tomato plants supported by sticks had made a miraculous appearance since yesterday.

At the center of the garden stood Monica and Willie dressed in work shirts and jeans. Hand them a rake and a pitchfork and you'd have American Gothic.

I looked at the equipment facing them—a camera that could dolly on a track, half a dozen tall reflectors, sound gear. The cameraman had an assistant, as did the sound man, who was wearing earphones and fondling his equipment. The director was a young man with granny glasses and a thick beard.

"Kind of a last-minute inspiration," Jim Quest told me. "Just got the tomatoes down from Oxnard this morning. All on a goddamn Sunday with everyone on golden time." He sounded both harried and proud. "But we've got a tight schedule."

"Why not just shoot it in someone else's garden?"

"I want to get a piece of the house for authentic background."

"Isn't it kind of late to bring out a political spot?" I asked him. "If that's what this is?"

"It's more than that. Watch."

The director cued Willie and Monica. "Okay. First positions."

They got down on their knees in the tomato patch, Monica digging in the earth with a trowel. Willie looked around and seemed to discover the camera, which was rolling. He climbed to his feet and walked toward it, slapping the dust from his jeans. He hit his mark and directed a level gaze into the lens.

"A little more than two weeks ago, an attempt was made on my life," he began. "Since then I've been asked by many

**107**

concerned friends whether I would continue to seek high office and—if I did—whether I could bring the same degree of dedication to bear in the fight for justice and in my sponsorship of causes unpopular with the proud and powerful."

He paused to glance fondly at Monica, still on her knees in the garden, then turned back to the camera. "I have a lot to lose, they point out, and I agree—"

"Aw shit, cut," said the director. "Someone prop up that plant, okay?"

An assistant ran out to where a tomato plant had keeled over on its side and rammed the stick supporting it deeper into the ground.

"Spontaneity," Quest said to me. "This will reek of it. Prime-time spot just before the election. Like an afterthought, a little final reassurance. It'll stick in the mind like Velcro."

"Okay, let's take it from the top," the director called.

Willie went through it again, working his way back to where he had been interrupted. ". . . I have a lot to lose, they point out, and I agree. But how much *more* is lost when we allow ourselves to be intimidated by assassins!" He raised his chin almost imperceptibly and I wondered if he was using the imperial "we." "No, my friends, I'm not quitting and I'm not wavering. I'm running harder than ever!"

"Cut!" The director walked over to the edge of the newly dug garden. "We're going to be tight on Bill for the rest of it, Monica. You're out of the shot."

She got up, tossing her trowel aside, and brushed past me on her way into the house, leaving me to trail in her wake. I caught up with her in a study with French doors overlooking the lawn where they were setting up the next shot. Willie was peering uncertainly in our direction, squinting against the glare of the reflectors.

Monica turned to face me, crossing her arms and resting her hip on the edge of a large oaken desk. "This is a bit much, friend. Showing up unannounced in the middle of a shoot. I'm trying to understand, I really am."

"I'll do my best to make it easy. You hired Gil, right? Probably over Willie's objections."

She shrugged. "It might have been my idea. He has other things to worry about."

"Nowhere in our heart-to-heart yesterday did it come out you were balling him."

She didn't move a muscle, just let the contempt slide over her face. "Was I? Your spies are everywhere, is that it?"

"This item is courtesy of Terri, Gil's wife. I talked to her last night."

She took her time, thinking that over. "And now you're going to tell me she's threatening to go public." The contempt deepened, etching itself into her voice. "This reeks of blackmail."

I watched her carefully. If she knew Terri was dead, she was giving an Oscar performance. "You're denying it?"

"Why should I deny it to you? Gil was an amiable stud. I was scratching an itch, just like you men do all the time. It doesn't have a damn thing to do with my relationship with Bill. I wouldn't expect you to understand, but it operates on a higher plane."

"Why, then Willie knew all about it and everything's okay. What was he, the towel boy?"

"You're disgusting." The vertical line appeared between her eyebrows and brackets formed at the sides of her mouth. Anger signals that coarsened her beauty. "He doesn't know anything about it, but if he found out he could handle it. As for any kind of public revelation, I'll deny it to the end. The voters won't buy it coming on top of everything else. They'll write it off as a last desperate dirty trick against Bill Clewes. So you and that little sneak better be reasonable. Keeping this quiet is worth a few dirty dollars, no more."

I took a step toward her, sorely tempted to backhand her off the desk. I longed to see her sprawled on the floor, stripped of all that poise and arrogance, but I kept my hands tight against my sides until the impulse passed. "Terri's not going to blackmail you." I had to bite back telling her what happened to Terri, in case she didn't know. "And you can't buy me."

"Then why are you skulking around here?"

"Because you were playing around with Gil and now he's dead. Because there's a kid in jail for a murder he didn't do. And because a husband wearing horns makes a great suspect. Especially when you consider the fringe benefits."

Monica slid off the desk but she still leaned back against it, gripping the edge with both hands. "You . . . are . . . absolutely . . . crazy."

"Three weeks ago Willie looked like a loser, I'm told. Now he'll walk into the Senate pretty much by default while Charlie Rydell takes a fall for murder."

"It was Bill he was trying to kill!"

"Someone nearly cuts Gil in half with a machine gun and then shoots up the office, but Willie never gets a scratch. That's choreography, baby. You ought to recognize it."

"That boy was drunk! The police investigated and that's what they found! He wasn't rational!"

I stepped forward again, towering over her. "That's what they thought because they never looked at it any other way except as an attempt on Willie. Well, I've got this whole new theory and I'm going to take Captain Kling by the neck and rub his face in it. He's not the world's brightest cop but with what I can give him he's going to take this can of worms and open it up from the other side. Then we'll see what comes crawling out."

She shook her head. "You can't do that. Not now."

"I can't think of a better time."

Her face went pale, making the freckles across her nose stand out. "You sick bastard," she rasped at me, her voice down to a harsh whisper. "You hate him. You have since we were kids but now it's out of control and you want to ruin him. You and Gil—the golden boys. You can't stand what Bill became, what he rose to be from nothing. While you turned into a beach bum after shooting a black man and Gil was nothing but hired help with all his brains below the belt . . ."

"I'll bet you got your money's worth."

She struck at me then, her fingers curled into claws. I caught her wrist in mid-air and jerked her against me, feeling the twin pressures of her breasts through the material that separated us, the nipples hard as buttons. She could have used her free hand, kicked at me or struggled. She just stared up at me, her face scant inches below mine. I thought I saw hatred and anticipation in roughly equal parts, as if she wanted to know what was coming next and was ready to challenge whatever that might be. Ready for anything.

It all came rushing back over me, all the anguished desire I'd felt for her when we were very young, the hollow ache in me when Gil had kissed her in the surf that time. I dropped her wrist and put both my hands on her slim waist. She let her arm fall, making no effort to pull away. Maybe she'd try to vamp me out of going to the cops, I didn't give a damn. What mattered was the moment. Everything else could wait.

Someone grabbed me roughly by the shoulder and yanked me around. I saw Jim Quest standing there and heard him start to say, "That'll be enough—" or something like that.

I punched him low in the belly, getting a lot of shoulder behind a fist that didn't travel far at all. Quest dropped to his knees, swayed, and then toppled onto his side. His breath sawed painfully in and out of his throat before he managed to say, "You'll . . . regret that, sport."

I looked down at him. "When?"

Monica walked past us to the open door. Before going out she turned and said to me, "You can't hurt us, because you're nobody at all. You and Gil . . . what a waste."

I watched through the window as she crossed the lawn toward the raw patch of garden where Willie was still facing the camera. The tomato plants stood in disciplined rows behind him, a captive audience.

The Guardrail squatted at one corner of a deep parking lot like an afterthought. The lot was full of cars but almost everyone was still on the beach, leaving the bar and patio nearly empty. I sat at a small table under an awning, facing the sand

and squinting against the glare bouncing off the sea. Everyone else seemed to be playing volleyball, throwing Frisbies, or baking in the sun. I was just drinking.

"You were sure an old smoothie out there today," Gil would have said.

"They belong under a rock."

"Even Monkey? For a minute there you could've fooled me." Sarcasm.

A waiter brought me another Moscow Mule. The vodka and ginger beer, tart and cold, reached for my extremities. "Why don't you just tell me what happened and save us all the hassle?" I asked when he left.

"What makes you think I know?"

Gil probably hadn't known what hit him, at that. The lights in his eyes and then a burst of gunfire out of the darkness. I could see it almost as if I'd been there. What I couldn't really see was Willie coolly tackling Rogelio when he heard the Uzi open up, lying there with bullets cutting the place to pieces. If it was a setup, it took the kind of raw nerve and timing I just didn't believe Willie capable of. Not Willie the Weege.

Could Monica be in on it, coldly arranging the murder of her lover and childhood friend for political advantage? Or Quest, the cynical manipulator? Or maybe all of them? Terri hadn't been killed by an angry lover or a trick. She'd been hit because she was a threat, by someone who knew how to make it look like suicide. Someone she'd been expecting. Murder by appointment.

And probably by contract. I'd seen the killer's face without recognizing him, but I wouldn't forget the peculiar set of the pale eyes that had looked at me calmly just before he committed murder. Eyes that made their assessment at a glance, the equipment of an upscale pro. But how had she known him and why did she let him in? Then I remembered that the call went through the receptionist in the lobby and he could give any name at all.

Someone played a Monica Loring oldie on the jukebox in

the bar and speakers blared it out over the patio. Mellow rock with overtones of country sung with a reckless lilt that suggested she didn't give a damn. I'd read somewhere she'd ad lib or blow a lyric at a recording session and insist they leave it that way. Statistically there wasn't a minute of the day or night when someone in the world wasn't listening to her. Now, that's clout.

I remembered we'd be driving along Sunset in Gil's bright red Pontiac convertible with Monica up front next to him, singing along with something on the radio. "Who're you supposed to be, Connie Francis?" Gil would shout. But if she was into it Monica would just shake her head and keep singing, snapping her fingers to the music, forcing the song to her own rhythms.

From where I sat now I could see the Moniquita just south of the Malibu pier with her likeness out front, bangs and all, holding a tray of Mexican junk food. At night her silhouette would light up in neon and she'd endlessly raise and lower the tray of tacos. Almost anywhere in the world you went.

She was ubiquitous, with all the power that implied. The way I'd handled it was to barge in and make a lot of angry noises, lose track of my mission long enough to grope her a little, and finally slug Quest for interrupting. It was a sorry performance prompted by helplessness and towering frustration. On more than one level. I wanted to pound on someone until I found out why Gil was dead. I wanted to make love to Monica Loring. Contradictions in themselves, you might say.

People straggled in from the beach and the Guardrail began to fill up. The sun sank toward the sea, an orange ball dropping into the smog bank on the horizon. The afternoon had passed, escaping my notice. As the patio got crowded, I took off my windbreaker and hung it over the back of Gil's chair so no one would take it away. Call it a gesture. We're all a little crazy.

"Maybe it's time to call the Marines," I could hear him say. "You've played it out as far as you can. You haven't got the juice. Like she said, you're no one at all."

I thought it over, counting up all the charges they could bring against me until I'd used up most of my fingers. Even if I could explain away the wake of corpses, the least they'd do was book me as a material witness. And that's just if they believed me. Finally I shook my head and took a pull at my drink, banged the mug down on the table, and muttered, "I could do *time!* It's easy for you to say when you're dead."

Everyone was looking at me; this wasn't Barney's Beanery. I glared back but I paid my check when the waiter brought it unasked, grabbed my windbreaker off the chair, and stalked out through the bar. There was a phone booth in the parking lot and I used it to call the West Los Angeles Police Department, only to learn that Captain Kling was out of the building but expected back momentarily. I hung up, declining to leave a message. West L.A.P.D. was on my way. Correction, it might be my last stop today. I hoped Pop knew a good lawyer.

I left the top down and drove through Santa Monica with the sly caution of the semidrunk. This wasn't Mexico. I could get a ticket. By the time I reached Butler Avenue the fresh air had restored perspective and I had to force myself to walk through the bright red entrance of the police station, realizing it might be a one-way trip. But I was fresh out of options.

Kling was still out and I wasn't about to lay my story on a complete stranger. To kill time I went over to the impound lot a block away and asked a civilian on duty where I could find the Plymouth belonging to Assemblyman Clewes. The man didn't speak English or Spanish and I don't have any Iranian or whatever, so he trotted along beside me gibbering while I walked between the line of cars. Finally I located a drab blue four-door that matched the photographs Kling had showed me. Basic transportation fit for Willie's proletarian image. I slipped behind the wheel, saw the key in the ignition, and turned it, watching the gas-gauge needle stop near the half-full mark.

It didn't prove anything. There's no law against topping off a half-empty tank, or even against parking where you can't possibly do it. Of course, it takes an idiot to behave that way, but the world is full of idiots. Gil just didn't happen to be one of them.

Kling still wasn't back, so I left my name and phone number and drove home to the castle feeling temporarily reprieved. I used my Genie to open the gate and parked in the driveway, wondering why the dogs weren't around. They usually come bounding over hoping to find an intruder to dismember.

It was dusk and the house was dim. I turned on a light in the den and built a drink I didn't need at the bar. The six o'clock news on TV featured a cross-eyed Oriental anchor person talking about the upcoming national Senate elections. A lot of interest was focusing on the California race, where a bizarre attack on candidate Bill Clewes that left his bodyguard dead was being blamed on the son of his opponent, State Senator Charles Rydell. Rumored close links between father and son were having a profound effect on the latest polls. Clewes had come from far behind to move into a narrow lead.

Another lamp went on behind me and I turned to see the man who had visited Terri sitting on the arm of a leather sofa in a far corner of the den. He wasn't wearing a hat today but he was holding a short rifle with a plastic stock that was unfamiliar to me. I wondered how long he'd been waiting there in the gloom.

"Tranquilizer gun," the man said. "It'll stop a big cat charging right at you in seconds. Some kind of nicotine extract. Works fine for dogs and people, too. Keep your hands on the arms of your chair."

He was about fifty, with short, sandy hair and a broad, pleasant face that didn't match the cold, wide-set pale eyes. "I'd like for you to get up and go sit behind that desk. Hands in sight."

I went over and squeezed in behind the desk. From his point of view, it made sense. I couldn't make any fast moves from there. Then I noticed a piece of stationary and a pen on the blotter in front of me I hadn't remembered seeing there before.

The pale-eyed man tossed over a crumpled wad of paper that

bounced on the desk and settled near my hand. "Copy that in your own writing."

I smoothed out the paper and read:

> Dear Pop,
>     I've done what I can up here. I can't prove Gil's death didn't go down like they say and the more I think about it, the more I accept the evidence. It's sad and it's lousy, but these things happen.
>     I'm leaving for Mexico this afternoon. Forgive me for not saying good-bye in person, but I'm feeling pretty rotten right now. I'll be in touch.
>
>                             Semper fi,
>                             Jonny

Semper fi. It was an abbreviation of "Semper Fidelis," the old Marine Corps sign-off, and an inside joke. I'd used it with Gil and Pop, no one else. Of course, Gil could have told Terri, and Terri could have told . . .

I tossed the note aside. "Then what happens?"

He stared at me for a moment as if trying to decide how to tell it. Finally he opted for the truth. "I inject you with this." The short rifle shifted in his hands. "You go to sleep and that's all you need to know."

My heart started beating so hard I could feel the pulse in my fingertips. "If you're going to kill me, why should I write your fucking letter?"

He shrugged. "I'm going to pack your gear and take you in your car and make you disappear. Or you can wake up again, way out in the desert somewhere, and we'll play around until you want to write the letter. There's an easy way and a hard way."

I thought it over while I looked into his indifferent eyes. There was no sign he cared one way or the other. "All right," I told him. "I'll write it if you tell me who set me up. And the girl, too."

"It's not going to matter to you, ace."

"It does now. There's an easier way and a harder way for you too, asshole."

He didn't react to the insult at all, just seemed thoughtful for a moment. "I'm a businessman," he told me at last. "Legitimate. I own a vineyard and I work it. A very few people know I do this, too. They call me and set up a meet. A lot of them are Vegas people, you know? Sometimes when I get to a place, they send along an envelope with half up front like I insist on and then call me with the details. Other times, they don't give a shit and it's face to face."

"And this time?"

He shook his head. "I go where I'm supposed to in Beverly Hills. I get in the front of a car, some kind of new Olds, the guy's in back. I don't look around. That's a no-no when it's set up that way."

"He told you to kill Terri."

"The girl, yeah. And how he wanted it done." Something crawled behind his spit-colored eyes. "She was a looker. I would've played around first, but I didn't want to leave a wad in her or any bruises for the coroner."

I hated him so much at that moment, I had to look away. "The punk," I said. "Did you take him out, too?"

He nodded. "It was a double-header."

"And how about me?"

"A bonus assignment. Write the letter."

I drew the paper toward me, picked up the pen, and wrote, "Dear Pop. When did they put me on the list?"

"This afternoon. By phone, but it was the same guy."

"He knew all about me."

"He knew where to find you and that the help leaves on Sunday. He knew about the dogs and he dictated the letter. Now write it."

A drop of sweat fell from my chin onto the paper like a tear. I wrote, "I've done what I can up here." Then I thought of something. "What name did you use to get up to Terri's apartment?"

He sighed, bored. "Bill. Just Bill."

Bingo! Why was I surprised? Gil could have told him what he needed to know. He liked to talk about the castle and Pop's eccentricities.

I wrote some more, talking just to stall. I didn't care what he answered now. I was thinking about survival. And about Willie. "How did you get it together so fast?" I asked.

"I had time left over. Been here for almost two hours. I saw your old man leave, I'd know him anywhere. Then I put the pups to sleep and waited. Write." He stood up. For the first time I noticed he was wearing flesh-colored gloves. And that he had an automatic stuck in his belt for a backup.

I wrote another line and when I looked up I saw my father standing at the top of the stairs that led down to the den. *It had been Rusty Naylor leaving the house!* I tore my eyes away and looked back at the pale-eyed man. "I hope this line of work pays better for three than for two," I said inanely, to buy time. When I risked a glance behind him, my father was gone. Did he think I was down here entertaining a friend, for God's sake? Or had he gone to phone for help that couldn't arrive in time?

"You better believe it does, ace." The killer moved toward me. "With a vacation thrown in. Finish that up, I've got a plane to catch." He leveled his weapon at me, bringing it in line with my throat, and I could see it had a slim barrel like a twenty-two and no trigger guard.

I wrote the last line slowly and a bit unsteadily, gathering my legs under me for a desperate lunge over the desk at him. He'd get me with his goddamn dart or whatever, but maybe I could do him serious damage before I went under. I guess he was close enough to see I'd finished because he said, "Now sign."

"Reach, you bastard!" The shout came from somewhere above and behind him. I looked up and saw my father standing spread-legged on the stairs, his hand hovering near a holstered revolver. *Holstered!* He'd gone back to put on his rig!

The pale-eyed man was fast. He dropped the rifle, drew his

pistol and spun around, firing without aiming, gauging his shot by my father's voice. The round didn't miss by much, splintering a section of banister.

Pop's .45 thundered like a cannon, echoes bouncing around the den as he fired twice. The hit man was blown back off his feet onto the desk in front of me and I heard the window behind my right shoulder shatter simultaneously. Bits of gore flew through the air to splatter my shirt. I caught a glimpse of Pop still frozen in the classic gunfighter's stance, holding the long, smoking frontier-model revolver at waist level, and I threw myself on the floor behind the desk in case he decided to do any more shooting. He wasn't taking prisoners today.

"Come on out, Jonny, he's run out his string," my father called and I recognized the line. It was from *Devil's Canyon*, the turkey he'd taken me along to on location in Colorado.

I got up and looked at the dead man sprawled face up across the desk, blood pooling under his back and running in streams down the wooden panels to the floor. Pop came trotting down the steps and crossed the room, blowing down the barrel of the Colt. I wanted to pick him up and hug him, but instead I shouted, "What the hell is this 'Reach' shit? Why didn't you just blow him away?"

"I've never shot a man in the back." He holstered his revolver with a flourish.

"You never shot a man before, *period,* except in the movies!"

He looked at me coolly, offended.

"Pop, *nobody* shoots *anybody* from the hip!"

I did grab him then, put my arms around him for the first time since I was a kid. "Thanks, Pappy."

He seemed embarrassed so I let him go. We looked at the man lying across the desk. The front of him was a mess; the back would be even worse. A smell of cordite hung in the air. "Forty-fives make a hell of a hole," my father said, then glanced up at me sharply. "How did he get past the dogs?"

I leaned down and picked up the peculiar little rifle. "Shot them with this. It's a tranquilizer gun."

"Damn!" Pop whirled and ran out of the room, heading for the front door.

I kicked aside a throw rug and rolled the dead man off the desk onto the hardwood floor. Then I peeled off his cotton gloves and put them on before searching him. An inside jacket yielded his wallet with a driver's license and credit cards in the name of Lawrence Murdoch of Sonoma, California. The wallet was stuffed with hundred-dollar bills, which I transferred uncounted to my pocket. There were two keys to a rental car, a single key with a plastic tab belonging to the Brentwood Motor Inn, a pocket comb, and loose change. He had four spare loads for the tranquilizer gun, dartlike projectiles powered by cartridge. I piled all the stuff on the desk and went upstairs to wash and change my shirt.

When I came back down, Pop was kneeling next to the couch crooning to one of the Dobermans stretched out on the cushions.

"Are they okay?" I asked.

"Herman's up and around outside. Heide here's just coming out of it now. The son of a bitch."

I put the dead man's motel and car keys in my pocket and went to the bar for some vodka over ice. Adrenaline had pretty well cancelled out the afternoon's drinking. On the couch, the Dobie looked up at Pop sleepily and yawned. I watched him lay her head aside gently and reach for the phone.

"Who are you calling?" I could guess, though.

"The cops, who do you think?"

Maybe there would never be a better time. The attempt on me should support the story I was going to have to tell Kling. Murdoch might even have a record or prove to be a known hit man. On the other hand, given my luck, he might turn out to be just good old Larry Murdoch, a grower from the Sonoma Valley, loved and respected by his neighbors. Either way, he was just as dead as a lot of people I'd associated with over the last three days. He couldn't bear witness against Willie or anyone else. But something he'd said gave me an idea, and there wasn't much left to lose by checking it out.

"Maybe we ought to wait," I suggested. "There's something I'd like to do first."

"Wait? It was clear-cut self-defense, no sweat. I dropped this bastard breaking into my house with a gun. Two guns. And he shot first." I knew he could see himself back in the headlines for his derring-do. "Movie Star Outdraws Intruder."

"I'd better tell you a story," I said. "Maybe I ought to take it from the top."

I waited until he put down the phone.

An Avis rental car was parked on the shoulder of Mulholland Drive, a hundred yards from the castle. My key fit, as did Murdoch's name on the contract in the glove compartment. I drove the car down Roscomare Road and along Sunset until I found the Brentwood Motor Inn, just beyond Barrington Avenue. It was the last of the old-fashioned motels in the area, a cluster of twenty whitewashed brick cottages with green shutters and roof shingles. A sign in the shape of a shield hung from scaffolding above the entranceway. Nothing gaudy or glitzy in this neighborhood. I drove past the office to unit six, the number indicated on Murdoch's key. It was early evening and only three cars were pulled up in front of the cottages. No one paid any attention when I parked in the allotted slot and let myself in.

The cottage had twin beds, throw rugs, cedar furnishings, and a small TV, all very homey. Before touching anything, I pulled Murdoch's cotton gloves back on. A suitcase on the spare bed held shirts, ties, socks, underwear, and a copy of *Hustler* magazine. In the closet I found his Panama hat, two pairs of trousers, and a light trench coat. In the top bureau drawer was a plane ticket to Mexico City.

He was scheduled to fly out on Mexicana Airlines at midnight. Scrawled across the jacket of his ticket was, *"Reservation Hotel Presidente—expect contact Monday."* It was already nearly eight o'clock, so he hadn't allowed a hell of a lot of time to dispose of me. Most likely he knew exactly where and how he was going to do that. A model of efficiency, friend Murdoch.

I sat on his bed and lit a cigarette. He'd said he had a plane to catch and he wasn't lying. They'd thrown in a vacation, probably to get him out of town. I remembered him saying he got paid half up front. It didn't seem impossible that the balance was waiting for him in Mexico. I pulled the money I'd taken from his wallet out of my pocket and counted thirteen hundred and seventy-three dollars. Unless he was pretty cheap that wouldn't amount to half his fee. The rest could be anywhere—in a bank, in the motel safe. He'd had time to take care of business.

*"Expect contact Monday."* It didn't say who the contact was, implying Murdoch didn't know. After all, he hadn't even seen who hired him. The idea that had seeded itself in my mind began to bloom, a disjointed notion ripening into a feasible plan. If Murdoch didn't know his contact, that individual probably didn't know him. Why not fly down to Mexico City in his place, check into the Presidente Hotel, and see who came calling? I could think of sound reasons why not. It was the stuff of spy novels. It was foolhardy and very dangerous. A fellow could get killed that way.

Or it just could work.

# N I N E

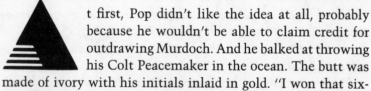 t first, Pop didn't like the idea at all, probably because he wouldn't be able to claim credit for outdrawing Murdoch. And he balked at throwing his Colt Peacemaker in the ocean. The butt was made of ivory with his initials inlaid in gold. "I won that six-shooter from Buck Rydell," he protested. "He had to break up a matched set. Hell, I used it in *Fort Doom*."

"Then you better find the round that went through him and out the window. Just in case they ever track him back here."

He was still grumbling as we cleaned up the house and then

wrapped Murdoch in three of those giant plastic lawn bags the gardeners use. By the dim light of the carriage lanterns we carried him out to the rented Buick and stuffed him into the trunk compartment, cramming his suitcase and trench coat in with him. I'd brought all the stuff up from the motel and left the key in the door of unit six. Chances were he was prepaid, so there shouldn't be any trouble there.

I backed my Chrysler into Pop's garage and hauled down the door. He had room for four cars including his cherished prewar Packard. "Anyone asks—I mean, anyone—I left you a note saying I was going back to Mexico," I told him again.

"Maybe I ought to go with you, kid," he suggested. "You know, as a backup."

"This has got to be a solo, Pop." I felt guilty as hell, making him an accessory instead of a hero, but I had to play this one out. There wouldn't be another chance.

"It's just like in *Match Point* where I took the place of the enemy agent, remember? Bill Bendix was my backup. I'd've been a goner without him." Pop's two worlds had finally merged.

I went back into the castle and up to my room. I showered and changed into a beige gabardine suit, packed a small suitcase, and took a topcoat out of the closet. Murdoch's wallet was in my breast pocket and I still wore his gloves. I kept his Panama hat too, though it was a little snug. It made me feel more into the part and, who could tell, it might even be part of some recognition signal.

Pop was sitting at the bar looking forlorn when I came downstairs. "You're taking a hell of a chance going down there alone, son."

"Better than staying up here playing target."

The phone rang and we both stared at it.

"Go ahead," I said.

He picked up the receiver. "Hello?" A pause. "Captain who?"

I took the phone from him. "Hello, Norman. I left a message to tell you I'm—"

"What the hell's going on, Storm? Monica Loring called and

123

said you were harassing and threatening her. And then you punched out their manager or somebody. That's actionable as a criminal or a civil offense, take your choice. You gone crazy, fucking that kind of people around?"

I couldn't believe it. They send a killer after me and then call the cops. The Clewes camp seemed to be at cross purposes, a gang that couldn't plot straight. Unless Willie had contracted Murdoch on his own. "Is someone bringing charges?"

"Not yet. She just wants you out of her hair. And I want you out of my business. I don't need this kind of pressure."

That I could believe. "It was a misunderstanding Norman, and I guess I lost my temper a little. I'm pretty strung out about Gil." I wasn't going to give him anything now. It was much too late for that.

"You're not a cop anymore, Storm. And I haven't forgotten what happened when you were. I was there."

"I remember that too."

He was quiet for a moment. I don't think he liked my tone. "You know, I could send a black-and-white to pick you up and we could finish this talk down here."

Indeed he could. My hands felt clammy inside the gloves. "No need to do that, Norman," I assured him. "I'm out of it. I'm going back to Mexico tonight. That's what I was going to tell you."

"Don't change your mind." He hung up.

My father walked out to the Buick with me. He stared glumly at the closed trunk. "I gave him a chance," he said. "I yelled for him to reach." It was getting to him now, the fact that he'd killed a man. This one wouldn't be getting up again to brush himself off, ready for the next take.

"That was your only mistake, Pop. He was a pro, a hit man. He butchered Gil's wife last night." I put my hand on his arm. "You saved my life, dammit."

"Yeah, I guess that's right." His chin came up and he straightened his back. "Good luck, kid. I'll hold the fort till you get back."

We shook hands and I had to smile. That's exactly what the place looked like, carriage lanterns splattering the cobbled drive with shifting light, turrets pale against the night sky. A fine setting for skulduggery.

I drove Murdoch's rental to L.A. International Airport and left it in Lot C, where you get a ticket out of an automatic dispenser and leave your car as long as you like. It was improbable that anyone would get curious before a couple of weeks or before the odor of decomposition escaped the plastic bag. I caught the airport bus to the terminal used by Mexicana, checked in with Murdoch's ticket, and got a tourist card in his name —all in plenty of time for the flight. The last thing I did was drop his gloves into a trash can.

On board the 727 I managed to keep my eyes open until they'd served drinks and dinner. After that I dropped off and didn't wake up until the stewardess insisted I place my seat in the upright position for landing.

At 5:30 A.M. even Mexico City was subdued. The cab ghosted through the empty streets of the sleeping giant, but I remembered the traffic and turmoil generated by seventeen million souls on my last trip here with Chispa. We hadn't been able to get out of town fast enough.

Someone had reserved a small suite for Lawrence Murdoch in the Presidente Hotel, high up in the tower. I made sure I was alone in there and then went to bed and to sleep again. The last few days had taken a toll, but I'd lost some weight by way of compensation.

The sounds of the city woke me at nine, a cacophony of blaring horns and porous mufflers. I stepped out onto my tiny balcony and watched flatulent buses toil along the avenue amid a swarm of taxis and private vehicles. The tops of the majestic mountains surrounding the city began to disappear as the ocherous fumes rose visibly from a thickening stream of traffic. The air, thin enough at eight thousand feet, worsened considerably under the petrochemical onslaught.

I would have walked over to Paseo de la Reforma and had breakfast at Sanborns, but I didn't know when to expect my contact. Instead I ordered juice, coffee, and eggs from room service. They threw in a courtesy copy of the *Mexico City News*, an English-language daily, and I learned that the body of Terri Buckler had been discovered by a maid and declared a suicide. The wire services had picked it up, making it an international item. I wasn't surprised, considering the nature of the California senatorial election.

There was a picture of Terri, smiling in happier days, and one of Monica and Willie, shocked upon learning the news. Jim Quest was with them, looking appropriately solemn. In an accompanying story, Willie called it part of an ongoing tragedy and said Terri was a victim of California politics, about as ominous an implication as he could make. I tore out the picture and put it away in Murdoch's wallet.

By noon I'd read every page of the newspaper, finished the crossword puzzle, and lost interest in the view from the terrace. Two hours later I had lunch sent up and took a beer from the fridge but ignored the well-stocked little bar the suite provided. I did three sets of push-ups and took a long shower, leaving the bathroom door open in case the phone rang. By five I was getting worried as well as restless, but hell, it was still Monday.

Just after six the desk called to announce the presence of one Lydia Ballesteros in the lobby. After being assured she was alone, I told the man to send her right up and then took a small precaution. I slipped on my jacket and went out of my room and down the corridor to stand around a corner from the bank of elevators. When one arrived at my floor I waited a moment, then stepped out and followed the lady to my door, reaching over to open it for her just as she was about to knock.

She gave a little start and her dark eyes widened slightly, not an overreaction under the circumstances. I gestured and she stepped into the suite without hesitating, looking around with bland curiosity, even with a hint of amusement. Then she fastened her eyes on me and I returned the scrutiny as casually as possible. Maybe this was the moment of truth, when I was supposed to give some password (The owl farts at midnight)? We stared at each other for a very long moment.

"I trust you are comfortable," she said at last, in tones that didn't care.

"Thanks, it'll do."

She stood in the center of the room and kept watching me with detached interest, the way you view a curiosity. It made me uncomfortable enough to go behind the little kitchenette bar and break out some ice and a bottle of vodka, but not incautious enough to take my eyes off her. Had I passed the goddamn test or not? Whatever I'd expected, it wasn't an emissary like this. "Would you like a drink?"

"If there's wine."

Her voice was totally integrated with her appearance, dark and cool, the English barely kissed by a Latin accent. She wore a charcoal business suit over a white blouse and had a black bag slung from her shoulder. The suit was severe but elegantly tailored to her small, solid proportions. She wore no jewelry and her black hair was pulled back from a high forehead in a style reminiscent of Chispa's, but there all resemblance ended. Chispa was fire and this one was ice.

Four splits of French wine lay next to the bottles of Mexican beer in the fridge. I pulled the cork on one and poured a glass before I mixed a drink for myself. "All the comforts," I remarked.

"Yes . . ." I got the impression she disdained her surroundings. She kept looking at me, not always in the eyes but as if to encompass the whole creature. I handed her the wine. "*Salud y pesetas*."

"You've been in Mexico before." She sipped at her glass.

"Just along the border." There was no point in giving anything away.

"I need to see identification."

Could it be that simple? Like cashing a check at your local supermarket? I put down my glass long enough to show her

Murdoch's driver's license, hoping that would do it. The bland photo looked enough like me.

She sat down on the short sofa, put her wine glass on a coffee table, and reached into her shoulder bag. I was beside her in an instant, close enough to intercept anything she might pull out of the bag. Her lips quirked in what might have been a smile and she slowly drew out a thick manila envelope, extending it to me. I opened it and pulled out four packets of American hundred-dollar bills, riffling through one of them. There were twenty bills to a pack. Eight thousand dollars in all.

"For the rest, you will have to wait a little." She shrugged in casual apology. "There is currency control here and dollar withdrawals are limited. I've been all day visiting banks to get this much together."

"You've had plenty of time before today," I told her, only because Murdoch might have said that.

"Not really. I was only informed Saturday. Banks are closed over the weekend." She kept watching me clinically.

I was going to have to be more careful. Too many details were locked away in the mind of a dead man. "How long do I have to wait?" Idly, I wondered how much money I was waiting for.

"Why the hurry? You have to stay here for the time agreed anyway."

Damn! Wrong tack again. I couldn't tell if she noticed. Her face gave nothing away. She had very pale, smooth skin that made it hard to judge her age. She might have been thirty, or close to forty. Her black eyes were large and thickly lashed under unplucked brows. The only makeup she wore was a peculiar dusky shade of lipstick.

"I like to tend to business before behaving like a tourist," I said, wondering what kind of deal Murdoch had made and how long I was supposed to stay down here.

"Well then, tomorrow it will be back to the banks. In the

evening you'll have all your money. Is that satisfactory?" Her eyes didn't leave me for an instant.

I nodded. "Look, I know I need a haircut, but didn't anyone ever tell you it's rude to stare?"

"Pardon me. I've never met an assassin before."

That riled me even if it was a case of mistaken identity. "I'll bet you only mingle with the Fortune 500 in your line of work."

She was unoffended. Her lips even twitched in what I took for a smile. "Oh, I know men and women who have killed. For their country or an ideal—but not as mercenaries."

"It's all the same once you get used to it. Just pays off in different coin."

"Don't misunderstand me." Her scrutiny persisted. "I find it . . . somehow fascinating."

It was time to talk about her. "I'm curious too. What kind of woman do they use to pay off assassins?"

"One who would rather remain a mystery. Is curiosity typical of your profession?"

She wasn't easy to draw out. I went back to basics. "What do I call you? My name is Larry."

"Larry." She tasted it with her lips. "How very American. You can call me Lydia."

"Larry and Lydia. Do you know many Americans, Lydia?"

"I knew at least one very well." For the first time I detected the absence of sardonicism. Well, now.

Lydia had hardly touched her wine but I went back behind the bar to rebuild my own drink. "Did he have a typical American name, like mine?"

"Yes. I didn't like it, so I called him by the Spanish version. Memo."

I excused myself and went into the bathroom, where I distributed the packets of money among my pockets, discarding the idea of leaving them in the hotel safe. Mobility was a prime consideration. Lydia was standing when I returned, the bag already slung over her shoulder.

"Maybe you can give me some advice," I said. Anything to keep her there.

She looked a question at me, a slight lift of one ropy eyebrow. She did a lot of business with her mouth and eyebrows.

"I don't like hotel food," I went on. "And I don't know my way around. Maybe you'd accept a dinner invitation and pick the place."

I watched her consider it, hoping her fascination with murderers would extend to a dinner date.

"I'll be on my best behavior," I promised. "No assassinations, even if the food's terrible."

There was that little tug around the lips to suggest she was smiling. I decided she had old eyes. "May I use the phone?"

"Of course."

She asked the operator for a number and I heard her tell someone in Spanish not to prepare dinner, she wouldn't be home. I looked at her suspiciously, as if I hadn't understood.

"Just my cook," she said. "Otherwise I live alone."

When we got outside a breeze was freshening the air, driving little gouts of rain before it, not enough to make me go back for my coat. We waited under the hotel awning until the doorman brought Lydia's car around. It was a small, drop-nosed Renault sedan that looked like a cat lapping milk.

Lydia didn't ask me to drive. She maneuvered through rush-hour traffic on the wet streets with ease, not showing off, just getting us wherever we were going. I saw we were on Insurgentes, a wide avenue that bisects the city from north to south, eventually leading to the tollbooths at the edge of the federal district and the highway over the hills to Cuernavaca. When she turned off Insurgentes, leaving the commercial area behind, the traffic thinned out. We drove toward San Angel, a suburb of cobbled streets and great stone mansions, and I guessed she was taking me to the San Angel Inn, a converted hacienda popular with tourists.

I was wrong. She swung onto a narrow, bumpy side street off Revolución and slowed, peering through the rain at the low buildings until she found what she was looking for. She parked in a lot that was no more than a gap between two small businesses long since closed for the night. I could see the street lights were far apart and the sidewalks deserted. It was a good setup for an ambush. I caught her wrist as she started to open the car door. "Where are we going?"

"Just across the street." I sensed my suspicion amused her. "It's not very touristic, but you can do that sort of thing on your own."

The place was easy enough to overlook. The name over the door, El Fundadór, was simply lettered on the white stucco wall, but warm light glowed through the window in modest invitation. I took her arm and we crossed the street quickly, ducking in out of the wet.

The restaurant was small and confining, rich with the aromas of food and tobacco. The candle-lit tables of rough-hewn wood were mostly unoccupied, but it was early for dinner in Mexico City. I saw a family with children at one table and a single man reading a book at another. A musician strummed a flamenco guitar and the menu featured *paellas*, so the place was Spanish.

I didn't object to Lydia ordering, figuring she had been there before. She chose a *paella* for both of us and a bottle of red wine. I thought the grizzled old waiter dressed like a Basque looked like Martins.

We drank rough red wine while we waited for the food and I smoked a cigarette, leaving the pack on the table. She looked at it and said, "Delicados. An odd thing for an American to smoke."

"I picked them up at the airport."

"Smoking will shorten your life." Spoken with irony.

"Did you come here with your American friend?" I asked, feeling for a thread leading back to the subject of herself.

I don't think I fooled her. She looked at me with her jaded eyes as if considering the merits of the subject. "No," she said finally. "I met Memo long ago, when I came here as a student with my father. We're Chilean, you see. Father went back when Allende was president, to serve the government. When the Fascists took over, he was killed."

"I'm sorry."

She shrugged. "I continue the struggle in his place."

"You met this Memo in school?"

"At the University of the Americas. A lot of Americans went there to avoid military service in Vietnam. I taught Spanish to help pay for my studies."

"Was Memo dodging the draft?"

I sensed disapproval. "He was sickened by the idea of fighting for imperialism. He wanted to work for the people, everywhere in the world. He wasn't one of the Americans who attended university in Mexico because the living was cheap and the poor could be exploited. I was . . . attracted to him."

Our food arrived and the *paella* was tasty, but someone in the kitchen had a heavy hand with olive oil. "Doesn't sound like a typical campus romance," I remarked.

"Not typical, no. I was fascinated by the quality of his mind, not by muscles or the ability to throw or kick a ball."

"A cerebral attraction."

"It became more than that. But I wouldn't expect a man like you to understand."

"I have my philosophical moments. So he became your guru?"

She smiled her tiny secretive smile. "No, I became his. I was quite advanced, you see, having been exposed to the revolution by my father. I believe I helped Memo to develop, to find a constructive outlet for his zeal. He learned it is not enough to posture, one must act."

I had her going. A little color was actually coming into her cheeks.

"But he's not around here anymore," I prodded.

Her animation ebbed. "No."

"Gone on to greater glory, no doubt."

"You're laughing at me, but that's exactly what he's done."

I took a guess and said, "Without you."

She didn't exactly come apart, but I saw some sincere emotion for the first time. Her expressive lips trembled and something came into the black eyes that I took for rage, or at least deep resentment. "Enough," she said harshly. "Enough of this!"

I hadn't had nearly enough. In fact, things were just coming into focus after hovering gray and shapeless on the edge of my consciousness for days. Individual bits and pieces were taking shape and merging. Translating from Spanish to English, the nickname Pepe becomes Joe. Paco becomes Frank.

And Memo is Bill.

More people came in and the smoke got as thick as the Castilian accents. The family group had been replaced, but the lone man still sat over his wine, squinting at his book by candlelight. He was youngish and balding, oblivious to the chatter around him. Maybe he just didn't want to go home. Rain splatted against the windows, hurled by the storm, making El Fundadór a cozy place to be.

Our waiter brought coffee and a Spanish cognac for me. I wished I could just reach across the table and choke the truth out of the enigmatic woman before me. She'd given me a glimpse of something beyond the obvious fact that Willie had set me up, and I couldn't let her slam the door. "Let me ask you something," I began carefully. "On the subject of philosophy."

She looked at me, waiting.

"If a man like your Memo, for the sake of argument, were to hire a man like me to eliminate a person or persons because their continued existence was a threat to him, would the purity of his motives excuse him?"

It seemed to me she grew rigid, inside and out. "That's not for us to discuss."

"Humor me. Who would the real assassin be? Would we both be guilty?"

"How can you compare yourself to him?" She was scornful. I was pushing the right buttons now. "You're nothing but an instrument of death!"

133

"Exactly! Just a weapon he loads, aims, and fires."

"I want to leave now."

"Do you know how many people I killed for him? Three. One was a young woman around your age. I cut her wrists."

Her chair scraped the floor as she shoved it back. People looked around. The lone man raised his eyes from his book to stare.

"I'm leaving," she said. "This instant." She stood up and so did I.

There was nothing more I could do here. Maybe if I could get her alone. "Let me have the keys to the car." I lowered my voice reasonably. "You don't have to get wet."

She hesitated, looking at the water streaming down the windowpanes before taking the keys out of her bag and giving them to me. I started toward the door and then thought, to hell with it. It was pouring. I went over to a young waiter who was leaning listlessly against the bar, strumming the air with his fingers to accompany the flamenco guitar. He took the keys and an American five-dollar bill, grinned, and ducked out into the wet night.

The man sitting alone stood up so violently that his chair crashed to the floor and the guitar died in mid-chord. I watched him struggle toward me through the tightly packed tables, leaving his book behind. Out of the corner of my eye, I saw Lydia watching him too, frozen in the act of slinging the bag over her shoulder. Someone who might have been the manager stepped into his path and was shoved roughly out of the way. As the man came closer, his attention focused somewhere beyond me, I saw the expression of frustration and dismay on his face. He pushed by me, got one hand on the heavy door, and pulled it open.

The blast blew him back into the restaurant. It knocked me off my feet and I saw the glass windows implode and the people sitting near them clutch at their faces, blood instantly coursing between their fingers. I rolled onto my knees and looked for Lydia. She was down too, crouching by a table.

My first thought was someone had tossed in a bomb, but

there was no fire or smoke, only panic. The explosion had been outside, somewhere nearby. I shoved my way over to Lydia and knelt beside her. She wasn't hurt, but her face was pasty with shock and fear.

I pulled her to her feet. "It's all right now. It's over."

She stared past my shoulder and her fingers dug into my arm like the talons of a bird of prey. I looked around and saw the man who had been sitting alone getting to his feet now, peering around him.

"It was meant for us!" Lydia hissed in my ear. "My car!" She let go of my arm and turned to run but I reached out and pulled her back.

"Let me go! He'll kill us!" Her panic was real.

I could guess who she meant, but there was no time to make sense of it now. Without looking back, I ran along the passageway next to Lydia, past the toilets and through the turmoil in the steamy kitchen, where people stumbled around flapping their arms.

We exited on a garbage-strewn alley under lashing rain. Lydia slipped and would have gone down but I caught her by the long fall of black hair and jerked her upright, ignoring her cry of pain. We reached the side street and turned away from the site of the explosion, scampering over slippery cobblestones, leaving behind even the meager urban lights for the darkened residential byways of San Angel.

She had to stop finally, hobbled by unsensible shoes, and I used the respite to look and listen. I couldn't see or hear anything following us through the curtain of darkness and rain. Just as well, because the walls around us were thick and high, protecting mansions built by grandees, their massive, timbered portals locking out the world. I pulled Lydia into one of the recessed entryways out of the downpour, shoved her against the doorjamb, and stood in front of her.

Her face was a pale oval in the darkness, unreadable. I leaned close and said, "Who's out there? I'm giving you one chance to tell me."

Nothing. Tight against me, she still seemed far away.

I put my hands around her neck. At that moment, I was just as dangerous as Larry Murdoch. "Good-bye, Lydia," I said, and pressed with my fingers.

"They were trying to kill me too," she whispered, because it must have been getting hard to breathe.

"You set me up," I reminded her. "The phone call."

"Yes, but they tried to kill me, too." She was incredulous, stricken. It was as if she'd given up. She didn't struggle against me at all.

I loosened my grip. Strangling her would have been an act of self-indulgence, solving nothing, but I think I came close to doing it. "Who?"

"Assassins. Like you."

"*Who!*"

"Russians." As if it no longer mattered.

I let go of her, glad she couldn't see my expression. I must have looked like an idiot with vacant eyes and mouth agape.

She raised her hand and palmed the wet hair away from her forehead. "Why don't you just leave me alone and run?"

"What was supposed to happen?"

"That man or one of the others was going to kill you. After we left the restaurant."

"But they wired up the car instead."

She nodded. "He watched us begin to leave together. We were both to die."

"It didn't bother you when it was just me."

"What loss would you be? A murderer."

I was angry enough to think about killing her again. "What about the others!" I shouted in her face. "What about the girl!"

"*La vida no vale nada*, the Mexicans like to say. Life is worth nothing."

"Except when it's yours!"

"Even then. Do what you like."

I couldn't, of course. She had me there.

"Who are you?" she asked. "You're not the man I was supposed to pay. He wouldn't care about the girl."

"I'm the man he was supposed to kill."

She was silent for a while. We listened to the rain come down, crammed into our niche, enemy breaths intermingling. "You can't get away," she said finally.

"Then neither can you."

"Perhaps I don't want to."

"Because Memo betrayed you." It was a guess.

"Yes. He must have known." I heard her anguish. "Otherwise they wouldn't dare."

"But what the hell, it was for a cause," I taunted her.

She shook her head violently. "No! I've always been loyal. There's no possible reason for an action against me!"

"Maybe it's just because he's married to a rich, beautiful celebrity now."

"No! That was necessary. It was his duty!" She didn't even ask how I knew.

"He gets all the tough jobs, huh?"

I don't know if she even heard me. "I made everything possible for him," she murmured.

"I'll bet he thinks about you all the time. Especially when he's in bed with her."

She clawed at me. "No!" she screamed. "No! No!" She found strength in despair and nearly broke past me. I hauled her back and slapped her face, just once but pretty hard. She shrank back from me, the breath sawing in and out of her.

At last I heard her say, "I want to survive."

"I want protection. Asylum. Will you help me?"

"That depends," I told her. "I'm not going to cover for you."

She nodded as if she understood. "I only want you to intercede with your embassy. I can't stay alive out here."

We were quite a pair, sitting side by side on a single bed wrapped in blankets. It had taken half an hour to get a cab, walking out of San Angel in the rain to Avenida Revolución. She explained we couldn't go to my hotel or to her apartment because they might be watching. At that hour of the night they could cover the train station and the airport as well. They could even check hotels, where guests had to show identification by law. The Russian embassy in Mexico City was one of the largest in the world and it had tentacles, a network of agents on call. Well, she should know.

They couldn't check the kind of hotel Lydia found us, though, the kind that rents rooms by the hour. I pushed money through a slot and got a key from someone in exchange. We saw each other's hands, that's all. The room itself wasn't bad. Maybe they catered to upper-middle-class quickies.

An odd couple indeed. I smoked damp Delicado cigarettes while she wrinkled her nose. Our wet clothes hung in the bathroom. I wished to hell I had a drink but didn't want to risk sending out for a bottle. And now she wanted me to help her hide in the American embassy. There was a lot more I wanted to learn from her.

"They'll want something in return," I pointed out, remembering her mention of the Russians. "Once they know who your friends are."

She shook her head. "I have never betrayed the struggle."

"Then you don't have anything to trade."

She stared at the pale-green wall as if she were already in a cell. "Perhaps I do."

"It better be good."

She nodded, but it was as if she were talking to herself when she said, "It is no crime to expose a traitor. I'll give them Memo."

I held back the sudden excitement rising in me. "I'm not sure they're interested in people who contract murder," I said casually, knowing that wasn't what she meant.

Her distant, frosty smile was aimed at the wall. "They are interested in the KGB. Memo is KGB."

Even braced, I wasn't ready for that. She went on as if I

weren't there, selling the idea to herself. "He betrayed me. If he would do that, he would betray the struggle. It's not difficult to see what happened. She seduced him with her wealth, made him a renegade. I am part of the past he wants to destroy so he can strive for himself. I'm not the defector, he is."

"Tell me about Memo," I said gently.

She looked at me and nodded again, as if to agree. "I was younger than he was, nineteen. But much older in political experience. Because of my father, I grew up in the party. The University of the Americas was still in Mexico City then. It was seething, a political potpourri. I know the CIA was there and many of our comrades were on the faculty." She stood up clutching the blanket around her and started pacing the small room.

"Memo was a visionary then, a young man on fire. But he was lashing out in frustration, without direction. Someone had to put the weapon in his hand and point out the objectives."

"And you did that."

"He was in my Spanish class. He hadn't much talent for languages, but an incredible thirst for knowledge. I remember he became letter-perfect in grammar and application." She shook her head and smiled. "But he could never master the accent. I'm sure it was the same with Russian."

"Russian?" I sat straighter, still capable of surprise.

"Yes, but to go back. I took him home to meet my father, before father went back to Chile. They spoke together for hours the very first night. I felt neglected, I remember, but proud. My father wasn't easily impressed. He became Memo's mentor."

"And you were his lover."

"Eventually."

"You recruited him."

"Father worked hard with him and was his sponsor in the party. Memo was accepted in less time than usual."

"Willie joined the Communist party," I murmured, and wanted to laugh.

She frowned. "Willie?"

"Memo in English."

She let it go. "It was more than just joining the party. He became part of a special cadre."

"An elite." I was fascinated by now.

"I despise that word. He was judged deserving of special attention. And advanced education." She stopped prowling the room and leaned a hip against the cheap, modern bureau. "He was awarded a unique opportunity. He was sent to Russia, beginning in 1969. There were several trips."

Nothing was going to surprise me again, I decided, waiting for her to go on.

"He received concentrated instruction at institutions for select internationals. Advanced political indoctrination, naturally. Paramilitary courses in survival and sabotage."

I shook my head. Well, it explained Willie's cool coordination under fire at the gas station. "How could he go to Russia and back without anyone knowing? Fake passport?"

"No need for that. It's simple enough, really. You take Cubana de Aviación to Havana and Aeroflot to Moscow. Then back to Mexico by the same route. Of course, no one's passport is stamped, so there's no evidence of exit or reentry. The Mexicans cooperate with Cuba."

"He just came back as a KGB graduate."

She gave me her twitchy little smile. I decided there was something sensual about it, something corrupt. "As a KGB officer," she said. "He's a colonel now, and a Soviet citizen." The smile turned decidedly bitter.

"Suppose someone checked up? He must have been away from that college a lot."

"His records would show that he took his complete curriculum. We covered his absences by assigning him research projects outside of the city. I was on the faculty, remember, and so were other comrades. He made no close friends among the students."

I leaned up against the wall and fired up another Delicado

even though the room was getting stuffy. "All that time and money. They must have had big plans for him all along."

"He came back here while we arranged a graduate degree for him in economics." Lydia looked past me, her eyes slipping out of focus. "He was changed, sure of himself and mature. I was happy then, and so proud . . ."

I let her maunder. It gave me time to get used to Willie as a KGB officer. When he finally retired from American politics full of age and honors after a lifetime of treason, would he go back to a dacha in the Crimea or opt to stick with Monica and her millions on an estate near Williamsburg? A real dilemma.

"He went back to America during the crucial period of the war in Vietnam, a very critical time. He joined and finally led a faction of the movement against the war. America had the capability to win, which would leave the Pacific Far East closed to Russia for the forseeable future. It had to be defeated from within. And it was."

I shook my head. "The campuses were crawling with kids against the war. Then the media jumped on the bandwagon."

"Exactly. Have you ever wondered who organized and guided them? Who controls your press?"

"A bunch of Americans who've all gone to spy school in Russia? Come on!"

"How many would it take? A handful!" She came over to the bed and leaned over me, incensed enough to be careless with the blanket. "Like everyone I've met from your country, you've got no idea how you're manipulated! Do you remember, more than a decade ago, how your own Congress gutted the CIA, practically abolished it? Do you know what that cost you from Iran to Central America? A few powerful members of your own Senate managed that!"

"Now you're going to tell me you've packed the U.S. Senate."

She laughed at me, her face flushed and animated for the first time. "You think it's impossible? Memo is going to be *elected* a senator! That tells you nothing?"

She straightened up and tucked the blanket more tightly around her, but not until I'd seen the swell and texture of her breasts. Perversely, I felt a visceral twinge of desire in conflict with a good measure of revulsion.

"Maybe you can understand this." She spoke more calmly, assuming the lecturing tone of a schoolmarm. "The Soviet Union does not want to inherit a barren planet. The strategy is to win by maneuver, if at all possible. When the United States has no friends in strategic areas, this will have been accomplished. You've lost China, Cuba, Iran, and Nicaragua—all strategic allies. A climate was created in your country that led to their abandonment by American governments without the loss of a Russian soldier. Will you please stop smoking? It's impossible in here."

I crushed out the Delicado, not wanting to interrupt the flow.

"Even your clever old president who so detests the Russians can only delay the process, not prevent it. Imagine what will happen when he's gone. And even he will fail to hold the Philippines. The Soviet fleet will take over your bases there as they did in Vietnam. After that, it will be South Korea and finally South Africa, whose minerals are vital to your weapons systems. All in the name of democracy, of course. All by the actions of your own Congress."

"And the Russians train people like . . . Memo to run for the Senate." I shook my head.

"Internationals are encouraged to enter politics everywhere, but Memo's opportunity is unique. Made possible by . . . that woman." She could hardly get her mouth around the word, never mind say the name. "You know about all that, don't you? That's why they want you dead."

I ignored her question. "Does she know he's KGB?"

Lydia laughed at that. "Of course not. She's a tool!"

"And he's one of a kind." Or were people like Willie crawling all over America?

"I don't know."

"Do you know why a man named Gil Buckler was killed in California?"

"I was simply told to meet an American assassin. Pay him to gain his confidence and then help arrange his termination. It was authorized by Memo, they said."

"A job for a woman, sure." Her unquestioning attitude toward taking life appalled me. Most murderers I'd dealt with were brutes, not polished ideologues. "But they decided to take you out, too. Maybe they went over his head."

"No." Her chin lifted proudly, in spite of everything. "They would never dare harm his wife."

That brought me off the bed. It also explained what she was beginning to see. Willie was looking forward, not backward. He didn't need two wives.

"It all makes a hell of a story," I told her. "But why should anyone buy it? From loyal comrade to informer in one day. What happened to all the dedication?"

"He's the traitor, not I!" Hatred gleamed in her eyes, the by-product of rejection. "If he can betray me, he can betray anyone! We're going to win, anyway. With him or without him—we'll win!"

I could see how she was rationalizing it. It was a state of mind to encourage. "Don't put it quite that way when you're asking for asylum. They won't understand."

"I don't have a future anywhere. I survive to see him destroyed."

"All right, but can you prove any of this? America isn't Russia."

She smiled her unpleasant smile. "I think so. He wrote to me. It was forbidden, but he did. Like any young lover. I have the letters. Stamped and mailed in Russia."

That made me smile, too. "Where?"

"In my apartment."

Which was nothing to smile about. They could be watching the place.

143

"Will you help me?" she asked again. "We have to get them and go to your embassy."

"All right." What else could I say?

"It will be safer in the morning." She walked over to the bed and pulled the sheet back. "And we'll be fresher." The blanket dropped to puddle at her feet. She bent casually to pick it up and flare it out over the bed. Our eyes met for a moment and I saw the look of casual invitation, maybe an offer of payment for services soon to be rendered. I won't deny I was tempted. They say physical danger heightens the libido, but I won't use that excuse. She was well made, smooth sheaths of muscle near the surface, firm sturdy buttocks that beckoned. But I had a notion she'd look at my dead body with more passion, so I settled down in the bedroom's single chair and stretched out my legs.

Whatever she read in my eyes didn't disturb her at all. She pulled the blanket around her, put out the lamp on the bedstand, and turned her back to me. In a moment I heard the altered rhythm of her breathing and knew she was asleep.

# T E N

round the corner from where she lived, we sat in a cafeteria that looked and smelled like it could have been in downtown Los Angeles. I studied a paper napkin on which Lydia had drawn the plan of her apartment and its location in relation to the others. The letters were in a box of blue stationery in her desk, between the sheets of paper. No one knew about them so there was no reason to hide them more carefully.

"Why didn't you put them in a bank vault?" I asked.

"I liked to read them."

Lydia's apartment was on the corner of Rio Lerma and Del

Prado in a slightly faded residential district not far from the Rose Zone, the fashionable hub of the city. At eight-thirty I walked by it on Rio Lerma and then turned down the side street for a look at the back. It was an older structure five stories high, as was its neighbor. The gap between the buildings was a narrow alley lined with garbage cans. There was no fire escape. People were coming out of doorways and heading for work, neatly dressed white-collar types. I kept moving, feeling conspicuous in my damp, unpressed suit.

"Do you know anyone who lives in the yellow apartments next door?" I asked Lydia when I got back.

"No."

"You don't know if they're alike?"

"I think they were built about the same time, so maybe they are."

"Can anyone get to the roof?"

"Yes. The maids have their rooms there. One for each apartment."

"All right, give me your key."

She gave me two keys. "That one is for the front door, this one for the apartment."

"Just the one to the apartment."

She seemed surprised.

"I'm not going in the front door," I explained. "That's where they'd wait."

"They'll expect me. They don't even know what you look like."

"Except for the guy in the restaurant. Listen, just wait here until I get back." I took the key I wanted and the illustrated napkin and stood up.

"For how long?"

"Give it an hour. If I'm not back by then, you're on your own."

There didn't seem to be anyone watching from a parked car or lounging behind a newspaper. I walked to the apartment

145

building next to Lydia's and rang half a dozen bells. A woman yelled, *"Quién?"* through the voice box but I just kept pushing buttons. Finally somebody buzzed me in and I slipped through the doorway, glad to be off the street. A small, cranky elevator took me to to the top floor and then I walked down a short corridor and climbed a single flight of stairs to the roof.

Up there was a small, square building surrounded by laundry lines, evidently where the maids lived. One of them, languidly stringing up sheets, looked at me with wooden indifference as I emerged. I smiled as pleasantly as I could and wandered around as if enjoying the view. Maybe she'd take me for a prospective renter.

Fortunately Lydia's building was on a side of the roof blocked from her view by the servants' quarters. It was a twin edifice down to the laundry lines, but there were no maids around. I climbed carefully onto the parapet and made the four-foot leap to the neighboring roof, pushing off hard enough to clear the wall, but banging my knee on landing. I limped over to the small blockhouse that accommodated the maids and found the door to the stairs. It was locked.

So were all the other doors. There was no one on the roof to-day. The girls would be working in the apartments or marketing and they had prudently locked their domain away from intruders.

I took out Lydia's napkin, oriented myself, and found the corner of the building directly above her apartment. From there I could lean over and look down on a small balcony the floor plan indicated was off her living room. It would be no big thing to hang over the side and touch down on the wrought iron railing below. Not for a stunt man. And even he'd want an air cushion under him.

The first thing I did was make sure no one was looking up from the street, like a cop or maybe some soldiers. There were a few cars and a man selling tacos from a pushcart to three customers, nothing threatening. I hiked a leg over the parapet and squirmed over onto my stomach, aware that I was in no condition for this kind of shit. Sweat popped out of my forehead and stung my eyes, which I kept away from the sidewalk five stories down. I didn't even want to think about what could happen if the individual I half-expected to find in Lydia's apartment happened to be looking out over the balcony.

I gripped the edge of concrete and lowered myself until I dangled, legs thrashing like a hanged man's to find purchase on the railing below. It was there and it supported me, but there was that god-awful moment when I had to let go of the roof and teeter, willing my weight forward toward the terrace rather than backward to the unthinkable.

Nobody shot me or pushed me off into space. In fact, curtains were drawn across the French doors to the balcony so no one could see me from inside. I couldn't see in either, but I felt the odds were leveling out a little. I had something under my feet again.

When my hands stopped shaking, I turned the knobs to the French doors and let them open slowly outward. A breeze played with the curtains and my heart paused. When nothing happened I slipped inside and drew the doors shut behind me, staying in back of the curtains, listening for anything at all above the distant grumble of traffic.

There was no sound nor any sense of presence, no trace of tobacco smoke or scent. I stepped into a modest living room furnished with a modern set of matching chairs and sofa, a dining alcove in one corner with the table under a cheap chandelier. The kitchen had the tiny refrigerator and primitive stove of typical Mexican kitchens, and a trace of foul-smelling local gas hung in the air. I looked into the bedroom, simply furnished again, and in the closet that held Lydia's small but tasteful wardrobe. The place was much more Spartan than the apartment Terri had shared with Gil, but there was the same peculiar feeling of absence. Even the prints on the walls could have been selected by a decorator for Holiday Inns.

I glanced into the bathroom and finally went in the small room serving as an office. Here, at least, she spent some time. There was a large desk made of rich mahogany with a comfortable chair behind it and an antique couch on bowed legs that looked both sturdy and valuable. The photos on the desk intrigued me. One of a stern-looking man with a tangle of graying hair who must have been her doctrinaire father and, in an oval frame, a young, burningly sincere Willie Clewes.

The desk wasn't locked and the box of stationery was easy to find. Sandwiched between sheets of blue writing paper were the letters from Willie, his neat, almost prissy handwriting unchanged since school days. The envelopes were coarse and cheap but the stamps bore heroic likenesses of Russian leaders with hammers and sickles prominent in the background. My hands shook as I carefully removed a letter.

It began conventionally, "Dear Lydia," and it was signed, "Your loving Comrade," but I wouldn't call it a love letter. Rather, it was a diatribe against America, "The rotten core of Capitalist Imperialism," a pouring out of bile over real or imagined grievances suffered in a society that was "a malignant racist cancer that we must cleanse by fire if it cannot be cauterized from within." The next letter, written two months later, contained more in this vein plus a résumé of his progress in Russian-language studies and in a course called "Sabotage and the Elimination of Imperial Puppet Collaborators."

There were six letters in all. I was tempted to read on but I didn't want to linger in Lydia's apartment. I buttoned the letters into a hip pocket, my jacket already being stuffed with envelopes full of money, and put the box of stationary back in the drawer. My heart was beating fast and my palms were sweating, not out of fear now but in anticipation. Willie had written his own indictment; I was going to make sure sentence was carried out. How about that, Gil?

I padded over to Lydia's front door and listened, then eased it open and stepped out. A man was standing there on the landing because this building, unlike its neighbor, had a staircase instead of an elevator. He was thin, with high, angular features, slick colorless hair, and a long corded neck. He looked just as surprised as I was.

I don't know if he was about to come in or was just stationed out there, but it didn't matter. He stepped back to gain space, reaching inside his gray jacket. I grabbed for his wrist and bulled him back across the landing into the railing above the stairwell. He was wiry and managed to get the little automatic out but couldn't point it at me. I clubbed his hand against the railing until the pistol dropped at our feet and then booted it skittering away from us. He clawed at my face and tried to twist free, but I jammed my elbow against his long, ropy neck and forced him backward until his upper torso was hanging above the stairwell. Then I reached down, got my free arm under his knees, and heaved. Over he went, thumping against the landings on his way down, making a thick, final sound at the bottom.

I followed him using the stairs, taking them two at a time despite the pain in my knee. This time a few doors opened timidly as I limped across the landings. The tentative brown faces probably belonged to the maids who lived on the roof.

When I reached the ground floor, the thin man was rolling around moaning. I walked past him, found a back door that opened on the narrow alley, and followed it to the street. No one trailed behind or paid me any particular attention as I took a circuitous route back to the cafeteria.

Lydia was there sipping coffee, giving the impression that only minutes had passed since I'd left her rather than the hours it seemed to me. Some stress must have showed as I walked up to her booth.

"What happened?" she asked, studying my face. "You're scratched."

"Let's go." I held out my hand to help her up.

"Did you find the letters?"

"Yes, come on."

The American embassy was within walking distance, six short blocks away on Reforma Boulevard next to the Maria Isabella hotel. I left Lydia under the hotel canopy and strolled past the embassy, glancing into cars parked nearby. They were empty. Two Mexican cops in blue uniforms carrying automatic weapons were stationed at the outer entrance under the high tines of the black iron fence guarding the perimeter. Within, I could see a United States Marine in dress blues on either side of the doorway to the building itself. Wire mesh screens protected the lower windows against grenade attack, and for all I know there might have been an antiaircraft battery on the roof.

I looked up Reforma Boulevard, often compared in grandeur to Paris's Champs Elysées. The traffic was already heavy, and fumes were rising around the tall, golden statue of the Angel. Between the side street in front of the embassy and the boulevard was a manicured strip of park, crisscrossed with walkways and shaded by tall trees. I sat on a bench and lit a cigarette, looking at the people passing by—young and smartly dressed for the most part, moving as if they had someplace to go. A bootblack polished the shoes of a business type, who sat on a stool reading a newspaper, his feet on a scarred red box. I got up and walked by him for a closer look, but he was just an elegant old man with a diamond pinkie ring and very thick glasses.

Lydia watched me come toward her and then followed me into the coldly modern, low-ceilinged lobby of the Maria Isabella. "It looks all right," I told her.

"Then let's get it over." She didn't look out of place in the charcoal suit. It had survived last night's drenching better than mine, and Mexicans in the capital are given to wearing dark colors day and night. Her hair was pulled severely back and there was that touch of dusky lipstick. At a glance, she seemed as cool and controlled as when I'd met her, but behind her composure I had a feeling she was drawn taut, ready to shatter. Tension peered out of her eyes.

"You go on ahead," I said. "I'll stay a little back and watch for anything unusual. Walk as if you're going right by the embassy and then just turn in."

She put out her hand. "Give me the letters."

I shook my head. "I'll take them in."

She looked as if she wanted to object, then turned away from me and went out through the revolving doors. I gave her a moment and followed, staying a dozen yards behind, watching for anyone loitering around near the embassy. Lydia walked along briskly, back straight and head held high, betraying none of the uncertainty she had to be feeling. For an instant she was my partner, no matter what had gone between us.

Nothing in her attitude suggested what she was going to do. She never glanced at the two cops until she was abreast of them. Then she turned abruptly and moved to pass between them, a quick lunge that should have taken her beyond the gate and out of harm's way. It didn't work because one of the cops slid quickly in front of her, incalculably efficient.

I suppose it was all the time someone needed. It looked to me as if Lydia had been clipped from behind by a tackle for the L.A. Rams. Her knees buckled and she flew forward even before I heard the chatter of an automatic weapon from somewhere in the little park. Either she took one of the guards down with her or he was hit, too. I saw him struggle to his knees, trying to bring up his submachine gun.

Getting into the compound seemed the best of some bad choices. When the firing from the park stopped, I grabbed the moment to run in and dive over the fallen like a ball carrier at the line of scrimmage. But the second cop clubbed the side of my head with the butt of his weapon and I was down too, sprawled over the shattered body of Lydia. I must have tried to get up, because they say he hit me again. I wouldn't know about the second time.

I woke up briefly in an ambulance, judging by the sway and the siren. A dark young man in white leaned over me, but beyond him I could see a fair-haired man wearing a grey suit. I guess I tried to get off the gurney or whatever I was lying on because he held me down while the guy in white gave me a shot that knocked me out again.

Then I was in a hospital room, all neat and antiseptic, white on white. I didn't have to feel my head to know it was bandaged.

The bandages seemed to have been applied to hold in the pain. When he saw I was awake, a short-haired man in a gray suit got out of his chair and left the room. He looked familiar, like a new friend you should remember.

He was back in moments with a doctor who went through the motions of consulting a chart, taking my pulse, thumbing up my eyelids, and listening for a heartbeat. "A mild concussion but no fracture," he said to the gray-suited man in Spanish-accented English, leading me to conclude I was in Los Angeles. "I recommend two days under observation here." Then he straightened up and left the room.

"How are you feeling, Mr. Murdoch?" the other man asked. "My name is Hood. I'm with our embassy."

Murdoch! That brought everything floating around in my head together in a sour lump. I licked my lips and looked around the room, trying to order my thoughts.

"You're in the British-American hospital in Mexico City. Do you remember what happened?"

I kept licking my lips until he held a glass of water so I could drink through a crooked straw. "Easy now. There we go."

I leaned back on the pillow and looked at him gratefully. His crew cut made him seem younger than he was and the tailored gray suit fit well but didn't belong on him. He should have been in uniform. "Now, then . . ." he said, prompting me.

"I was on my way to Sanborns for breakfast," I began, letting inspiration dictate my words. "I was walking past the embassy when someone started shooting. Then I saw this woman fall down . . ." I shook my head. "Jesus!"

Hood nodded. "And you came charging right at the gate. The guard thought you must be one of the attackers. You're lucky he didn't shoot you instead of just slug you a couple of times, Mr. Murdoch."

"Well, dammit, the American embassy suddenly seemed the safest place to be. I guess I should have hit the deck."

"That's what I would have done."

"Guess I panicked a little. I saw those Marines in there and the place looked like home. You know."

"Yeah."

No one said anything for a minute. "What was going on anyway?" I finally asked him.

"Guy giving shoeshines took a machine gun out of his box and opened up."

The shoeshine boy! "Did he get away?"

"Not quite. A motorcycle cop ran him down and then blew him away. The woman's dead, too." He pulled his chair up close to my bed and sat down. "You looked like you might be American and you were kind of half on U.S. territory, so the Marines came down and pulled you in. They checked your I.D. and then went and got me. I'm a security officer, by the way." He looked at me to see if I wanted to say something. I didn't.

"Well, then I got into the ambulance with you. Some of those crews will steal your socks before they deliver you to the hospital and it seemed the thing to do for a fellow citizen."

"Thanks." I felt around under my blanket and discovered I was dressed in one of those white night shirts they give you in hospitals everywhere. *Where was all my stuff?*

"We took charge of your belongings," Hood went one, reading my mind. "Nothing to worry about." He rose.

"When can I get out of here?" I asked him, never thinking it was going to be that simple. "Where do I find my things?"

"Almost nine thousand dollars in cash is a lot of money for a tourist to be carrying around, don't you think?"

Here it comes, I thought. "Is there a law against it?"

"Nope." Hood walked to the door and opened it, letting me see a man in civilian clothes sitting just outside in a chair. "Rest easy now, you hear?" He went out before I could say anything more.

They left me alone for the rest of the day. Nurses checked my vital signs and attendants brought food. I had a private room and bath, a pretty good view of the city through a screened window, and lots of time to think. I got out of bed and prowled around to find that my clothes weren't in the small closet and there was indeed a permanent guard outside my door, an American who wouldn't speak to me. All this bother over a few thousand dollars didn't make sense. Did they think I was trying to attack the embassy barehanded? Or had the real Murdoch been found, leaving me under suspicion for murder?

Gordon Ellis of the Central Intelligence Agency came to talk to me early the next morning, when I was barely awake and still groggy from sedatives. He let me play around with his credentials, hold them up to the light, whatever I wanted. When I was ready to concede he was the genuine article, he pulled up a chair and sat next to me, just as Hood had done.

"Mr. Murdoch," he began, "you haven't been forthright with us."

"I haven't?"

He sighed. "Among your things, along with all that money, were letters to Lydia Ballesteros, the woman who was shot to death in front of the embassy. She was a Communist party member known to Mexican authorities, as was the man who killed her. Naturally, we're intrigued."

For a moment I considered concocting a story about an attractive woman I'd met in a bar who had charmed me into helping her deliver some documents to the American embassy. The moment passed and I worked myself into a sitting position with Ellis helpfully cranking up the hospital bed. "Can you get me a pack of cigarettes?" I asked him.

"Sure."

I didn't leave much out of the story I told Ellis, except for Pop's part in Murdoch's death; I said I did it with his gun. It took a long time because he'd take me back over parts of it in detail, trying to catch me in contradictions. We had breakfast and lunch together, commiserating over the rubbery hospital food. I grew to like Ellis. He was about sixty, with a trim white mustache, thin hair, and a debauched, handsome face. When he was younger he must have looked like the secret agents in old movies. You could tell he liked to drink, readily picture him in a trench coat.

At last, late in the afternoon, he turned off his tape recorder and massaged the purple circles under his eyes. "That's one of the wilder fucking stories I've heard in my thirty-some years in this unlikely business. Just one of them."

"You don't believe it."

"Oh, I believe it. Liars seldom incriminate themselves to the extent you have."

"Will it hang him?"

"No one hangs anymore."

"You know what I mean."

"Authenticate the handwriting in those letters and his act might unravel some."

He wasn't cheering me up. "What happens now?"

"It's not for me to say. We share jurisdiction with the FBI in matters involving domestic espionage. They'll want to study the tape. Maybe there's something to act on, I don't know."

"Maybe?"

He stood up. "Meanwhile I'll get this stuff typed up so you can sign a statement."

"The tape's for your information, any way you want to use it. But I'm not signing statements yet."

"Suit yourself."

Nurses fed me, removed my bandages, and smiled patronizingly when I inquired about my future. I had contusions, some stitches in my temple, a little swelling, nothing more. My pupils looked normal and I felt reasonably well physically. But my rest was uneasy despite the pills they gave me.

I'd see Lydia Ballesteros as she walked away from me toward the embassy, her back rigid as if anticipating the bullets about to shred her flesh, and wondered if she'd known more than I did and gone under the gun willingly. She had no future, she'd said. Or had I set her up coldly, sent her in to draw fire in case someone was waiting for us, as proved to be the case? Not consciously, I decided. I never thought it would happen.

"The hell you didn't," Gil contradicted from the foot of my bed. He was sitting there with his legs crossed, one Gucci loafer swinging idly. Or maybe it was just the pills. "But then she did the same for you, old chum," he added. "And one good turn deserves another."

"I didn't want her dead, for Christ's sake!"

"But she is and you're not. She must have had some great stories to tell. Too bad."

"Can we get him without her, Gil?"

"I dunno . . ."

"Handwriting experts can confirm he wrote those letters."

"Let's say everything meshes and he goes to jail . . ."

"Yeah?"

"Maybe long enough to write his memoirs, like the Walkers. He'll probably get out while he's still young enough to star in the movie."

"You're as bad as Ellis."

"Well, you know how things are nowadays."

"What the hell can I do about that?"

He grinned at me, a smug flash of teeth to tell me he was way ahead of me. "You'll think of something," he said.


My next visitors were FBI agents, two of them. Lionel Meers was assigned to the embassy in Mexico City and Jim Constantine had just flown down from Los Angeles. Constantine was the one who gave me a jolt.

"Your friend Gil Buckler worked with me on the Clewes thing," he said as we shook hands. I'd been walking around my room in the hospital gown digesting breakfast, but now I sat down on the bed.

Meers took the only chair in the room while Jim Constantine paced around. Constantine was a young man in a three-piece suit whose Mediterranean good looks reminded me a little of Gil, but he was shorter. "I work in Soviet counterintelligence," he told me. "Out of the federal building in Westwood. I recruited Gil personally and I was his contact. My supervisor sent me down here to talk to you. We don't usually discuss anything with people outside the bureau, but you seem to have stumbled into a unique situation."

I had no comment on that one. *Gil working with the FBI!*

"Background is this. You probably read about a Soviet defector named Yurchenko who changed his mind, slipped his leash, and went back to Russia. More than a year ago."

I nodded. It had been pretty embarrassing for U.S. intelligence at the time and got a lot of publicity from a gleeful press.

"He underwent extensive briefing before he changed his mind, if that's what happened. There's a school of thought that he was fako from the beginning, planted to make us look bad, which he did. Thing is, he fingered some authentic Soviet agents, so we could never discount his information."

"Like that ex-CIA guy in New Mexico who got away from you and turned up in Moscow?" The story was coming back to me. It had been a badly bungled case.

Constantine soured at the recollection. "Howard, yeah. Well, anyway, Yurchenko's switch back to the other side left us with several names that could be red herrings or the real thing, we had no way of knowing. After all, he ran a lot of agents in the West. It was his job."

"Let me guess. He named Willie Clewes."

Constantine stopped stalking around and stood in front of me, hands in his pockets. "He did."

"You've known about him all along."

"Not 'known,' just accepted the possibility. That's why we recruited his bodyguard to help us find out. Buckler had been a Los Angeles police officer and that made him good material. When I found out he'd known Clewes for years and didn't seem that fond of him, I thought I had the right man."

I offered my cigarettes around, but there were no takers. I lit up and said, "Did Gil give you anything on Clewes before they killed him?"

Constantine shook his head. "Nothing we could use. It's no crime to be a radical. We'd have to catch him in a criminal act and we didn't have much hope of that as long as he stuck to politics. He's programmed for deep cover. Gil's job was just surveillance."

"Suppose you could get him for murder. Gil's."

"That would be nice."

"That's what he did. Don't you believe it?"

"Personally, I do. Gil was having too much fun on the job."

I knew what he was talking about. "He killed Terri too. So maybe Gil told her something he didn't tell you."

"Maybe. And of course Gil's murder sets Clewes up to win the election."

"So pick your motive. You just mentioned three."

"It's a matter of proving it." Constantine sighed and walked over to the window to look out at the smog. "We've gone over the tape Gordon Ellis made with you. It's not evidential. Unless, of course, we wanted to lock you up."

I sat up at that. "Then go back to the other angle. The letters are in his handwriting! I'd know it anywhere. Has spying gone legal?"

Meers got into the conversation. "This may be hard for you to believe Mr. . . . ah, Storm, but even if we could prove he attended an academy allegedly for spies in Moscow, we don't have anything to indict him with unless he actually commits an act of espionage. You know . . . steals information and places it in foreign hands, something like that?"

I detected the sarcasm and began to dislike Mr. Meers. "You mean you're not going to charge him with anything?"

"We don't want to shatter any cherished illusions, Mr. Storm, but we live in an age of legal technicalities and litigation, not in the hallowed days of Jack Armstrong, the All-American Boy. Clewes wasn't even charged when he broadcast enemy propaganda in wartime."

Constantine put in quickly, "Thanks to you, though, we know he's a mole now and we'll watch him. He's been placed to work his way through our system, not gather information by breaking the law. This thing has been all the way to the top in Washington, by the way. We've got an assistant director in charge of counterintelligence and he's taken it to State, so don't get the idea no one's paying attention."

I began to experience a feeling of deflation. "At least it'll finish his political career, won't it? The papers will have a field day, right?" I hated to hear myself plead.

Constantine looked uncomfortably over at Meers. The pale man answered. "People in the high places of responsibility Mr. Constantine just mentioned have decided that any such leak to the press might prove counterproductive at this time. If the letters can't be substantiated—and believe me, both sides will introduce their 'experts'—Clewes will yell 'Smear!' and the administration could face a real disaster if we're traced as the source of the leak. As a former police officer, you should be familiar with the laws of evidence. With the Ballesteros woman dead, we can't even charge him with bigamy."

I couldn't believe what I was hearing. "You're going to let him become a United States senator? Where he can head committees and vote for enemy interests? He's favored to win, you know!"

Meers said, "The people in Washington have other options. I don't try to second-guess them. They may confront him with what we've got and try to turn him, can you understand that? He must know quite a few alumni of this international spy school he's supposed to have gone to. I suggest you leave this whole matter to professionals."

I turned away from Meers in disgust and addressed Constantine. "You're going to turn around a fanatic? A KGB colonel? You pressure him and he'll catch a flight to Moscow like the guy from New Mexico!"

Constantine snapped, "It's not our decision, Storm!"

"What are you guys going to do when he runs for president? Just not vote for him?"

"Don't be silly," Meers scoffed.

"Silly? That's the goddamn plan!" I turned to Constantine, getting angry. "He killed Gil while Gil was working for you and you're going to sit on your hands! Maybe you're voting for Willie after all."

Constantine's mellow hide turned to deep ocher as he took a step toward me. "Okay, try this on—if you hadn't let the woman get killed she could probably have given testimony that would really put that bastard away! You could have called the embassy for a meeting instead of just trying to walk in. But that would have been out of character, wouldn't it? You'd rather start a war, like you did in California!"

I got off the bed and stood over him. "Sure," I snarled, "and the war's not over! What I leak to the papers and TV and any other individual or institution who'll listen is going to turn into a flood that'll wash Willie down the toilet!"

Constantine turned his back on me and went over to stand by Meers's chair. He shook his head. "Backed up by what?" he asked, reminding me I didn't even have the letters anymore.

Meers said to him, "I was afraid of something like this. That's why we wanted you to come down."

"What the hell, I tried," Constantine shrugged. I might as well have been in another room.

"Well, Storm," Meers said to me at last, "I suppose you've read a lot of those novels about how ruthless we are in the FBI and the CIA. How we operate just like the Russians, blah, blah, *ad nauseam*. So you're steeling yourself to be locked up or murdered." He broke off to sigh. "Sometimes I'd like to have that option, I'll admit. Just be able to do away with nuisances like you.

"However, the reality is much more mundane. We elected to share information with you, hoping you'd understand how delicate this matter is and how it's got to be handled. We haven't succeeded, which is unsurprising considering your actions up until now." He looked at me judiciously, his hands steepled over his midriff, legs stretched out and ankles crossed. "Fortunately, you've been frank with us, too. Decimating the state of California by three citizens last week . . ."

"Self-defense in every case," I cut in, but I felt moisture start on my forehead. This ponderous man was acting like an enemy.

"Chap stuffed into a car at the airport comes to mind," Meers murmured. "Grape grower, wasn't he?"

"A contract killer with a good front."

"He owns a vineyard, Storm," Constantine said. "You were right about that. We checked quietly. Kind of a loner, no family. His neighbors and workers liked him. We confirmed he's missing."

"No record?" I held my breath.

"You luck out there," Constantine admitted. "Brig time in the navy for assault. Armed robbery indictment. But no conviction."

"That ought to tell you something."

"He's been clean for years," said Meers. "But no doubt he is what you say he is. Point is, if you force us, we'll regretfully forward your taped statement to California and you along with it. Let them sort it out up there."

I smiled at the stuffy bastard, couldn't resist it. "Groton or Andover?" I asked. "Or just wishful thinking?"

Meers reddened. "We'll throw your ass to the wolves, is what I'm saying!"

Constantine tried to put it more politely. "You'll tell your story, which you've got to admit is pretty wild. Clewes, who'll probably be a senator by then, will be alerted and have a chance to cover himself. We'll lose him and you'll be in jail. Is that what you want?" He came back over to stand in front of me. "I liked Gil. He was a lousy operative because he talked to his wife, it seems. He was out of his depth, and maybe that's what got them both killed. Or maybe not, it doesn't matter. But I know Clewes is responsible, thanks to your information, and I want him very badly. We all do."

"How does that translate into action?" I sat down on the bed again, feeling bitter, thinking of Charlie Rydell waiting in purgatory.

Meers said patiently, "We are hindered, Storm, by a system of justice that operates very much in favor of the accused and over recent years has added a labyrinth of new obstacles to frustrate prosecutors even when the national security is at stake. But we are a large organization with formidable resources and we are going to vector in on this individual until we have him, in a manner of speaking, by the balls." He liked to talk in measured tones reserved for addressing the semiretarded, pausing now and then to let his words take effect. "Now, in your case we are sticking our necks out to the maximum in not sending you back to California in a package with that tape to let the locals deal with a series of crimes that were committed, after all, in their jurisdiction."

I was tired of listening to him. "You've been over that. What's the option?"

Constantine had the answer. "You live in Mexico, Storm. In Puerto Vallarta, right? Go back there and paint or whatever you did before you got involved in this. Let us handle it based on the very valuable information you've given us. We've convinced the Mexicans you had nothing to do with the Ballesteros woman; Hood never showed them the letters. They don't even know your name, so you're clean down here. Hood's going to take you right out of here straight to the airport. Your things will be returned to you, including, of course, the money found on your person."

I had to admire his timing with the carrot after he'd worked me over with the stick. He stuck out his hand. "Thanks for everything. I'll keep in touch personally, I promise."

I smiled at him. "Don't call us, we'll call you. Right?"

"Exactly," said Meers from his chair, sounding bored.

# ELEVEN

was sitting on my terrace with a bottle of tequila waiting for the sun to sink low enough so I could start bar-hopping at a respectable hour. No Hay was shuffling around with her broom looking intimidated, and even Fred kept his distance, peering at me with solemn saucer eyes. I guess I wasn't very good company, drinking and carrying on conversations with Gil. I knew he wasn't really there, but these were things I couldn't discuss with anyone else.

"Well, can you think of any good moves?" I'd ask, and try to guess the answer.

"Shit, they've got you pretty well boxed in." He began to pace the terrace and I swear the cat got up and moved out of his way. "Who would have thought the cavalry would fail us?"

"Who, indeed?"

"You know what day it is?"

"Lessee. Sunday." A week ago I'd gone to Monica's brunch. It seemed a lifetime.

"Sunday, the second of November," Gil reminded me. "Willie gets elected on the fourth if everything goes as expected."

"They're just going to let it happen." It was still hard to believe.

"What are you going to do?"

"Maybe I'll just stay down here and paint like I was told to."

"You'll never get rid of me that way."

"Maybe I don't want to."

"Okay, consider this. Someday Willie's going to find out Murdoch's dead and conclude you're alive. He can't afford that, can he? You're a loose end and you've seen how Willie handles loose ends."

"Maybe he'll figure I'm harmless now and leave me alone."

"Don't kid yourself. He'll send the Russians after you."

"What?" Jan's voice asked behind me. "Russians?" I hadn't heard her come in.

I turned my chair around and said, "Hi."

She looked at me for a moment and shook her head. "What a mess. What happened to you?" Whatever it was I'd brought it on myself, her tone implied.

I remembered the stitches on my forehead and touched them. "A whole tribe of things . . ."

She waited for a moment but I didn't elaborate. "Okay, be mysterious." She dug into her mesh shoulder bag and put a stack of American bills next to the bottle of tequila. Everyone was throwing money at me lately. "I sold *Semana Santa* and *Day of the Dead*, both of them, so we're low on your stuff. Better go back to work while you're hot."

"Oh, I'm hot all right."

She studied me for a moment. "We're not talking about the same thing, are we?"

"No."

"That's all you're going to say?"

"Except if anyone calls, you haven't seen me."

"Don't be silly. You went to El Farolito last night. People know you're back. Why do you think I came over?"

"I don't mean the locals."

She scowled. "You're not going to tell me what's going on?"

"Sorry." I poured some tequila into my glass and looked around for another one. "Want a drink?"

"Keep that up and you won't be any good to yourself or anyone else," she snapped. "Chispa knows you're back, by the way."

"Fine."

"Don't expect her to come running right over." She adjusted the net bag over her shoulder and strode out of the house, visibly annoyed by my evasions.

• • •

Chispa.

I knew I was in no condition to visit her, but I needed to badly. It was a selfish need to be reassured there was something or someone worth prevailing for, if that's what I decided to try and do. Someone who was alive, that is. I showered, shaved, and changed into my tropical best—a *guayabera* shirt, white linen trousers, hand-crafted sandals. I walked carefully around the tequila bottle on my way out the door. Not a bad start.

Chispa rented a bungalow a few yards from the sands of Los Muertos beach. When I'd met her, over two years ago, it had been in a quiet nook of the town, smelling of night-blooming jasmine and the sea. Now a half-built condo towered over it, a hive of noisy workers by day, an ominous black skeleton at night. She was looking for another place.

I'd have stopped somewhere and called her first, but that might have invited a rebuff. Of course, if she had company, that could be embarrassing too. If Carlos Freebaker was there and he smirked, I decided I'd give him a knuckle sandwich on the spot.

I rang her bell, heard the corresponding "bong" inside and then Chispa's voice asking, "*Quién?*" That would probably be Pepe the parrot, who could imitate her perfectly. Pepe had been my first gift to her. I'd rescued the seedy bird from a dissolute life in El Farolito, where patrons thought it was fun to buy him tequila and teach him to curse. Most evenings Pepe ended up hanging upside down from his perch, barely able to squawk. I didn't think it would be a good idea to take him home to Fred the cat, so I bought him for Chispa. She'd changed his name from Pendejo to Pepe and tried to clean up his act. As far as I knew, he was off the sauce but still spouting obscenities.

Chispa opened the door reluctantly when she saw who it was. I think the stitches in my head got me in. She looked at them and shook her head much as Jan had, and with the same implication. I went by her quickly, before she could change her mind, walking a straight, careful line until I smacked my temple against one of her hanging plants. After that, the stuff I'd gargled with wasn't going to make any difference.

"I'm not offering you a drink," were her first words.

"I don't want one," I lied.

"You've lost weight."

"I've been under stress." She'd never looked lovelier to me. She wore a short robe, her favorite outfit for lounging around home, and her hair was pulled back and cinched with a fuzzy twist of red yarn. I thought for an instant of Lydia Ballesteros, how different they were despite the hair. "I've missed you, Chips."

"So you got drunk and wandered on over."

"A lot has happened."

"*Quién?*" Chispa's voice queried again.

I peered up to see Pepe the parrot clutching a rafter below the beamed ceiling and reached up to touch his molting coat. He tried for my finger and screamed, *Chinga tu madre!* in the voice of the bartender at El Farolito.

Chispa sighed. "You can have him back. He's an embarrassment."

"You don't mean that."

"I mean the second part."

The place was homey. Throw rugs over warm brown tiles, copper pots suspended from the kitchen ceiling. One of my paintings hung on a stucco wall next to a multihued carpet too precious for the floor. From the front you could see the ocean and a corner of Tacho's, the palm-thatched beach bar at the edge of the sand. Too bad about the damn condo looming above.

But it gave me an idea. "Find a place yet?" I asked.

"I've been too busy."

"Think Pepe and Fred could learn to get along?"

"Probably better than we could." She went to sit on the sofa, giving me a glimpse of splendid golden thigh, and looked up at me curiously. "You made some oblique suggestion like that just before you went away. We've been over it."

I sat down next to her. "I've been blind," I said. "It's been you all along." They were the right words but I had to wrap them in flippancy so they'd be easier to take back in case they didn't play.

"Same old silver tongue." She looked at me without rancor. "Something's different, though. You're older. You said a lot happened."

"Oh hell." I wanted to tell her, but not the whole thing. It could be dangerous knowledge. "Gil was murdered, as you know."

She nodded. "I read his wife committed suicide. How sad."

"No, she was murdered too, like Gil. By a future United States senator from California. Willie Clewes. Sound crazy?"

She stared at me. "You know that?"

"I know it. The highest powers in the land know it. But they're not going to do anything. Not now, maybe never. They took away the evidence I had and told me to go home and forget it. Or else."

"Or else what?"

"They could send me to jail."

"For God's sake, why?"

"I broke a lot of rules putting things together. They know where the bodies are buried." Literally, I thought.

"I mean, why would they want to stop you?"

"Politics. Fear, maybe." I put my head back on the sofa and closed my eyes, feeling as if I'd fly apart if someone hit the right button. It wasn't the drinking. Just everything catching up to me now that I'd stopped moving ahead.

I knew she was watching me but I kept my eyes closed. "You see, I don't know what to do now. No one cares a damn about Gil or about justice or any of that shit. They're all playing games and we're just pieces they move around." I was grateful for Chispa being there to listen. It would have been easy to let it all pour out, but I kept it short. "So I came back here like a good boy to set up my easel, maybe catch a few sunsets. Only I don't think it's going to work. Gil won't let me alone." I opened my eyes to see if she was tracking, because I sounded maudlin to myself.

But I had her attention. "From what little you've told me, you've done what you can."

"It almost makes it worse to know that."

"What would *he* do?" she asked.

It was a good question. "I think he'd try to get close to Willie and kill him." I said it aloud for the first time.

She sat up quickly. "Please don't do anything like that. Don't even think about it."

It was the way she said it. With concern. "You asked me what he'd do."

"He's dead. I don't want anything to happen to you."

There it was again. "You're worried about me."

"Of course I am. I care about you. There, you see? It's easy to say what you mean."

I felt a rush. We'd laughed, played together, made love. But since she'd decided my life-style inhibited a long-term relationship we'd managed to keep things light, even when we were fighting. Now she was bending the rules and that was my cue to say something smart-ass and put things back in perspective. I didn't. "It's not easy for me, Chips. Never has been."

"I know. The macho creed."

"Not really. I think it's a defense mechanism. I can't stand rejection."

"Take a chance."

I took a deep breath. "Well, I think it's kind of silly that you live in one place and I live in another. Think of the overhead."

She smiled a little but her eyes were narrow. "Very romantic, but you can do better."

Why not? Suddenly it seemed like the right thing. A place out of the storm. We could be good for each other and I wouldn't have to go out into the night again or stay here alone with only dark memories for company. I shifted around on the couch. "Well, I guess I love you." Jesus, it sounded awkward, but she nodded approval and I rushed on. "We could get married if people still do that. I can mend my ways within limits, and you can even invite your friends from Gringo Gulch to the wedding. Is that what you want?"

She sighed and rested her head against the cushion. "I don't think so, not just now. But it's nice to hear you say it."

I struggled off the couch and stood over her, too tired to think of an appropriate remark.

"Oh, sit down. You're swaying."

"Hell with that." I pointed myself at the door and took a couple of palsied steps.

Then she was in front of me, her hands resting lightly on my shoulders, a tall girl who fit against me very well. "You're in no shape to travel, Jonny."

"I'll manage," I growled.

"Stop pretending to be offended when you're relieved."

"Balls. You set me up."

"I'll admit I was fishing. But you're not ready, Jonny. There's this other thing."

"Carlie Freebaker?" I asked between my teeth.

"Don't be silly. Where have you been the last ten days?"

Now *I* wasn't tracking. "You pretty much suggested I stay out of it."

"I want you to stay out of danger, that's all. Isn't there another way? Some alternative to violence?"

"Sure. Lay everything out and maybe do time!"

That gave her pause. Finally she said, "I don't have an answer. You didn't tell me enough for me to figure out what's going on."

"I can't do that. You'd have guilty knowledge. It's not your problem."

"It will be if you crawl into a bottle and brood. That won't work for either of us."

I stepped back from her. "I'd better go."

"No." She planted herself. "I'm not going to stand in as your excuse to go stumbling around town on a morbid drunk."

"What is this? A mercy lay?"

169

"Who said anything about getting laid? I'm just taking you off the streets."

"I was going straight home." But I didn't protest as she led me down the little hallway to the bedroom. She turned me around and gave me a light shove so I toppled back to sit on the bed, a tower with shaky foundations.

"Take off your own shoes, Jonny," she called on her way to the bathroom.

"I'm tapped out," I told myself aloud, and fell over sideways.

I woke to a warm insistence tucked against me, as naked as I was. At first I didn't know where I was, and I sat up with a hell of an adrenaline start. Moonlight was pouring across the bed through the louvers, striping us both like a couple of tigers, and I could hear the sea slapping gently against the shore, tame within the semicircle of the bay. Then disorientation gave way to the notion that I was exactly where I belonged, in fact that I'd never left. Where else was there, anyway?

I looked at the mound of her hip and traced the full, familiar line with my hand. She stirred, her breathing skipped a beat, and I guessed she was awake. I nestled closer, cupping a firm, warm breast, feeling the nipple harden like a tiny creature apart. She turned in my arms and I felt her breath play across my cheek before I found her mouth with mine. Then she was stretched full length against me, her hands locked at the small of my back, tugging, and I remembered the remarkable strength of her and knew what was in store for me and wondered for an instant before it began that I could be such a fool as to risk losing her.

I didn't wake up again until ten o'clock and she was gone by then. The hammering and yelling of a score of little brown laborers swarming all over the scaffolding of the condo next door prodded me out of a deep sleep. Once there was nothing to hear but the murmur of the surf and the tolling of a distant church bell. Once, they say, it was like that all the time.

170

Showered and dressed, I wandered into the kitchen to put on coffee, then decided to have breakfast at Tacho's instead. Maybe take a walk along the beach afterward. Simple pleasures were becoming important.

On my way out, I removed the cover Chispa had thoughtfully left over Pepe's cage. *"Puta madre!"* screamed the parrot as soon as he was unveiled. *"Hijo de la chingada!"* I decided I liked him better when he was drunk.

It was too early for tourists and there was no one in Tacho's but a few waiters lounging around drinking coffee. I took a table on the beach under a palm-thatched *palapa*, kicked off my sandals, and dug my feet in the warm sand. A waiter named Chucho came over and said with a grin, *"Andas muy elegante, Don Juan."* They weren't used to seeing me wearing a pleated *guayabera* shirt at Tacho's.

I ordered a beer and the special, a sort of bastard version of *huevos rancheros* consisting of tortillas under a layer of refried beans topped by eggs and smothered with cheese. The sky was an improbable blue and the sun bounced off the incoming ranks of breakers. Some kids had a small fire going and were barbecuing fish impaled on sticks they'd sell to the tourists later on.

I finished breakfast and sipped my beer, daydreaming about life in the slow lane with Chispa. Perhaps I'd begin painting the stark contrasts of Mexico, a project I'd had in mind for some time. Condominiums nudging aside the jungle, thatched huts in the flight paths of jetliners, stuff like that. Not exactly a new concept, but an expression of the vague resentment I'd begun to feel toward progress in most of its forms.

Maybe they really would let me alone down here now that they'd won. That would be what mattered to them—neutralizing the enemy, not playing revenge games. But I knew Gil wouldn't buy that. I could see him shaking his head, raising an eyebrow at my naiveté. "You're still an unknown quantity. They can't afford it."

"What would *you* do?" I asked him Chispa's question, feeling testy. He was the fly in the ointment of my content.

"If I were you?"

"Yeah."

He sighed and looked out at the ocean. "I don't know. Maybe I'd take the lady and run. But you'll be looking over your shoulder until you get a crick in your neck. I'm sorry I got you into this, old friend."

I left some money on the table and walked back to Chispa's cottage. Pepe greeted me with an obscenity, but I felt at home. When I came back it would be to stay, not to run. The note I left Chispa said, "I'm going for the alternative. Don't worry. Love." Then I added, "P.S. Stay away from Carlie Freebaker. He's after your money."

If I hurried I could catch the noon flight coming from Mexico City.

# T W E L V E

stole back into my own country like a thief, taking the Aeroméxico flight to Tijuana and walking across the border. The only I.D. I carried belonged to Larry Murdoch and I wasn't about to use it without knowing whether or not he'd been found. In San Diego I caught PSA to Los Angeles and then cabbed up to the castle on Mulholland, arriving at mid-afternoon California time. I didn't plan to stay there but I needed my car and I wanted to talk to Pop.

Martins let me in the gate, and when I asked for my father, he said, "This is Sunday, remember?"

Of course. Ladies' Day. "What are you doing here?" I asked him.

He shook his head, looking surly. "Your old man won't leave the house empty anymore, so I gotta stay on Sundays. Then I gotta replace a window and get a lotta tough stains off the floor, which isn't my job. I don't know what the hell's going on anymore. Pardon me, I just work here."

As I started past him he added, "Guy's called you about four times. Name of Tom Grayson. I left the number on a pad in the kitchen."

I'd forgotten about the Jolly Green Giant. My plan, if that's what you could call it, didn't include him. I was going to look up a columnist with the *Herald Examiner* who had written a decent item about my case when everyone was after my badge and give her the scoop of a lifetime—an exclusive on Willie Clewes. Then I was going to go to Norman Kling and tell him why so many people were dead and where one of them, Larry Murdoch, could be found. After that, I was going to hold out my wrists and let him put the cuffs on them. Let the F.B.I., the C.I.A., the State Department, and the local police do their worst, I was through with playing games. Sometimes you have to burn down the barn to kill the vermin. Which, some part of me whispered, is pretty stupid when you're inside. But my mind was made up, because when it was over maybe I could go back to Chispa and live in the slow lane without looking over my shoulder. Someday.

I went upstairs, took a shower, and changed into California clothes—chinos, a windbreaker, and topsiders. I pocketed my own wallet as well as Murdoch's and decided to take along his .38 Special, loaded except for the round he'd fired. Then I packed a flight bag with shaving gear, a change of underwear, and cigarettes, on the reasonable assumption that I'd be detained. After a moment's hesitation, I crammed in my ill-gotten eight thousand and some dollars and finally I went to Pop's bedroom, took the .45 six-shooter from the holster in his closet, and threw that in the bag too. All the evidence Kling would need to really stick it to me.

That left me with nothing to do until I'd talked Pop into backing my story instead of trying to star in the shoot-out with Murdoch.

Meanwhile, it couldn't hurt to return a phone call. The Jolly Green Giant hadn't tried to reach me four times for nothing. I didn't want to use a phone in the castle in the unlikely case we were bugged, and there were no near and friendly neighbors, so I took my stuff down to the garage and put it in the Chrysler, shoving it well up forward in the trunk compartment. The battery was weak but the car started up after a moment of suspense and I pulled out to head west on Mulholland.

I turned again on Roscomare and drifted down through Bel-Air, past sleek homes with aquamarine pools out front and box hedges to guard the driveways. The sun was still well above the horizon because of the time change and the hot Santa Ana wind was at work again, blowing the smog out toward Catalina Island. On Sunset I headed toward the ocean, driving aimlessly through Brentwood and Santa Monica until I found myself back on the mean streets of Venice, taking a right on Washington and parking in front of the burned-out shell of the Pit Stop. They'd roped off the area and there weren't any Harleys around, but nothing else had changed. People still pedaled or roller-skated along the bike path next to the beach, dodging bums drinking out of brown-bagged bottles and hustlers trying to sell dope or stolen software. I found a pay phone and dialed the number the Giant had left for me.

"'Allo?" I recognized the furry voice of his live-in and asked if Tom was there.

"No. Be back soon. Few minutes."

I gave her the number of the phone I was calling from and went to buy a copy of the *Times* from a dispenser, tossing most of the bulky edition into a trash can. A couple of punks wearing dreadlocks coiled to their shoulders gave me the hard eye. Only lames use the trash cans in Venice.

I glanced through the news section of my paper leaning against the phone booth. With the dirtiest campaign in California history coming down to the wire, all the other state races were being eclipsed by the scandal surrounding the alleged attempt

174

on Willie's life by Buck Rydell's son. Willie had taken a commanding lead in the polls.

The Jolly Green Giant called back in about the time it took four ghetto blasters to go by. "Where you *been*, baby?" he wanted to know. "I been callin' for days!"

"Here and there. What's up?"

"What's up is I got a fuckin' witness! But I can't keep her on ice forever!"

He picked me up ten minutes later in the kind of cross-country vehicle with opaque windows favored by Central American death squads. "How come you just fuckin' disappeared, man?"

"Couldn't be helped. What about this witness?"

"Felix's chick, baby. After he got hit by the truck, she stayed in his place, 'cause the rent's paid up. I got next to her 'cause she already knows I dealt with Felix, so I'm righteous, see? I give her some ecstasy too, so she's been floatin' free."

"You shot her up?" He had to be talking about some drug.

"Ecstasy's oral, where you been? I don't do needlework. Anyway, she knew Felix'd get burned someday 'cause he's a hitter. I said, 'Shit, I don't believe it!' real surprised, you know?"

"She didn't buy an accident?"

"Guys like Felix don't die accidental. Not being chased around by pickup trucks, for chrissake." We were driving up the Coast Highway toward Malibu against the last of the weekend beach traffic, a steady stream of Japanese plastic headed for L.A. "So I tell her Felix never worked anything but iron for me, which is true. She says that's what she thought too, iron and dope, until she found out different and that's why she figures Felix had to get it. He was over his head, too far uptown."

I was confused about exactly what the girl had witnessed. "You mean she saw the pickup truck take out Felix?" I asked, disappointed.

The Jolly Green Giant took his eyes from the road and looked at me patiently. "No, baby. She saw the guy who put out the contract on Gil."

175

•  •  •

The El Rancho Motel was just past Topanga Canyon on the inland side of the Coast Highway. The sign advertised thirty units for rent by the day, week, or month. Three rows of identical white plank cottages with red roofs, backed up against the foothills and separated by gravel drives. In front of them, a wide concrete apron served as parking space for a seafood restaurant and bar called the Swagger Inn.

As we crossed it, the Jolly Green Giant said, "He was walkin' right along here on his way to get some cigarettes, the chick told me. Fuckin' truck must've been waitin' for him. It run up on him and knocked him maybe fifty feet against that wall." He motioned toward the restaurant. "They hadda scrape him off with a trowel."

Felix's cottage was in the second row, behind the motel office. Up close the buildings looked dilapidated, as if they were held together by the thick layers of paint that covered the rotting wood. The steady tenants would be surfers, beach bums, assorted drifters. Maybe a few tourists on tight budgets.

The Giant opened the screen door without knocking and I followed him in. The place was dim, with the shades drawn and the windows closed. I made out a single main room, a kitchenette, bath, and closet. Just the bare essentials. A small color TV pantomimed soundlessly in one corner.

"Hey, Iris! Hey, darlin'!" the big man called.

A figure leaped through the sleazy, beaded curtains veiling the kitchenette onto his broad back. He gave a great yell and I jumped a foot or so off the ground. Then I heard the giggling and saw the girl clinging to him like a monkey. The Giant went along with it, roaring and bouncing up and down. Finally he peeled her off of him and set her on a sofa. "Goddamn, you scared me, darlin'!" He went to the windows and let the paper shades roll up.

She laughed, delighted, until she noticed me. Then she inspected me with round eyes that scurried over me like a pair of gray mice. Her blond hair was parted in the center and hung limply to her shoulders, but it had a healthy gloss and her skin was clear. She might have been twenty.

"Who is he?" she queried. "I don't want to party."

"He's my pal."

When she held still she was nearly beautiful. Her legs beneath the cut-off jeans that climbed her buttocks were long and smoothly muscled, the breasts perky against her T-shirt. Her features were perfectly integrated—slightly up-tilted nose above a cupid's-bow mouth, full, even brows over darker, curling lashes. A California girl.

But when she moved or spoke, she was out of sync. Her eyes lost focus; her mouth worked at inexpressible thoughts. She was a lovely structure built around a vacuum. Finally, she took her eyes off me and looked at the giant. "Give me a tab, daddy. I want to get back on the plane."

"You're higher'n the fuckin' Concorde now, darlin'. You gotta come down." He got up and lumbered into the bathroom. When he came back, he handed her a glass of water and two pills. "Drop them both," he commanded.

"I don't want to! No downers, come on! Not yet."

"Hey, I don't wanna hafta break your skirts, okay?" He glowered down at her convincingly until she took the pills. "Quaalude," he said to me. "It takes a few minutes."

I felt disgusted with the Giant. "Did you have to drug her?"

"I hadda keep her from splittin'. Look, this is designer shit. New since your time. It's harmless."

Maybe he believed that. I shook my head. "I can't do much with a freaked-out witness."

"You want her to go to court?"

"What the hell do you think?"

"I thought you just wanted to know personal. I don't know if she'll testify to anything."

"I'll take what I can get, Tom, but it's got to stand up."

The girl had been chuckling and humming to herself, looking from one of us to the other, still half out of this world. "Testify to what?" she asked suddenly.

"Nothin', darlin'," he told her. "I just want you to tell my pal what you told me about Felix takin' a contract the other day."

That sobered her more than the 'ludes. "Oh, come on! What is he, some kind of cop?"

I sat down across the coffee table from her. "Let me be straight with you, Iris. I'm not a cop, but I want the guy who killed Felix for my own reasons. Don't you want to see him pay?"

She didn't say anything, just stared beyond me as the thoughts gathered as slowly as clouds behind her eyes.

"Did you love him, Iris?"

She kept looking past me, perhaps searching for Felix. "I was crazy in love with him. He gave me what I wanted and he took me places, down to Mexico. This dump is just a crash pad. We were free, do you understand that, man? Free! Like the wind in those Mexican deserts down there."

"But someone took him away from you."

She shook her head violently.

I sighed. "Well, maybe it wasn't who you think anyway."

"It was! Felix said it was a big deal with very important people. He didn't know how big until he read the papers after he did it. After that, he wouldn't tell me anything, but I'm not stupid. I can read too. Then he said we were going away for a while. Just before . . ." She stopped and tried again. "Before they . . ."

"Who is they?"

"Whoever hired Felix. The one I saw."

"Did you recognize him?"

"No."

I wondered if she was lying. "You said Felix was dealing with very important people."

Her eyes evaded mine. "That's what he said."

"And you read something, too."

"Yeah, but I'm not going to talk about that."

"How did you see who contracted Felix? They just let you sit in?"

"No. It's because Felix was standing right there in the door and saw him coming. He told me to get in the can and stay there until he came for me. Later he told me he wanted me to hear what they said, just in case. He trusted me, see?"

It wasn't hard to guess why Felix wanted her there. Later he could use a witness as leverage. Except he never got the chance. "That was risky," I said. "The guy could have insisted on looking around before they talked." Anyone but an amateur would do that.

She shrugged. "I thought of that, but Felix laughed. 'So what?' he said. He wasn't afraid of anyone. He was very physical."

I remembered that about Felix. "Did he tell you who it was?"

She shook her head. "No. I just heard what they said and later I saw him."

"Well, what did they say?"

She looked at the Jolly Green Giant. "Why should I tell him anything? I don't know who he is."

He rasped, "Because I told you he's righteous, goddammit!"

"Not because I'm righteous, Iris. Because they killed Felix. If you help me, maybe we can do something about it."

"Felix is dead. I'm alive! I want to stay alive!"

I took out my cigarettes and lit one. It wasn't going to be easy after all. "I don't want to lean on you, Iris, but the guy Felix killed was my friend. And the guy that hired Felix really killed them both. So we have something in common, you see?"

She didn't. "Those people are dead!"

I tried looking behind those clear, gray eyes, but nobody was home. "I thought you loved Felix."

"Nothing's gonna bring him back."

I stood up and looked down at her, rocking on my heels, fairly menacing. "Okay, then here's what's going to happen. I'll get the word out that you heard them make the contract if I have to take out an ad. Who you are, and where you are. Then, like somebody said once, you can run but you can't hide." I turned and started for the door. Slowly.

"Wait!" I heard her yell. And then, "You going to let him do that to me, Tommy?"

"You're doin' it to your own self, doll," he growled.

I turned and looked back from the door, waiting.

"I don't know who it was," she said.

"Just tell me what happened." I came over and sat back down.

She drew her legs up on the couch and sat on them. "He came in and didn't want a drink, just wanted to talk business. He told Felix he wanted this guy killed. He asked him if he could handle an Uzi and Felix said yes but it was going to cost more than inciting riots. The guy said okay and told him when he wanted it done. A Thursday night around eleven. At a gas station on Sepulveda. He said an eighty-two Plymouth four-door, dark blue, was going to pull up to a gas pump with two men in it. When the smaller one went into the station office, Felix was supposed to hit the other one. Then he was supposed to shoot up the station. 'Shoot it to pieces,' the guy said, 'but aim high and don't hit anyone. 'Repeat,' the guy says. *Don't hit anyone!*' He told Felix to rip off a car for the job and wear a ski mask, too."

I reached for my cigarettes again. "So Felix had worked for him before. Inciting riots."

"You could tell they knew each other the way they acted, you know? But afterwards, Felix wouldn't talk about him or tell me who he was."

"What else did they say?"

"Well, this man told Felix they were going to plant the gun and some other stuff on Chick somebody, who Felix knew, because he laughed. And he said Felix was going to have to organize it. Felix says, 'Man, that's *really* going to cost you.' The guy didn't seem to mind." The girl added bitterly, "Now I know why."

"Did he ever give Felix any money?"

"I don't know. They were going to meet again to work out details. Coordinate everything, the man said. This time was just to agree."

"So they met again."

"They must have, but I wasn't around. Felix was jumpy and we fought a lot. I told him he was crazy to kill someone, but he told me it was a one-time deal for real money and afterward we could go away. Do Mexico on the bikes from one end to the other."

The Jolly Green Giant grunted, "He killed people before."

"When did you see this man?" I asked her.

"Well, when he left. He'd parked in back. He walked around the house and he went right by the window of the john. I could see him as close as I am to you and I could even hear his feet crunching on the stones. He was dressed in a suit and looked like maybe a banker, I swear."

The Jolly Green Giant grinned proudly. "What'd I tell you?"

"What did his car look like?"

"I don't know about cars, except maybe 'Vettes. It was new, I guess. Kind of light blue or gray, a sedan. And it had a bumper sticker."

"What did it say?"

"Somebody's name and then, 'If you care.' I thought it was kind of funny. Care about what?"

I put my cigarette in an ashtray, took out my wallet, and fished for the photo I'd torn out of the *Mexico City News*. I smoothed the scrap of paper and put it on the coffee table in front of her. "Was it one of these men?"

She frowned down at the picture and then pointed without any hesitation at all.

And I'd thought nothing would ever surprise me again.

# THIRTEEN

hen we left the El Rancho Motel, it was dark and a hot wind still blew down the canyons to the sea. The Jolly Green Giant drove me back to my car, which was still there because it wasn't shiny enough for anyone to steal, even in Venice. I opened the trunk compartment, dug around, and separated five thousand dollars from the wad of money stuffed into my flight bag.

The Giant's eyes shone when I handed it to him. "Hey, it's nice to know someone who's holdin'. Who do I hafta kill?"

"Go back and get that girl and don't lose her."

"Fuzz'll go crazy."

"You can handle it."

"I mean, she really digs young blondes."

I sighed and got into the Chrysler, making sure it would start. "I need her as a witness, Tom. Space cadets make bad witnesses. Can you get her clean?"

He looked at the clump of money in his big paw. "Hey baby, anything you say."

It took me twenty minutes to get to L.A. International Airport using Lincoln Boulevard. I turned into Lot C, pulled my ticket from the machine, and went looking for Larry Murdoch's Avis rental. I'd forgotten the row number, so I spent another fifteen minutes searching for the right Buick, half expecting to find they'd towed it away. Murdoch would be pretty gamy after a week in this weather, and someone could have smelled him.

The car was still there. I circled it without touching anything, sniffing for the telltale scent of death. We'd doubled him over and triple-taped the necks of the big lawn bags, each inside another, but decomposing bodies tend to bloat and he could have burst the plastic. I had to be certain he was secure. The policy at airport lots is to leave cars alone for thirty days, but they'd sure as hell investigate an odor.

At the exit I fed my ticket into the reader, which registers no charge for the first two hours. I drove to Santa Monica and checked into a Travel Lodge motel under the name of L. Murdoch, paying cash in advance and giving a phony address and license plate number. That way no connection could be made to the late hit man. No matching signature or auto license. Just a name, in case anyone asked for Murdoch later in the evening.

In my room, I got out the telephone directory and looked up the number I wanted, relieved to find it listed even without an address. Had it been unlisted, I would have had to try going through a few old channels I wasn't sure were still open. It was only eight o'clock, too early for what I had in mind, so I went into the bathroom and splashed cold water on my face, then came back and turned on the TV.

With nothing to do but wait, I tried to concentrate on the old movie plodding its way across the screen, but thirty-second political spots kept interrupting the story line. One of them featured a corroded drainpipe sticking out of a mudbank, leaching bilious green slime into a stagnant pool. Drip, drip, drip. The voice-over, spoken in hushed confidential tones, revealed that Senator Charles Rydell had taken $750,000 from polluters in return for fighting an antitoxics bill. As a result, California water was hazardous to your health. Cut to a charming little girl with blond tresses raising a glass to her lips. Freeze it for two seconds and then cut to a still shot of Willie Clewes framed by an American flag over the legend IF YOU CARE.

In forty-eight hours it would be over. Polls would be closed across the nation and the candidates would be sweating blood as the results dribbled in, preparing speeches of victory or concession, probably both to cover themselves. I closed my eyes and tried to doze off, but it was no use. Would he be home tonight? Certainly not until late, if then.

At nine o'clock I went down and got the medicinal tequila

out of the Chrysler and filled a plastic ice container with cubes from the motel supply. I made a single drink last an hour while I watched the movie without seeing it, rehearsing in my mind the one move that was left for me to make.

At ten-fifteen I stuffed some Kleenex into my cheeks, covered the mouthpiece with another sheet of the tissue, and made the call.

"Hello?" I was surprised that he answered personally.

"This is Murdoch. The man you sent south," I said nasally, with no inflection whatsoever.

He made no reply, but I could hear him breathing.

"I don't like what went down in Mexico City. We got to meet. Now."

"I don't know who you are or what you're talking about."

"Now. Or you're the target."

"You're crazy!"

"I'm in a motel. You can come here."

This time the pause was longer. I could imagine what was going through his mind and wished I could see his face.

He said finally, "No. You come here."

"Where?"

He gave me an address and hung up.

I didn't like it but I'd allowed for the possibility that he'd set the place. Or even refuse to meet. I got there as fast as possible, racing along the night streets and over the Santa Monica mountains on the 405, keeping an eye on the rearview mirror for cops. His place was in the hills above Tarzana on a street called La Mirada, overlooking the valley. I drove past it once, then turned and parked three houses below him and walked back.

It was a contemporary two-story home in an upper-middle-class suburb, the residence of a successful but not ostentatious man. I saw a pale Oldsmobile four-door with a Clewes bumper sticker parked in the driveway as I walked to the front door. There were no lights on upstairs but a dim glow showed through the window by the door. I saw a key-operated burglar alarm next to the jamb as I reached for the doorbell, holding my other thumb over the peephole.

He opened the door almost immediately, as if he'd been waiting. He was dressed in a black silk robe over lime-green pajamas. Nothing moved in his face when he saw me; the consternation was in his eyes. His lips worked at framing the words before he got them out. "You can't come in," he said, and started to close the door.

I stepped forward, compelling him to move back. "Because you're expecting someone else? No one else is coming, Jimbo."

Quest's eyes flickered, the only sign of life amid doughy features. "Are you alone?" I asked him.

"No. My wife and daughter are upstairs asleep."

"Where can we talk? You lead the way."

He didn't know what to do, just stood there with one hand in a pocket of his dressing gown, probably clutching a gun. If I hadn't hated him so much, it might have been funny. "Let's go," I prompted.

He turned and I followed him into a dimly lit den paneled in walnut. There was a large desk in front of the curtained window, a long leather couch with a matching chair, a TV, and a wet bar. Only a desk lamp was burning. Quest stood in the middle of the room as if he didn't know where to go.

"Sit down." I waved him toward his own desk and pulled the leather chair over in front of it.

He went behind the desk slowly, taking his time, but I knew his mind would be racing. He sat down and put his hands on the green blotter in front of him. "You're the one who called and said you were someone named . . . Merrick?"

"Murdoch." I glanced around the den now that his hands were in sight. Framed pictures hung from the wall. Jim Quest grinning at the camera, cheek by jowl with one politician or another. Then I saw the old Colt six-shooter suspended from two pegs under a photo of Quest with Senator Charles Rydell.

His eyes followed mine. "It's not loaded," he said, trying to smile. The one in his pocket would be. "Want to know where

I got it? From Buck Rydell himself. For a job well done back in eighty. Small world, isn't it?"

Smaller than he thought. My father had its twin, the other piece of the matched set. There was no difference except for the ornate handles Pop had put on his. I looked away from the wall and leaned over to pluck a business card from the holder on his desk. "Consultant," I read aloud. "Your clients get a lot more than that for their money, don't they? Including murder."

Quest sighed. "Tomorrow's election day. On top of it all, we've got the funeral. I can't give you much time."

"Funeral?"

"Monica's mother died Saturday. They opened her up and she was full of cancer. Died right after surgery of shock or something."

"Goddammit." I hadn't seen anything in the paper.

"It was good timing. Gets the sympathy vote. I gave out the release this afternoon. He looked at his watch. "I don't know or much care what you want, Storm, but I'll give you five minutes."

I crowded Aunt Kitty out of my mind. "But you're curious or you wouldn't have asked me—or Murdoch—over."

"I don't know any Murdoch." And perhaps he didn't, by name. "Keeping potential nuts away from my client is one of my responsibilities. I'm the lightning rod, so to speak."

"You're right about that. Willie will walk away clean while you sit there on death row. By the way, the smart money thinks the California gas chamber will be back in business after this election."

"Three minutes." He had regained his equanimity; it was time to give him a jolt.

"Okay, I'll be brief. Remember the El Rancho Motel? Where you contracted Felix Hubner to murder Gil? Well, Felix's girl-friend was in the head, listening to the conversation. Didn't it occur to you to look around? Afterward you walked out in back, right past her window. She made you and the car right down to the bumper sticker." I leaned back in my chair watching him closely. "She's on ice. She'll testify."

Nothing about him really changed but his color. He couldn't control that.

"And Murdoch. Attempted murder, with a witness to the deed. He even got off a shot before I took him. I can't prove the bastard killed Terri Buckler or Felix, so he can plea bargain on this charge. They'll probably reduce it to simple assault in return for a name." I grinned at him. "Your name."

He showed me his teeth in return but it was more of a grimace. "What've you been smoking? I don't *know* any Murdoch."

I took a small chance. "That old gag, having him sit in front of your Olds. Amateur night. They've got mirrors, you know. He saw you clearly and he looked at the plates, too. People like that remember things, it's part of the profession. Of course Murdoch screwed up, but he's smart. You know he wants to say he came straight to me with the information that you tried to contract him? That way he couldn't even be held, except as a witness. They might even go for it, I don't know."

Quest's eyes grew bright and shrewd. "They?" he pounced. "Are these people you're talking about in police custody?"

"The girl's safe. She'll keep. So will Murdoch. Did you know he's quite a respectable businessman? Killing's just a tax-free sideline for him. He's got a lot to lose if he runs, and I told him I'd back his story about coming to me up front. You think he'll turn that down?"

Quest's hands fidgeted and dew broke out on his forehead.

"It's not that hot in here, Jimbo. Or is it?"

He swallowed and cleared his throat. "This is all a fanciful pile of bullshit," he decided. "If you had any kind of hard evidence, you'd have taken it to the cops. You wouldn't be sniffing around here. There's something you ought to learn, Storm. Never kid a kidder." He shoved himself back in his seat, his keen little eyes on mine. He reminded me of the kind of bull a matador hates to face in the ring. The clever, dangerous kind that chooses a terrain to defend, bellowing and hooking at the man instead of charging clean and straight. After we'd stared at each other for a moment, he leaned forward and shoved the phone on his desk at me. "Now call the cops or get out of here."

I reached for the phone. "Then you're it, and I lose Willie. For now, anyway. So be it. You were closer to the trigger."

His big paw shot out to cover mine. "What do you mean?"

I got my legs under me and backhanded him across the face as hard as I could. He fell back against his chair with a small, startled cry and I went around his desk fast, caught a handful of limp hair, and yanked his head back while I took a small automatic from the pocket of his dressing gown. I shoved the barrel into his neck and thumbed down the safety.

"Jesus!" he mumbled and raised his hands to cover his shattered nose. Blood began to course down between his fingers.

I let go of his hair and sat on the edge of his desk looking down at him. I'd been ready to kill him, and that wouldn't do. Not yet. "I was going to trade your life for Willie, Quest. I was going to let you face a jury if you'd give me Willie because I know what he is and what he can do. But you had Gil hit and I know that for sure. So I've changed my mind."

He took his shaking hands from his face and stared down at them as if he'd never seen his own blood before.

"Here's what happens," I went on softly. "I came here and confronted you with all this evidence, for my own satisfaction before calling the cops. When I reached for the phone, you pulled out a gun. You ate a slug before I could stop you and then you fell forward and hit your face on the desk . . ."

He looked up at me and I'd never seen such fear on a man's face. His mouth opened to form an "O," but no words emerged.

"I was a cop for a long time, Quest. I know what they look for, and I can set it up perfectly." I slid the clip out of the little automatic, saw it was full and there was a shell in the chamber. "Trouble with these twenty-five-caliber jobs, they don't have much power. The slug could lodge in your head and leave your brain dead instead of killing you outright. But hell, it's a chance I'm willing to take. How about you?"

"Jesus God!" he sobbed. "It was Clewes who wanted Gil dead! I set it up, yes, but it was Bill . . ."

I put the gun against his bleeding nose and he closed his eyes and whimpered, "Please, Jesus, please . . ." I saw the stain against his green pajama leg and smelled his urine.

"Why did Willie want him dead?"

"He always hated him, you knew that." He kept his eyes shut as if nothing could happen if he didn't look. "And then, I'd bugged the beach house with his knowledge and I had all this tape on Monica and Gil. They spent a lot of time in bed together when he was out of town. I played him the tapes and he'd listen with no expression, like he didn't care. And then he got this idea . . . He was way behind in the polls in spite of all her money . . ."

"Who got the idea?"

"He did! He did! He could turn around the election and get rid of Gil at the same time—"

"But you're the consultant. You told him it was feasible. You hired the killer."

"I was under his influence . . . You've got to understand this. You've got to know what he's like—"

"Oh, I know what he's like. Open your eyes, you sack of shit!" I prodded the swollen flesh of his nose with the pistol and he cried out, blinking against his tears. "Tell me how it went down. All of it. Start with Felix."

He searched for his voice, blinking away. "Can we deal?"

"For your life, maybe."

He nodded, jerking his head as if palsied. "All right. All right."

"Felix," I reminded him.

"I used Hubner for shit details like disrupting rallies, biking through crowds wearing Nazi gear, strong-arm stuff. It gets good press for the candidate who's the victim. Then I found out he knew Rydell's kid, or at least they hung out in the same place. I knew young Rydell too, since the campaign I'd run for his father in eighty. He was a surf bum even then." He looked past me with slitted eyes, trying not to see the gun.

"So you gave Felix the package."

"Bill saw the possibilities."

"Have Felix hit Gil while A-Frame and his other chums kept track of Charlie Rydell and built a good tight frame around him, right?"

"Yes."

"And you gave Felix the typewriter and the poison to plant on Charlie along with the Uzi."

"I got them from Bill! I mean, he gave them to me. You've got to know that!"

"Sure, I know that. That's why he's covered and your neck is hanging out a mile. No one can connect him with anything."

"Except me." His wet eyes grew crafty again. "You need me alive, Storm, if you want him."

"Why did you bastards have to slaughter Terri, too?" I could feel the blood pounding behind my eyes. Now I knew it was his idea, because he'd made the connection between Felix and Charlie Rydell. He'd sold the plan to Willie, who'd patted him on the back and said, go to it, son.

"She told Clewes Gil had been working for the FBI, spying for them. She said he'd told her enough so she knew why we'd killed him. And she knew about him and Monica. She wanted money. I didn't begin to believe it. I advised him to forget it, she was lying, but he was all worked up."

"You don't know why?"

"No. What the hell would the FBI be doing planting someone on us? They check you out but they don't go that far even if you were a radical years back. Recruiting someone he grew up with? That's out of the movies." Maybe he really didn't know about Willie's other life. "But Bill was acting crazy. He said find someone to kill her and make it look like suicide due to grief. I fought against it, you've got to believe that!"

"But you did it."

"I was already in too deep because of the . . . other matter. It was too late to split away from him. I used a contact I had from way back to set up a meeting with this man. I relayed what Bill wanted him to do and how to do it, that's all. Meanwhile, Bill stalled the girl. He never admitted anything about Gil, just told her he understood why she was upset and he wanted to help her out, set up a fund for her. Damned if he didn't charm her." He shook his head in wonder. "I think he even had something going with her. She was pretty venal, and he was headed for the Senate. She was going to replace the unfaithful wife, she might have thought."

"Until Murdoch killed her. And Felix, too." Now I knew why the hit man had used Willie's name to get up to her apartment.

He gave another jerky nod and sweat dripped off his chin onto the blotter. "Whoever. I never knew his name. Bill said with the FBI involved we had to wipe the slate clean. Everything had gotten out of hand, and you were nosing around too. I tried to get him to back off, but it was like being sucked into a riptide. You just keep getting pulled further . . ."

"So after Murdoch killed all of us, he was supposed to go to Mexico."

"That was Bill's idea, telling him he'd get the rest of his money in Mexico."

"But you knew he wasn't ever coming back, right?"

Quest's shoulders twitched in what might have been a shrug. "I didn't know. Bill said he had contacts in Mexico. He said leave that part to him. I just gave the guy his tickets and upfront money. I was past caring about that kind of detail anyway. I had a campaign to run."

A campaign to run. I stared at him, thrown off for a moment. "But you knew something went wrong in Mexico," I said at last.

"Yes, but I didn't know what. Bill got a call from down there and he's been strung out ever since. When you called, I figured I'd find out."

191

It made sense that Quest was still in the dark about Willie's career in espionage. Even Monica didn't know about that, according to Lydia Ballesteros, but I wondered if she was in on the rest. "Did Monica help you with all this?"

"No." He seemed surprised. "After what happened with Gil, how could he trust her?"

Quest fascinated me. He meant what he'd just said about trust. It was as if some key element had been left out in the process of his assembly, some vital gene omitted, leaving the reasonable facsimile of a man with all his faculties intact save the one designed to recognize evil. I had to ask him, "Why? Why did you do these things?"

I could almost see the flawed brain at work behind the slivers of his eyes as I watched them grow shrewd, perhaps even hopeful.

"Don't bother to lie," I told him. "It won't make any difference."

He saw me take up slack on the trigger of the automatic so close to his face and he knew it was over for him, as I wanted him to. The beads of sweat on his forehead merged and formed a trickle that ran down the side of his nose to mix with his blood. He began to weep in earnest. "You said we could *deal!*" he sobbed.

"Why?" I asked him again. "An answer will buy you time. Isn't every moment precious?"

He swallowed his sobs, hiccuped, and drew in a deep shuddering breath. "I can make him president of the United States, do you understand that? Not next time, but soon. Everything will be exactly right for him. In two years there's going to be a vacuum and the pendulum is going to swing with a vengeance! Scandals, deficits, disillusionment will be his allies. He'll have the money and the momentum . . ."

"And you to whisper in his ear?" I thought Quest might be certifiably insane.

"How can he cut me loose? After what I've done and what I know . . ."

Just like he does everyone else, I could have told him. But I didn't care what he thought or knew anymore. I'd come here trying to persuade myself he could be used against Willie, that I could have them both. But Quest was a coward, not a fool, and without a gun against his head he would recant and take his chances with my "witnesses"—one of whom was flaky and the other dead. The time to settle his case was now.

"I'll give him to you!" he cried as if he could read my mind. "I'll testify to everything I told you!"

I wasn't even listening. Inside my head Gil's voice urged impatiently, "What are you waiting for?" and I looked at Quest clinically now, judging the choreography and the ballistic implications of the situation. The bullet should enter through his mouth, I decided, and I caught his hair again, pulling back his head while he gibbered on. I began to press the muzzle against his lips, cutting off the sound, trying to get past his teeth. Then it would look like suicide, just as I had promised him . . .

I heard the motor of a car as it turned into the driveway, but saw no headlights. A door closed first and then a thin beam of light swept the drapes, visible because the den was so dimly lighted. "Who's that?" I grated in Quest's ear, taking the automatic away from his mouth and pressing it into the soft flesh below his chin.

"Bel-Air Patrol," he croaked. "Panic button . . ." His little eyes glittered with a desperate hope.

The Bel-Air Patrol is a private security outfit that operates in the western suburbs of Los Angeles. I know their rules of response. A regular alarm signal brings them to your front door. The panic signal means they have to inspect the grounds first and then approach with caution. Quest had a panic button rigged to his alarm system that connected with their station, probably under his desk somewhere.

I very nearly pulled the trigger anyway. Reason interposed itself reluctantly. The patrolman would hear the shot and box me in. I wasn't here to shoot it out with security officers. I let go of Quest's hair, gathered him by the lapels of his dressing gown, and yanked him to his feet. We crossed the room and I looked out into the corridor. To my left was the front door and to the right, beyond the living room, sliding glass doors that led to a patio. As I watched, the beam of a flashlight danced along the flagstones and caught the blue edge of a swimming pool. He was checking out the back.

I hauled Quest to the front door and said, "You can do a couple of things after I go. Yell for help and everything I told you goes into evidence if they pick me up. Or say you fell down and hit your face, then freaked out and pushed the panic button when you saw the blood. 'Ha-ha, sorry to bother you, officer. All I really need is a cold washcloth.' "

I opened the door and pulled him out with me. He stood swaying, wiping at his face with a handkerchief he fumbled out of the breast pocket of his robe. He was still stunned, but I thought I saw a beginning gleam of triumph in his eyes. "It isn't over," I promised him.

I could have shot him down and run for it, but somehow the moment for that had passed. The situation had changed and I'd lost the keen edge of resolve I needed to perform his execution. As the flashlight beam preceded the security guard around the corner of the house, probing the lawn, I dropped Quest's pistol in the pocket of my windbreaker and ran down the driveway past his Olds and the patrol car, getting on the far side of the hedge between his property and the street. Keeping on the grassy side of the curb, I moved in the direction of my car, careful of any gaps that might exist in the hedge. Behind me, I heard their voices.

"You all right?" the patrolman asked Quest.

Quest mumbled something I couldn't understand.

Passing the next house I could hear the security man call in on his radio but couldn't make out what he said, except that his voice was calm enough and he acknowledged the static that came back at him with a casual "Ten-four." I had to assume Quest had taken my suggestion in order to give himself time to think. Otherwise the Bel-Air guy would have been boiling around gun in hand, yelling into his radio or racing his unit up and down the street, code three. I stole along toward my Chrysler, looking back over my shoulder, trying to decide whether to take cover until he left or just drive away.

He made up my mind for me. I heard an engine start and saw his lights splash on. Before he could back into the street I dove for the lawn of the low, ranch-style house I was passing and rolled behind a redwood fence that was overgrown with ivy. There was no light showing and I hoped no one was peering out of the dark windows and no dogs roamed the property at night. The patrol car came nosing down the street and stopped next to my Chrysler, directly across from where I hugged the ground. I held my breath, but it was understandable. They take a second glance at any car they don't recognize in the neighborhood, and my rust bucket was worth a longer look. They don't ticket or tow, of course, because the car almost certainly belongs to someone's guest, but they might jot down a license number. I stayed tucked down and kept very still until I heard him roll on, engine barely turning over.

Still I didn't move. The Santa Ana wind blew against my face, as hot and dry as the African sirocco that's said to drive men to violent, irrational deeds. Maybe they both do. I'd been within a second of killing a sniveling coward as he cringed and pissed himself while his family slept upstairs. With good reason, to be sure, but then what? Why, go and blow Willie away too, of course. Jon Storm, the Crimson Avenger. Until they finally reeled me in like any common murderer and let me explain my lofty motives to an incredulous jury of my peers.

I lay there in grass that was damp in spite of the arid wind, and contemplated my failure. When he recovered, Quest would hang tough and get a pricey lawyer who'd make Iris look terrible—if I could get her to court. Even if she didn't show up zonked out, it would be her word against his, and of course I couldn't produce Murdoch. Quest would walk and Willie would remain beyond reach. Unless I simply assassinated everybody, and I decided I'd come as close to doing that as I ever would.

Lights flared again in Quest's driveway and the Olds came backing out. I stayed down on the turf as the headlights swept over the ivy in front of me and the car went rushing down the hill. A fair guess was Quest didn't trust phones either or else he'd been summoned to brief Willie personally on recent developments. He never slowed as he passed my Chrysler, but then he wouldn't have any reason to associate it with me unless he remembered seeing it outside of Willie's beach house.

When he was gone the night closed back in and the desert wind went on whispering in my ear. But the idea came to me because I was thinking about the coincidence in Quest and Pop both having one of Rydell's old Peacemaker Colts. As it took shape and began to make a modicum of sense, I chuckled out loud. The mechanics were on the chancy side, but there wasn't much left to lose.

Once again I rummaged in the trunk of the Chrysler, this time coming up with my father's six-shooter and the smallest screwdriver I could find in my old tool kit. I stuck the gun under my belt, pocketed the miniflashlight I kept in the glove compartment for mechanical crises, and walked back up the hill.

Quest's house was dark now, but there was an outside light on over his door. I reached up and unscrewed the bulb, so at least I wouldn't be visible to the whole neighborhood while I worked. There was also a likelihood that the Bel-Air Patrol would come by at least once in the time it was going to take me, but that was just another element beyond my control.

There isn't much to disarming a key-operated alarm. The newer systems are all coded now; you just punch in numbers and the odds against an intruder coming up with the combination are out of sight. When Quest's house was built they were probably unavailable and, fortunately for me, he hadn't updated.

I put the little flashlight between my teeth and knelt down so the narrow beam was focused on the control panel where a tiny red light showed the system was armed. With the screwdriver I loosened the plate, then inserted the tool behind it to depress the tamper while I removed it. Carefully I peeled the wires leading to the tamper and crossed them to produce a short circuit. When the alarm was disconnected, I put the outside light on again and moved around to the back of the house.

Sliding glass doors are usually no problem either. Most of them can simply be lifted off their runners, as was the case with Quest's. He was as careless as the average homeowner, so I was inside his house six minutes after I went to work.

No dogs, please, I mouthed as I ghosted through his living room toward the corridor behind the front door, where a single weak night light burned. I turned left into the den and thumbed the flashlight on again to locate the Colt .45 mounted on the wall. Then I sat on the leather couch and worked on both revolvers with my screwdriver, holding the light between my teeth again. I screwed Pop's fancy handles onto the butt of Quest's six-gun and put it away under my belt. My father's .45 went up on the wall with simple wooden grips after I'd carefully wiped it clean with my shirt.

Ten minutes after I'd removed them I was lifting the heavy sliding glass doors into place, teeth clenched with the effort of doing it quietly. There could be a live-in servant downstairs or a light sleeper almost anywhere.

As I started back around the corner of the house, a set of headlights came creeping up the hill. I stepped back into cover and watched the Bel-Air Patrol car glide slowly by. Then a slick of moisture broke out on my forehead despite the dry heat because I remembered I'd left the metal plate to the alarm on the ground near the front door rather than take time to screw it back in place. He wouldn't spot anything from the car, but he might just decide to check on Jim Quest's condition after the earlier incident and come to the door. I took very shallow breaths while the unit drove on by, turned around in the cul-de-sac at the top of the hill, and went drifting past me again.

Hooking the alarm back up was a matter of reversing the earlier process, unraveling the wires I'd crossed, repositioning the tamper, and replacing the plate over it. I worked very carefully by the thin beam of the flashlight between my teeth, listening for any breach of silence in the dark house. When I was finished, I put the outside light back on once more and got the hell away from there.

It was ten past two when I drove into Lot C at the International Airport complex for the second time that night. I prowled past the dark rows of cars parked like markers in some automotive graveyard, searching out Murdoch's Buick again. This time I found it quickly, but I pulled into a slot several spaces away and looked around carefully before I went near it.

Lot C was deserted at this hour. No buses trundled people too and from their flights. No one seemed to be around except the attendants who would be manning the exit booths. I got out Murdoch's wallet and car keys and went over to the Buick. Standing near the trunk compartment, I put Quest's card in the wallet along with two hundred and twenty dollars. I removed a few other business cards that might be distracting and the parking ticket for his rental car.

Still I hesitated, knowing what was in there, wondering if I only imagined a taint in the air. When I finally leaned forward and let the rear panel spring up the smell hit me, a putrid whiff that rocked me back on my heels. I stood back gagging, my eyes watering, remembering how the pathologists enjoyed the indoctrination sessions when they got to cut open a floater and watch the rookie cops pass out as the trapped gases reached them. Holding my breath, I tossed Murdoch's wallet in and slammed the trunk shut. Then I smoked a cigarette while I wiped the surfaces I'd touched with a handkerchief.

I chose a different exit booth so no one would remember seeing me twice and handed over Murdoch's ticket, paying for a week of parking. The attendant had coarse sable hair that grew back from his eyebrows and a blank, baleful stare. I hoped to hell he understood something besides Urdu.

"Row P-18, man," I said as he handed me change. "There's a Buick back there where I was parked. It really stinks."

He grunted.

"You understand? It smells like maybe there's a stiff in it. Black Buick two-door."

That seemed to bring him around a little. "Aw, shit," he said. At least he spoke English.

As I drove out I watched my mirror and saw him leave his booth and start walking slowly back into the lot. Dead bodies aren't a complete novelty in the parking lots around LAX.

# FOURTEEN

The Santa Ana wind had swept the night clean and the castle stood out under the stars, as dated as a forties Hollywood postcard with its rococo turrets and towers. The gates swung open to the Genie's signal and Herman and Heide came bounding over, two shadows darker than the night, silent but for the thrum of their pads against the cobblestones. When I was sure they recognized me, I got out of the Chrysler and scratched their ears.

Inside, most of the lights were on. I climbed the stairs to my room and tossed the flight bag on the bed. Then I dug out the Frontier Colt and went down the corridor to Pop's suite. He wasn't there, so I put the revolver in the holster hanging in his closet and went looking for him. After trying everywhere else, I finally thought of the projection room. Hell, it was only 3:00 A.M.

It took a moment for my eyes to adjust to the dimness and then I saw him sitting alone in his usual place, bottles, glasses, and an ice bucket on the wheeled cart at his elbow. But in the picture on the screen, an old western in early Technicolor I vaguely remembered seeing as a kid, he was at a green felt table holding a hand of cards, dressed in the elegant waistcoat and pleated shirt of a riverboat gambler. A seductive Kitty Mars

199

leaned over his shoulder, showing quite a bit of cleavage for those days.

I walked down the aisle and took the seat next to him. He didn't say anything, just gestured toward the bar. His eyes looked puffy in the weak light that reflected from the screen. I poured Jack Daniel's over ice and bummed one of his cigarettes. "I guess you heard about her."

He nodded as if he didn't trust his voice.

"I went to see her not long ago, Pop. She sent you love."

He turned to look at me, surprised.

"There was something else. She said to ask you about it when she was gone."

I heard the ice rattle in his glass as he took a pull at his drink. He cleared his throat. "Ask me what?"

"I don't know. She wouldn't talk about it then, but it was about Willie."

My father reached down beside his chair and hit a switch that cut off the sound track. We sat watching the silent images of a handsome young man with steely eyes and a flashy redhead. You couldn't hear what they were saying, but anyone could guess. It wasn't in the lines anyway; it was in the way they looked at each other.

Finally my father said, "Such a long time ago."

We kept watching, lost in our own thoughts.

"Your mother had died," he went on. "I was lonely. Kitty was so much like me in many ways. It wasn't just that we were both small people physically, but that helped. I didn't have to stand on boxes and she didn't have to walk around in slit trenches." He stopped, and I knew it cost him to talk that way. He had more than his ration of pride.

"You loved her." I could see it on the screen. My old man wasn't that good an actor.

"We both came up the hard way, no one gave us anything. It made us rough with everyone else, sometimes even with each other. But see, we understood why and that made it all right. Christ, how we used to laugh!" He let out his breath and reached for his glass. "I can't explain it, kid. I'm no good at words without a script."

"Why didn't you marry her?"

"She was already married to Oliver Loring. He was crazy about her even though he hated everything about Hollywood except Kitty. And, yeah, she loved him too. Not the same way as me maybe, but now I think just as much. He made her feel like a lady and I made her feel like a woman, she'd say. I guess she wanted it both ways. And then there was Monica. They both adored her.

"Anyway, we were together when we could be. It wasn't easy because we were both famous—the only time I ever wished I wasn't. We had to be careful. Christ, we even wore disguises. I said, 'Divorce him and let's get married, to hell with this.' But she didn't want to hurt Loring, so I went along with it."

Up on the screen, the young gambler took such exception to something a rawboned cowpoke said to the redheaded saloon girl that he knocked the bigger man through a glass window.

"Maybe I could have changed her mind, I don't know. But she had this goddamn chauffeur, Burton Clewes. She trusted him even though I thought he was slimy. Kitty couldn't drive, so Burton had to take her everywhere, even when she was meeting me. What he did was keep a journal of every place we went, the little out-of-the-way hotels up here and down in Mexico. He got the names of some of the help in these places, people who'd remember. He even got some pictures, the bastard. Not in the act, but once in a pool, naked. Jesus, that was just as bad in those days!"

"Like father, like son."

Pop turned his head to look at me in the gloom. "How did you know? I thought she didn't tell you."

I was confused. "She didn't tell me anything." I'd just been using an expression.

He leaned back and muttered, "Well, that's truer than you think. But long before that, Kitty decided to fire Burton. He'd been getting obnoxious—rude to her and lazy. That's when he told her about his fucking journal. She called me up in tears and I went over there ready to kick the shit out of him. Before I could get started he showed me a bunch of photocopies he'd made. He'd stashed the originals in a bank or somewhere. He figured he could get a pretty good piece of change from a scandal sheet, and he was right. But that would be a one-shot deal, so he settled for keeping his job at a higher salary and money to send his kid to college. When I asked him why he was doing this to Kitty when she'd always treated him right, he laughed and said he hated us rich bastards. Can you beat that? We probably started out poorer than him."

"So Aunt Kitty paid for Willie's education in Mexico. Or maybe you did."

He shrugged. "Burton had us. But it wasn't the money. Kitty changed when he began blackmailing her, and maybe I did too. We didn't see each other much after that, and it wasn't the same when we did. We grew apart. I went back to playing the field. Hell, I could have anyone I wanted in those days."

I looked up and watched a white riverboat plying the Mississippi, smoke billowing out of its tall stack. Cut to the afterdeck, where the gambler and the redhead promenaded together. Impulsively, he stopped and caught her by the arms, drawing her to him.

"But you wanted her," I said.

"Yeah."

"What does it all have to do with Willie?"

"Burton died of peritonitis and we thought we were off the hook, even if we couldn't get back to the way we were. That was in the late sixties, I guess. You were still in the Marines. Monica was already a big name in music, marching around protesting Vietnam while she was pulling down seven figures a year, according to Kitty. About that time, Burton's kid came back from Mexico and made a play for Monica. He was some kind of radical too, so she started going with him. You'd see them on TV at anti-Vietnam rallies, waving commie flags. It upset Kitty, but she couldn't do anything about it."

"It wouldn't be easy to handle Monkey."

"Except for her father. She worshipped Loring. He had no use for the Clewes kid and when he told her not to see him, she listened."

I thought I remembered what happened to Loring. "He finally killed himself, didn't he?"

"I'd say he had some help. Young Clewes found Burton's journal in a safe deposit box when he inherited his father's personal stuff. He took it straight to Loring. I guess he figured he could blackmail the old man into letting up on Monica. But Loring flipped out instead. He told Kitty what the little bastard had showed him and then went into his study and blew his brains out."

I reached over for the bottle of Jack Daniel's and poured for both of us. There wasn't any reason to be surprised. It fit Willie's M.O. Lydia Ballesteros had said an American disaster in Vietnam was at the top of the Soviet agenda back then, and Willie was programmed to contribute to it. Monica was much more than a source of financing for him. She was his access to radical circles and media coverage. He couldn't let her get away.

"Why did Kitty let Monica marry Willie?" I asked Pop. "She could have told her what he'd done."

"Because she couldn't face telling Monica she'd cheated on Loring." My father knocked back most of his drink. His voice was getting thick. "She was ashamed. She stopped working and just locked the world out. Stayed in that house alone for years before she moved into the Motion Picture Home. I never saw her after Loring's funeral. Almost twenty years ago."

The picture was ending. The gambler leaned glumly against the railing looking back at the dock where the redhead stood, heartbroken. Huge paddlewheels churned the water as the riverboat pulled away, widening the distance between them. As a final gesture, the gambler took the flower she had given him from his lapel and dropped it overboard, where it bobbed around in the wake.

Music up.

# FIFTEEN

t was a hell of a day for a funeral. The warm wind had stopped but the sky was scrubbed blue and the rolling green acres of Forest Lawn Cemetery with its myriad white markers and monuments looked as idyllic as advertised. In Pop's old pictures (and Aunt Kitty's) it always rained when they planted someone on Boot Hill.

Six hours of sleep and a big breakfast prepared by Martins had restored me. In fact, I'd slept so soundly I awoke in untroubled innocence of preceding events and lay in bed blinking at the old pennants on the wall, content to speculate on nothing whatsoever. Then an image intruded, followed by another, and the grace period was over. Bits and pieces joined ranks and marched through my head to remind me I wouldn't be going to the beach today.

Last night had been full of sound and fury, mostly mine. I'd been on an adrenaline high, pushing hard, moving things along. But what had been accomplished beyond panicking Jim Quest and perhaps causing some consternation in the enemy camp? They'd regroup under Willie's discipline, and even if I'd managed to create a pretty unique set of problems for Quest, Willie was as far out of reach as ever. Unless Quest cracked wide open, and I couldn't count on that.

Somehow I had to get through to Monica. Quest had said she wasn't involved and he'd been in no frame of mind to protect anyone last night. Lydia Ballesteros had called her a tool. That left her in the middle of a nest of snakes, as well as the only person who might help me unravel Willie. If they were telling the truth, and if I could get her to believe me. But when I tried the number Norman Kling had given me, I got a friendly recording instead of a frosty secretary.

I found what I needed in the morning edition of the *Times*

—a page-three item, nearly lost in the election coverage, that announced a memorial service would be held for Kitty Mars at the Forest Lawn Cemetery today. It wasn't specific, but once I got there a panel truck with the call letters of a local TV station indicated which chapel was holding the service. Jim Quest wasn't going to miss a photo opportunity, so I could assume Monica wasn't going to miss her mother's funeral.

I sat in my car, dressed in a gray gabardine suit out of respect for Aunt Kitty, and watched the press watch the chapel. They lounged around with their hand-held cameras, kept at bay by two security types, probably plainclothes cops paid out of Willie's campaign funds. They had stationed themselves on either side of the path leading to the beige slab house of God. The *Times* had said the service would be for immediate family only, and there were few cars in the parking area. One was a stretch limo with opaque windows that would be for the principal mourners. It stood at the foot of the path, in front of the two bodyguards.

The trick was going to be to get anywhere near Monica. Pop said he'd never go to a funeral, least of all this one, which scotched my idea of bringing him along as a diversion. The fourth estate would have had a ball with him, and I might have been able to cut Monica out of the herd in the confusion.

I got out of the Chrysler when I saw them coming out of the chapel. Monica, in a charcoal suit with a black armband, was flanked by Willie and Jim Quest, who wore sunglasses and a broad strip of bandage over the bridge of his nose. The dozen or so reporters started around the security detail, which fell back to keep from being outflanked. On the steps of the chapel, Willie made a statement I couldn't hear, while Monica just shook her head and started moving forward with Quest clearing the way.

Opting for the direct approach, I simply walked up the path toward them. Quest stopped cold when he saw me, but I looked past him and said, "I'd just like to talk to you, Monica."

"I have nothing to say to you. Stay away from us." Her face

was set and stony, her eyes hidden by dark glasses. "Get him away from me, Jim."

Quest's forehead went suddenly greasy, but he didn't move. "Sure, Jim, do that," I encouraged him.

"This time," Monica told me evenly, "I'm going to swear out a complaint the police can act on."

"Give me a few minutes of your time and you can do what you like."

Behind them Willie was easing past the reporters, his body-guards running interference. He came up to us and I saw rage in his eyes, but he forced a hairline smile. "What's going on here? What do you want, Jonny?"

"I'd like a few words with Monica, Willie. Just take a minute."

"I told him to leave us alone," Monica put in. "Can't any of you get him to do that?"

"Take her to the car," Willie snapped, and the larger cop caught Monica's arm and bulled past me. The other one, a cool youngster with insolent eyes, stood in front of me for a moment in case I wanted to make something out of it. When I didn't, he followed them to the limo.

"Go stroke the press, Jim. Tell them thanks but that's it." Willie waited until Quest left us. "Now, then. You wanted to talk."

"To Monica."

He shrugged. "She won't see you. You can't force her."

"Mexican standoff. Sooner or later something's going to give. I think it'll be Quest, Willie."

"You're making a fool of yourself. A spectacle."

I looked past him and saw the limo pull away, leaving the security detail standing at the curb. "There goes your ride."

"I've got another one. What do you want, Jonny? What do you really want?" He stood blinking at me with his small, muddy eyes. As usual he looked as if he'd dressed and groomed himself in a closet. He wore a suit but his narrow tie was askew and his shirt collar curled up. Untrimmed hair fell over his forehead. Everyman. I put my hands in my pockets to keep them off him.

"Didn't Jimbo tell you last night?"

Willie nodded, looking around. The handful of mourners were getting into their cars. I hadn't recognized any of them and wondered who they could be. Probably the last of Aunt Kitty's aging clan.

"I've been worried about Jim," Willie said, watching Quest chatting up a few straggling reporters. The panel truck had already left and the bodyguards stood watching us from a discreet distance, smoking and rocking on their heels.

"So have I."

"He's been working too hard. Did you really barge in last night and accuse him of arranging Gil's murder? And then having the killer killed? He said you gave him a wild story about having witnesses, evidence."

"That's right, Willie."

"That's fantastic, as you know."

"Just suppose they can make it stick. Where would that leave you?"

He shook his head, frowning as he thought it over. "He's very dedicated but, my God, this would be hard for me to believe."

I could only stare at him.

"I suppose it's conceivable he could have become . . . over-zealous. He might have decided to help me win the election by any means, I suppose. He's brilliant at his work, but I can't deny I've noticed a ruthless streak. Even so . . ." He shook his head again. "It's too bizarre."

I saw how he was planning to handle it, but the sheer gall of the man was incredible. He projected the shock and concern of someone who has just discovered a terrible flaw in an associate or friend, but no anxiety. He was't going to come apart. Then I realized he wouldn't know about my trip to Mexico in Murdoch's place or my talk with Lydia Ballesteros. I'd never told Quest about that. Willie could only speculate that Murdoch had inexplicably skipped with the money without doing his job and survived the ambush in Mexico to come back enraged and go into collusion with me. He was assuming he was still covered up. Quest was expendable and now it was a matter of damage control.

"If anyone in my campaign is guilty of criminal behavior on my behalf, it'll be embarrassing to me," Willie went on, developing it. "I'll deplore and condemn it if an investigation warrants that. But I'm not involved, and it won't keep me from taking my seat in the Senate. It's too late for that, Jonny." He gave me his stingy smile.

"He says it was all your idea, Willie."

He nodded his understanding. "I was told you forced your way in and threatened him with a gun. You were hysterical, he said. Acting like a madman. He simply told you what you wanted to hear in fear for his life."

"Why didn't he call the cops?"

"On the night before the election?" Willie shook his head.

"It'll be interesting to hear what he says when he's arrested. See if he'll take the heat alone."

"Arrested? Why *hasn't* he been arrested, by the way? Why all this charging around if you've got a case you can take to the authorities?" He raised puzzled eyebrows. "Or are you just running a bluff, Jonny? Trying to settle some old grudge?"

I would have enjoyed jolting him with the news that Lydia had blown his cover in Mexico and the FBI had the letters he'd written from Russia. Except that Meers and Valentine had made it clear the government wasn't going to act on the information very soon. I might succeed in making him panic and run, but that was no solution. No one would ever get to Willie in Moscow. I decided to save my last bullet.

He broke in on my hesitation. "Why did you stick your oar in, Jonny?" he asked softly. "Whatever gave you the idea I had anything to do with Gil's death in the first place?"

That was an easy one. "Because I've known you and Gil all my life. People run true to form, like horses. I remember you wrote him a note when we were kids saying you were going to get him if it's the last thing you ever did. Then there were the threats you wrote yourself, the dog you poisoned. All in character, pieces of a pattern. Gil wouldn't stop for gas and then park where the hose wouldn't reach the tank. That's out of character, so that's not why you stopped. I don't know why you lied about it. Maybe just stopping to take a leak didn't seem convincing under the circumstances, and you just threw the other in." I paused to light a cigarette. "Little things, Willie. Not evidence. Just indications to a guy with a cop nose and all that inside knowledge of the people involved."

Willie showed his teeth and his head bobbed a little, as close as I'd ever seen him come to laughing. "That's the sort of deductive thinking that led to all this nonsense? That's funny, really funny."

"It'll be even funnier when Quest opens up like a brand new shopping mall." I dropped my cigarette on the lawn and walked away, tired of talking to him.

Quest and the two watchdogs stood near a black sedan, the last car on the lot except for mine and one in a reserved parking slot that could belong to a clergyman. The two men assigned to Willie gave me bored glances to let me know the whole incident hadn't offered much entertainment.

I ignored them and paused to wink at Quest. "I guess it's going to be you after all, Jim," I told him pleasantly, and watched him blanch.

The look on his face was the high point of my day so far.

The FBI keeps offices on the seventeenth floor of the Federal Building in Westwood, on Wilshire Boulevard near the San Diego Freeway. The reception room has rust-colored carpeting and paneled walls featuring photo portraits of J. Edgar Hoover on the left, Ronald Reagan and William Webster on the right.

The secretaries sit behind bulletproof glass, uninterrupted except for a slot you can slide documents through. It's hard to converse with them.

I hadn't made an appointment with Jim Constantine because I didn't want him to be ready for me. When the secretary told me he was out to lunch I went down to Wilshire Boulevard and killed an hour getting a sandwich and a haircut rather than sit around waiting.

He wasn't happy to see me when I got back, but he took me to a small conference room off reception where we sat in Spartan chairs on either side of a metal table with some kind of acrylic finish. He heard me out while I watched his skepticism turn to anger and finally disbelief.

"I think you might be coming unwrapped, Storm," he said when I was through.

I felt pretty together, actually. With a new haircut and a suit that fit almost perfectly now that I'd lost weight, I looked almost as much like an up-scale yuppie as he did. Maybe a little further over the hill, though.

"You made a statement on tape," he reminded me, "implicating yourself in the death of Lawrence Murdoch. I have that statement here in the office."

I shrugged. "It isn't signed."

"We can still use it."

"The validity would be in doubt."

"You were warned in Mexico, Storm. This can go hard on you."

"Why don't you call the Venice Division? The airport cops'll have turned it over to them by now. They'll confirm an ongoing investigation. They'll tell you Murdoch was shot to death by a large-caliber revolver more than a week ago, if the coroner's had a look at him. Of course, they may have found a card or something belonging to Jim Quest, but there hasn't been time for them to go out there and ask questions. When they do, they'll see that big, single-action Colt hanging on his wall, but they won't make a connection until ballistics has had a crack at it. Someone in an official capacity with inside knowledge could kind of goose them along, nudge 'em in the right direction. Like you. I mean, you're all working for uncle, one way or the other."

Constantine got up and strode out of the room, leaving me to wonder if he was going for the cops. I noticed the conference room had only one window and that was set in the door so the secretaries could see if anyone was freaking out in there. I got a cigarette going and waited instead, hoping for the best. At least I wasn't dealing with an asshole like Meers.

Constantine came back in about five minutes, no less angry than before but very controlled. "You rigged this Murdoch killing," he stated. But he'd come back alone, and he sat down.

"The card and the gun will make a strong circumstantial case," I said, "but that's just part of it. There's a reliable witness ready to come forward and testify she heard Quest put out a contract for the murder of Gil Buckler with one Felix Hubner." At least, I hoped to hell she would. "Then Murdoch killed Hubner for Quest, but that's immaterial because it's probably unprovable. The important thing is this witness, who I've got under wraps, will give hard evidence against Gil's murderer. One of them. The other one's Willie Clewes."

"You're obsessed, Storm." He shook his head. "You've lost any sense of perspective or legality."

"How well did you know Gil?"

"I was his contact."

"Did you like him? I mean, even if he was a lousy agent and got himself killed working for you?"

For a few seconds I thought he'd swing at me, and then he subsided. He had a Latin temper like Gil, but I think he could understand what he couldn't condone. "I liked him."

"I could have gone to the officer in charge of Gil's case, Constantine. A captain at West L.A.P.D. I know him pretty well and I think he has a middling level of competence at best. Besides," I added frankly, "he'd have me held as a material witness or anything else he could come up with."

211

"And we wouldn't."

"Oh hell, no. First of all, it seems the government doesn't want to move against Willie Clewes right now, and the first thing I'd do is hold a press conference about his education in Russia and the letters he wrote Lydia that you're suppressing. Second, the evidence now accumulating against Quest on the Murdoch killing makes my unsigned statement pretty weak." I looked around for an ashtray.

"Just put it on the floor." There was no carpet in the conference room.

I said to him, "Gil worked for the FBI, Constantine. Maybe he was just an informant, but it got him killed. Doesn't that give you some kind of jurisdiction?"

He looked up at the ceiling and thought about it for a moment. "Yes. We can ride herd on the case." His eyes came back to me. "How about the rest of your revenge, Storm? What about Clewes? How do I know you'll get out of the political side and leave that to us?"

"Because I know Quest. He's shrewd and he's a coward. He'll never take this fall alone. He'll try to cop a plea on the basis that a United States senator is much bigger game than a political consultant. Anything to stay off death row." I leaned back in the uncomfortable chair. "He'll cancel Willie's ticket and I'll settle for that. Shove politics."

"What makes you so sure Clewes will win the election?"

"His campaign headquarters is at the Mirador Hotel in Santa Monica. Why don't you go over there tonight and watch him do it?"

But his mind was elsewhere now. He sat watching me for a full minute before he asked, "If the witness you have can make such a tight case against Quest, why the hell did you go to all the trouble of setting him up on the Murdoch thing?"

I gave him my best simulation of honest surprise. "Well hell, Constantine, you guys were going to hang it on me!"

# S I X T E E N

The Jolly Green Giant and his girlfriend, Fuzz, were pumping iron in his garage, while Iris watched. The blonde sat staring in awe as the diminutive Arab jerked an incredible amount of weight off the floor and heaved it above her head. Ridges of muscle bunched her thighs, rippled and coiled along her shoulders and down her back. Tendons and veins stood out in her throat, her eyes bulged, and her mouth strained open in a rictus of total effort. I didn't find it sexy, but when she finally let the weights fall with an impact I felt in my feet, Iris went over with a towel and dried her off tenderly.

"Who the hell you supposed to be?" The Giant stared at my suit. "Even cops don't dress like that anymore."

I held up the copy of the *Herald Examiner* I'd bought on Wilshire Boulevard after leaving Constantine's office so Iris could see the picture of Jim Quest grinning at the camera. I'd folded the paper so Willie and Monica, giving the thumbs-up signal during a weekend rally, weren't visible in the frame to distract her. Iris gasped and stopped rubbing the other girl's shoulders.

I tossed the paper on the folding chair she'd been sitting in and said to the Giant, "Let's take a short walk."

We crossed the bike path and stepped onto the beach. The Giant had a towel around his neck and his sweat suit was soaked dark. "How's she doing?" I asked.

"Great! We're like one big family. Fuzz really grooves after that chick. She's cookin' Ay-rab food again and doin' them kootch dances I get off on."

"You keeping her off drugs?"

"Trust me, bro."

"Well, I'm glad everyone's happy."

"A family that lays together stays together."

I knelt down to take off my shoes and socks. The warm sand felt good between my toes. For a moment we watched a volleyball game, a girl and a guy on each side of the net. With just two on a team you really have to hustle, especially on sand. These kids had the perfect California bodies, supple muscles under golden hides, and they were living the California dream. I remembered when Gil and I had played the game up on State Beach in another life. In those days the girls just sat around and watched.

"I want to move on this thing, Tom," I said. "Will she testify?"

He nodded. "I talked to her about it. She feels a whole lot better now she's got me for protection. She knows she can't stay here if he's on the street and she don't want to run away anymore."

"Okay, then here's what you do. This afternoon you take her to the West L.A. Police Station and find Captain Norman Kling. She's just seen this picture in the paper and she's realized he's the man who put out the contract on Gil. She's been too scared to come forward but now she wants to do the right thing. She came to you for advice and help and you remembered Kling was in charge of the case and brought her over."

"I gotta go with her?"

"Yes. You've got nothing to worry about. She's telling the truth, remember? And that's pretty much what you do. You used to live next door to Gil, true? So you followed the case even though you hardly knew him and you remembered Kling's name from the publicity. Look, I don't want her wandering around alone, Tom."

"Okay. You're paying top dollar, baby."

"Kling should move on it right away, but I can't count on that. If you can work it into the conversation that Quest is going to be at Clewes's campaign headquarters in the Hotel Mirador tonight, he might just take her down there and get a positive I.D. He might even be inspired to make an arrest."

Someone spiked the volleyball hard and it bounced out of the court and rolled to my feet. I picked it up and tossed it to

214

a blonde nymphet with a scrap of material around her loins to match her wisp of halter. She gave me an automatic smile of thanks and ran back to the game, pert buttocks pumping. I don't think she really saw me, and that gave me a pang.

"You ought to come back to the beach, baby," the Jolly Green Giant said.

"I live on a beach."

"Like this?" He was watching the blonde, whose snippet of bikini was mostly caught up in the cleft between her buns.

I thought of my own postage-stamp-sized beach and the clear, warm water that raked the gravel. Where Chispa and I liked to catch some late-afternoon sun and horse around naked in the mild surf. "No, it's different," I told him, feeling better about the detached little beach bunny now.

The afternoon was as hard and sharp as a new beginning. Driving along Mulholland I could see the snow-clad mountains surrounding Los Angeles and the expanse of the San Fernando Valley. The orange groves and horse ranches Pop had looked out on when he built the castle were long gone and the valley was one vast city all the way to the foothills of the Sierras. But then, I couldn't remember it any other way.

I found Pop at the bar with his back to the view. He wore a black armband around the sleeve of his white shirt and he was in the third day of a running drunk, according to Martins. The drinking was supposedly prompted by Kitty Mars's death, but he had never needed much excuse. When he was a younger man he got into fights when he drank and he was still unpredictable, but I couldn't remember seeing him out of control. Which meant he could walk, drive, and fake a conversation.

"Doesn't surprise me," he said when I told him what had happened in Mexico. "His father was a commie, too. Hated anyone with money."

I sighed at his boozy logic. I would rather have told him the story another time, but I didn't know when I'd get a chance and I didn't want him acting on his own. Not with a skinful

215

of vodka and his penchant for close-ups. And I had to hang around anyway because Martins told me someone had called three times. Each time Martins said I'd gone back to Mexico and the man replied he understood, then called back within half an hour. I had an idea who it might be and I wasn't going anywhere until I got that call.

"I should have told you, kid. About Kitty and me. About Burton and his prick son." Pop peered into the depths of his drink. "But she didn't want that."

I shook my head. "It wouldn't have mattered unless someone could get Monica to believe it. And they're not going to let me through to her even if I could convince her of anything."

"Maybe I could talk to her."

"You won't get anywhere near her either."

"Maybe Kitty said something to her before she . . . died."

"I can try to find out, but Monica didn't act like it at Forest Lawn."

"What are you going to do, then?"

"Shove on everything until something gives. And try to get Monica out before it all comes down on her." I told him how I'd set Quest up and that I expected an arrest pretty soon.

"No good," my father said glumly.

"No?"

"No. It doesn't take care of Clewes." He gave me the flat stare that had carried him through so many pictures. "Somebody ought to shoot the cocksucker."

The phone rang and Martins called out it was for me. I left Pop at the bar and went to take the receiver from Martins.

"Jon Storm?"

I recognized Quest's voice at once. "How did you get this number? It's unlisted."

"Right out of Bill's black book. Listen, I want to meet."

"We did that, remember?"

"Bill Clewes is going to kill me if he can. I know that now. Goddamn you, Storm!"

216

"Sure he will. You're all that connects him to murder and soliciting murder."

"He doesn't believe I'll keep him out of it. I know him. I can read his face."

"Will you? Go to the gas chamber for him, I mean? Contract murder is a special circumstance that permits the death penalty. Give evidence against Willie and the D.A. might go for life."

"I need a better deal than that!"

"The girl saw you. Life comes out to about seven years." Not if I could help it, it wouldn't.

"I'm not going to just walk into some police station, Storm. You could be conning everyone about this witness."

"Willie won't take a chance on that. Can you?"

"That's why I want to meet. You want Bill or you would have produced this witness by now. I want a better deal."

"You're right, I want Willie. What can you bring to a meeting, Quest? Besides more talk?"

"Tapes. The tapes I've got on Gil and Monica. They're evidence of a motive."

I held the receiver so tightly my hand hurt. "That would be a beginning."

"Then meet me at the beach house at nine o'clock. Bill and Monica will be at campaign headquarters by then."

"Won't they want you along? This is the big night."

"I'm on medication because you broke my nose. I'll tell them I'm going to be a little late. Anyway, California returns won't even show a trend until around ten. They'll just be watching television until then."

"Why the beach house?"

"Why not? That's where the tapes are."

"All right." I hung up.

It was the first real crack, but it ran the length of the wall. If Quest would give me the tapes, he'd go the rest of the way; he was committed. The tapes would back any testimony he gave against Willie, and I didn't think a D.A. would back away from that kind of *prima facie* evidence.

I went back past the bar, where Pop was telling Martins somebody "oughta shoot the sumbitch," and upstairs to my room. I changed out of my suit into a comfortable shirt, slacks, and cat-burglar shoes. Then I got Gil's gun case from the closet and took out his accurized .45 automatic. It was an awkward carry—actors like Pop and Humphrey Bogart made it look easy because they never actually had to lug one around—but if Quest was setting up an ambush I wanted to be ready. The heavy pistol was the best possible handgun the way Gil had it refined. I shoved in a loaded clip and left it on the bed.

Four hours was a long time to kill, but sleep was impossible even though I'd picked up the siesta habit in Mexico. I prowled the room trying to plan my meeting with Quest, but there were too many variables. He'd be there or he wouldn't. He'd be alone and ready to deal, or . . . Maybe a wiser man would call Norman Kling, who probably had a statement from Iris by now, and turn it over to him. Tell him to go out to the beach house and reel in Quest along with the tapes. I couldn't do that. With everything coming down to the wire, I had to make the score. Constantine had called it an obsession.

I turned on the TV and got a flurry of early election returns from the eastern states. Then I learned that the weather was unseasonably warm and a peculiar line-up of the Earth, sun, and moon was producing record high tides. Fully a third of the bus drivers in the L.A. transit system possessed no license, the reporter went on, and a somewhat smaller percentage of air traffic controllers at the busy Palmdale facility were allegedly stoned out of their gourds most of the time. As if in descending order of importance, the latest slasher had killed his seventeenth black prostitute downtown, while the state supreme court had preserved its record of refusing to invoke the death penalty by reversing the sentence of a veteran child molester convicted of raping and torturing a four-year-old girl to death as he recorded her screams. Warfare among Latino gangs had claimed a record number of victims this year in the ongoing battle to control the drug trade, but the city council had still voted to declare Los Angeles a legal sanctuary for any and all illegal Central American refugees. I detected no irony in the bored tones of the anchorperson, to whom such events and statistics seemed unexceptional. Maybe you have to leave town for a while and then come back to know when a city is dying even as it grows. Or, in the case of L.A., erupts.

It was dark outside when I went downstairs to build a very light drink. Martins was tidying up the bar, wearing the sullen expression that was becoming habitual. I asked him where Pop was.

"He went out."

I frowned at him. "You let him go out? He was pretty drunk."

"Look, I work for him, not the other way around."

"How long ago did he leave?"

"Maybe half an hour. He was wearing a hat. Christ, he never wears a hat." Martins wagged his head. "Everything's been really weird around here the last couple weeks."

"Where would he go?"

"I don't know, Jonny. Sometimes when he was drinking, he used to hang around a place in Malibu called Moby's Dick. I had to go get him there once."

"How about his girlfriend? Would he go and see her?"

"Usually just on Sundays."

I didn't like the idea of my father out driving around drunk in his frame of mind. "Well, how can I get in touch with her?"

"I think this one's name is Laurel, but I don't know her. She never comes here and I don't even know where to look for her number."

I carried my drink outside and saw that the garage doors were open and the old Packard convertible was gone. It was a car Pop saved for special occasions or when he wanted to grandstand a little. I went back inside and ran up the stairs and down the corridor to his suite. Even before I opened the closet door, I knew his six-gun would be gone.

# SEVENTEEN

oby's Dick was a ramshackle tavern on the Coast Highway in Malibu, just north of Rambla Pacifica Drive. It was built on piles over the high-tide line, and more sawed-off piles connected by heavy hawsers roped off the parking lot in back and gave the place a seedy, nautical air. I'd been there once over a dozen years ago and nothing had changed. It still looked like a gunfighters' hangout, with a brass rail and cuspidors that received frequent, inaccurate use. The clientele consisted mostly of movie people, stunt men and actors. The kind who made action pictures and lived their roles. You wouldn't want to bring your girl.

When I got there, the creaky building was taking a pounding from the freak high tide, shuddering as waves crashed against the pilings and flung spume against the windows that faced the sea. A dozen customers were sitting at the bar staring at the frothy regiments of combers advancing through the clear night.

I ordered Jack Daniel's on the rocks with a drop of water and asked the bartender, just for something to say, "How'd you ever get a name like Moby's Dick past the state licensing people?"

He was a big-bellied, bearded man with a fringe of red hair and a purple explosion of broken blood vessels on his nose. He sighed as if he were tired of hearing that one. "Got friends on the board," he said shortly.

"My father used to come in here," I told him. "Maybe you know him. Robert Storm."

The bartender squinted at me with insular suspicion but a man on the neighboring bar stool turned and peered at me closely. "You Jonny Storm?" he asked. "No shit?"

"No shit." But I recognized him, too. He was built like a

fireplug, and his profile under an inch or so of forehead had been flattened by years in the ring. He'd played heavies in about every second western made in the fifties and sixties until finally his boozing and brawling got him blackballed at the studios. His last and worst offense had been to pick a fight with the leading man on a picture he was working in, get him in a headlock, and pull out all his hair. A few old-timers like Pop thought he was a riot and got him jobs whenever they could on independent productions, but I hadn't seen him in anything for years.

"Yeah, I guess you are," he decided. "Goddamn, I remember when you was knee-high. Your old man took you with him on *Devil's Canyon*. He stuck out a square hand. "Kirby Rand."

We shook. "Sure, I remember that."

"Hey, Red. Get Stormy's kid another drink."

I hadn't started the first one, but I didn't want to offend him. "Thanks."

"Jeez, *Devil's Canyon* seems like a hundred years ago. Fuckin' Henry Hathaway directed, the mean bastard. Stormy and me borrowed a stagecoach and drove into that hick town we were shootin' near for a few pours. We got shit-faced and wrecked the stage so Hathaway tried to fire me, seein' as I wasn't on much film yet. Stormy says, 'If he goes, I go,' so I stayed.

"But we hadda get even, right? Well, we dug like a fuckin' tiger trap, took us all night. We filled it up with horseshit from the corral and soaked it down to keep it soggy. Then we camouflaged it real good and went and stole his favorite walking stick he couldn't go nowhere without, while he was sleepin'. In the morning he gets up and looks all around until someone tells him it's stickin' right in the ground over there, then takes off before the prick can tell him to go fetch it. Hathaway steps on this dirt we stuck the cane in which is sprinkled over nothin' but cardboard and goes into the shit up to his ears ..." Rand leaned over wheezing with laughter that ended in a hacking cough.

I finished my first drink. "I've been looking for him."

"Well, you just missed him by maybe half an hour. First time I seen him in here in years. I tried to get him to stick around and hoist a few more, didn't I, Red?"

I almost grabbed him. "Did he say where he was going?"

"Naw, just that he had business. He was pretty juiced, but hell, he can handle it." Rand bashed his glass into mine almost hard enough to break both of them. "Drink up, kid."

I took a swallow. "Listen, Kirby, it's pretty important. Did he give you any idea? Can you remember exactly what he said?"

Rand's inch of forehead furrowed in concentration and his bleary eyes stared past me. "Well, we were talkin' about old times, you know? How everything was better then. Simpler. He was sayin' how back then we'd just shoot a thief or a killer. Or take him out in back of the jail and hang him. I was thinkin' he was confused because we weren't around back when they did that, we just made movies about it. When I told him so he got sore and said he wasn't talkin' about acting now."

Oh, Jesus.

"I didn't laugh or nothin', because Stormy can break bad when he's had a few. I guess he thought I was jackin' him around, though, because he said if I didn't believe him all I had to do was read the fuckin' papers tomorrow."

I dropped a five-dollar bill on the bar and headed for the swinging doors. Behind me Rand called, "He was wearin' a hat. I never seen Stormy wear a fuckin' hat. Except in the movies!"

Outside, I stood in the parking lot and watched the traffic go by on the Coast Highway. The surf boomed behind me; the stars lit up the sky overhead. Where the hell had he gone? Did he know where Clewes lived in Beverly Hills or about the beach house? Would he go to the hotel, which would be crawling with security? Pop was out there living one of his old scripts, carrying live ammunition instead of blanks. I didn't know how to stop him and there wasn't even time.

In half an hour I had to meet Jim Quest.

• • •

I left my car on Zumirez Road, just beyond the cinder-block bungalow with the rust-buckets parked on the overgrown lawn, and walked to the beach house. The sheet-metal gate stood slightly ajar in dubious invitation and I would have preferred another way in, but I remembered that the high wall enclosed the property completely and the only other access was by way of the steps climbing the bluff from the ocean.

The earlier desert wind had swept away the customary coastal fog and I felt like a slow-moving target as I walked up the long driveway through the clear night. Light glowed dimly downstairs, and Jim Quest's Olds was the only car parked on the semicircle of gravel.

I kept a hand on the heavy pistol that dragged at my jacket pocket as I rang the bell and then moved back into the shadows when I heard steps approaching. The door opened and Quest asked, "Is that you, Storm?"

"Come out here."

When he walked out on the stoop and peered around I grabbed his shoulder, spun him, and shoved so he had to place his palms against the side of the house, "Spread 'em."

"This isn't necessary." He tried to mask his apprehension with contempt.

I patted him down carefully. "Okay, let's go inside."

"You're getting a little paranoid, Storm." But he led me through the dim living room to the study, where a single standing lamp burned. The French doors leading to the terrace were open and I could hear the surf crashing against the base of the bluff.

"If you want a drink, there's a bar." He already had a glass standing near the edge of the heavy oak desk.

"Let's get right down to it. Where are those tapes?"

"They're here, but first we've got to talk about a deal."

"I told you if you turn state's evidence you can probably plea bargain."

223

"Life in prison, instead of death? No way. Not even if it's seven years."

"What do you suggest? The witness saw you."

"This witness isn't in police custody, am I right? *You* control the witness."

"Yes."

"Then the witness doesn't have to come forward. I'll testify Bill told me he was going to have Buckler killed, leaving myself out of the rest. I tried to reason with him and didn't expose him out of loyalty, but I've had an attack of conscience. I can testify how he did it and the facts will jibe. That way I'll be guilty of nothing more than withholding evidence or some other lesser form of complicity. I could bargain for probation."

I wondered if he could be serious. I'd judged him as being intelligent, although murderous and possibly insane. But if he thought I'd go along with his scheme or he could get off with probation, it could work for me. He was dead meat anyway, and I had to move past him at Willie.

I pretended to give it some thought. "That could fly. It depends what's on the tapes."

"I'll let you judge for yourself." Quest went to the wall where a tape deck sat on a shelf breaking a row of books. He took a cartridge from a stack of three on top of the machine and shoved it in.

I kept my back against the same wall, where I could look out the French windows and watch the entrance to the study at the same time. Quest went back to rest a haunch on the desk and picked up his glass.

The tape whirred along for a few seconds and then I heard what sounded like the hiss of a shower in the background and the muted babble of a radio or TV set. Much nearer, Gil began humming "On a Clear Day." I knew it was him because it was his favorite song and he never could carry a tune worth a damn.

"Where was the bug?" I asked Quest.

"Lamp on the bedside table."

The hissing sound in the background stopped, and then the

murmur of the TV or radio. "Hey, don't turn it off," I heard Gil protest.

"We don't need it, do we?" came Monica's voice.

"Willie's on in a couple of minutes. I want to make sure he's where he's supposed to be." I could hear the banter in Gil's tone.

"Don't be silly." Monica was closer to the bug now.

"I think it might be kind of fun to make it while he's here with us on the tube." He would, too.

"You're a perverted bastard." But she made the accusation sound like a caress.

I reached over and stopped the tape. "When was this?"

"Last July. Bill was on a panel show in San Francisco, re-butting the governor on a toxics bill."

I switched the tape back on and heard the mattress protest as she sat or lay down on the bed. Then there was the pop of a match after two scratchy tries and the sibilant, sucking sound of someone taking a hit on a joint. The quality of the tape was excellent.

"Don't be greedy," said Monica, after another long drag.

"Gotta get my chemistry balanced," Gil whispered, holding in the smoke.

"Mmm."

He exhaled. "You really think Willie's got a chance to win?"

"Stop calling him Willie, goddammit!"

"All right, all right."

"I've told you he's got a chance. A small chance. This is the year of the Fascist in America."

"Why does he waste his time going to places like Silicon Valley? The high-tech crowd isn't going to vote for him."

"Because they give him money. Not as much as they give Rydell, but substantial money. They're scared of him and they want to hedge their bets. The defense industries do the same thing."

"Knowing he's going to clobber them?"

"Hoping he won't. Hoping he's just talking."

"But we know better." Well, well. Gil was in there working.

"We know better. Gil, you don't give a damn about politics, so what do you care?"

"I don't, Monkey-face. Not really. But I might as well learn something while I'm around experts. Nothing wrong with an education."

"Your talents lie elsewhere."

"Sometimes I think that's all you want me for." Gil contrived to seem hurt. Someone took another long toke at the grass. They were beginning to sound like Cheech and Chong.

Monica burst out laughing. "A classic case of role reversal! Of course, that's what I want you for. Here, I'll give you a sample . . ."

"Hey!" For a moment all we could hear was his heavy breathing and small, mewling sounds from her.

"Come up here," Gil growled at last. "Keep that up and I won't have anything left to do but say thanks."

She gave a throaty little laugh that was more of a gasp and then there was a lot of thrashing around as if they were in a wrestling match. She cried, "Oh, God! ohgod, ohgod, ohgod . . ."

Suddenly there was a meaty whack and she screamed, "No!"

"No?" Gil's voice was silky. "No?" Another good smack and her answering cry. "Now, over you go," he said, as if talking to a child.

"No, you bastard!" Her breath became a coarse rasping, sawing in and out of her throat. "Goddamn you!" she yelled, and the rest was mumbled as if smothered in a pillow.

"Now we re-reverse the roles, you see?" Gil whispered to her between his own grunts of effort.

"Ah . . . aah . . . aah . . ." She set up a monotonous, high-pitched keening and Quest cut off the tape.

"Nothing but mattress pounding for the next half hour," he said. "Then there's some more talk, but I think the point's been made. Bill had a reason to commit murder."

"I want to hear what they say afterward."

Quest shrugged and pushed the fast-forward button, stopping the tape twice amid a medley of cries and groans until he found the right place.

"—needed that," Monica murmured. "My God, I did."

"Oh, I believe you, Monkey," Gil said breezily. "Old Willie would never guess what gets you up there, would he? Too busy trying to save the world. Or maybe run it."

Her voice tightened in anger. "That's right, Gil. He works at saving the world while you give stud service. Some comparison in values, wouldn't you say?"

Gil sighed. "Everyone makes their own unique contribution."

"You're very droll, Gil. You're even a good lover in a cruel sort of way."

"Well, I simply tailor the supply to the demand," Gil said innocently. "Isn't that what studs are supposed to do?"

Sounds suggested she was shifting position or getting off the bed. "Stick to that, Gil. It's your whole bag of tricks."

"I disagree. I play excellent tennis." He chuckled. "C'mon, Monkey, don't go away mad. We've been pals too long."

"Why do you work so hard to infuriate me?"

"Because that's what you want."

No one said anything for a while, but finally she laughed. "I think you're right. I use you to get it out of my system. Any complaints?"

"Hell, no. But I must admit it hurts that you think I'm a dummy. A curious intellect lurks behind this lecherous mask. I wasn't being facetious when I asked if Willie ... Bill has a chance in this election."

"And I told you he does."

"This is the one he has to get past, isn't it?"

"Yes. To go all the way."

"But hell, Monkey, I know you guys are both pretty committed, but what can a junior senator do to change the world? I mean, they don't get to head the big committees, do they? I know he can run for president from the Senate—"

227

"He'll do that when the time comes. Right now he can get on the important committees, even if he doesn't run them. Bill has sponsors for the Joint Intelligence Committee . . ." She paused and the fire left her voice. "Look, Gil, I live this every day of my life. When I'm with you I want to forget it. It's the only time I can."

"I'm strictly for R and R, then." Again Gil tried to sound offended.

"Isn't that what we agreed?"

Gil gave it one more shot. "Sure, Monkey. It's just I'm curious about a point. If Bill gets on this Joint Intelligence Committee, does that give him access to government secrets?"

"I'm not going into this with you, remember?"

"Well, we've got to be able to talk . . ."

She interrupted him. "Do we really? You think so?" More sounds of a tussle and Gil said, "Christ, give me a chance to smoke a cigarette, can't you?"

"Okay," I said. Gil may have been a clumsy agent, but he'd enjoyed his work. I felt a rush of jealousy that surprised me, but I had to smile, too. Why did they all go for him? Because a hard man is good to find, he liked to say . . .

Quest punched a button to eject the cassette and I caught it coming out of the slot and put it in my pocket. I took the other two off the top of the tape deck and kept them too. He just shrugged and said, "They're all pretty much the same."

It was the wrong reaction. He should have protested, because now I had his tapes and he had nothing. He knew I hated his guts, so why should I make a deal with him? But he just stared at me as if he were afraid to look anywhere else.

"There's another thing." His voice sounded strained when he finally raised his eyes to the bookcase behind me and lifted a hand. "Bill kept his appointment books up here . . ."

I began to turn my head to follow his gesture. It was the natural thing to do. What was unnatural was his whole attitude, from his strange detachment about the tapes to the slight tremor I could detect in his voice. It kept me from completing the automatic response and I caught the movement of one of the curtains framing the French doors in my peripheral vision. Just one of them. On a night without the slightest breeze.

I dove past Quest toward the sheltered slot between the desk and the wall, hitting the floor hard, spinning around, and jerking the big automatic out of my jacket pocket. Quest was my priority because he'd rigged this and he could have a gun close at hand.

But the instant I could see him again, I heard two sharp coughs from the terrace and he stepped back into the shelves with a look of utter astonishment on his face. Then he raised his hands toward his chest and abruptly sat down next to me, amid a cascade of books.

I swept aside the standing lamp, snapping the cord from the wall outlet, and the room went dark. The silenced weapon spat twice more and I could hear bullets chiseling through the desk above where I lay.

Quest began to scream as I rolled back over on my stomach and used my elbows to drag myself where I could peer around the edge of the desk. There was no target so I aimed at the curtain I'd seen moving. The roar of the big automatic echoed around the house and I saw a slim figure break cover and flit across the terrace toward the lawn.

Quest was still screaming as I got my feet under me and, keeping low, plunged across the study and through the French doors. From the terrace the gunman was easy to see, a dark form racing through the pale night toward the bluff. Until then I'd assumed it was Willie, but Willie would know better than to trap himself. The bastard hadn't studied the layout or, more likely, hadn't planned to fail. By waiting on the terrace he'd cut himself off from the front of the house, and with the wall sealing off the property from the road, he was out of choices.

I went after him, but by the time I was halfway across the lawn he had reached the stairs leading down to the private beach. He turned and I threw myself flat on the ground as he fired three times. The muzzle of his gun flared like a cigarette lighter and the shots were close enough for me to hear their passage. I guessed he was using a target pistol and I stayed down while I steadied the .45, but before I could line up a shot he was gone as if he'd dropped off the edge of the world. I got up and ran for the scrub brush fringing the bluff, working my way toward the head of the stairs under cover. If he was waiting there, I'd see him before he saw me.

But the stairs were empty. As far as the first landing, anyway—beyond that they angled out of sight down the face of the cliff. The surf was a steady roar now, shaking the timbers under me as I started down the steps. Which meant there would be no beach and no place for him to go. He couldn't leave the stairs because the sides of the cliff were too steep and rocky, and I didn't think anyone was going to swim away in this surf.

On my way down to the landing I stayed low and held the .45 extended in both hands, cocked and ready. When I got there, I went all the way down on my stomach and peeked over the platform, presenting the smallest possible target.

I was right; he had no place to go. He was standing on the second landing, maybe fifty steps above the angry sea, aiming his gun where he expected me to appear. I could see the pale blur of his face and the bald crown of his head above his dark clothing.

His best shot nicked the wood a foot from my hand, not bad considering how little he had to shoot at. Two more rounds went high, smacking the steps behind me. I shoved out my arms and drew down on him, aiming high on his chest, taking time to squeeze the trigger slowly.

The heavy report of the .45 was muffled by the thunder of the surf, but he flew backward like a rag doll, tumbling and rolling down the last flight of steps. I could see him crumpled near the bottom, the ocean lapping at his upper torso, but I went down after him cautiously, keeping the automatic leveled.

The heavy, hollow-point bullet had hit him in the throat, nearly decapitating him. His head rolled in the foam at the high-tide line and the water carried away the spurting arterial blood, black as oil under the starlight. One leg was crooked

230

awkwardly around a wooden upright supporting the rail, which kept the sea from sweeping him away. His right hand still clutched a long-barreled Colt Woodsman equipped with a silencer. An assassin's weapon.

I went through his clothes and found a wallet, car keys to a rental, change, cigarettes, and a passport. I crammed the stuff into my own pockets, though I doubted it would be worth much. This one would have a carefully crafted identity leading nowhere. The last time I'd seen him was in the smoky little Spanish restaurant Lydia Ballesteros had taken me to in Mexico City just before her car blew up. He was a pro.

# EIGHTEEN

used my foot to kick his leg free of the stanchion that had snagged him and roll him into the sea. Then I pitched his target pistol into the waves after him. It wouldn't float like his body, but it didn't matter if they found it or not. What mattered was whether he'd managed to kill Jim Quest.

I tried taking the long flight of stairs two at a time, but I wasn't in that kind of shape yet. At the top, I had to pause for breath before walking across the lawn to the darkened house. If Quest was still yelling I couldn't hear him, but then the booming surf would have drowned him out even as it had muted the sound of gunshots. I crossed the terrace and slipped through the French doors. I felt around for a light switch but couldn't find one, so I waited for my eyes to become accustomed to the dim interior.

Quest was a dark shape against the hardwood floor, huddled by the far wall, making no movement or sound. I went over to him and held my fingers against his throat, feeling a weak but steady pulse. He groaned when I touched him. There were two dark stains high on his stomach, over his diaphragm. Enough

231

to produce a serious, possibly mortal wound, even given the light caliber of the ammunition. There was nothing accidental about that kind of shooting. The gunman had wanted us both. When I drove out of range, he'd simply dealt with Quest first. It was pointless trying to speculate how Willie had planned to handle it. We could have been dumped in the ocean or driven off to some convenient landfill. It was a pretty good bet we weren't supposed to be discovered here.

I found my way to the wet bar in a corner of the study and took a long drink of Scotch straight from the bottle. It was good stuff and the glow emanated from the core of me to reach for my extremities. A couple more and I'd probably be ready to play host to the cops when they broke down the door, though I didn't think that would happen. Tonight any sound from the beach house would be cut off from the world by the high wall and an angry sea.

I wiped the bottle off with a bar rag and put it reluctantly aside. I was still alive, but this was no time to celebrate.

My car was where I'd left it, near the house with the junkers blocked up on the lawn. A grotesque antenna rose high above the roof and I could hear the babble of TV before I got to the Chrysler. They were listening to the election returns.

Quest was a heavy burden. I'd locked his arm around my neck holding on to his wrist and I had him by the waist, but his legs barely moved and tended to buckle under him. His eyes were open and he wheezed, forming little bubbles of blood at the corner of his mouth, so I guessed a bullet had nicked his lung. I got the door open on the passenger side and worked him onto the seat, where he slumped over against the dashboard like a sack of laundry.

Merging with the sparse, fast traffic on the Coast Highway, I turned south and stole five miles an hour on the speed limit. I didn't want to get stopped with a shot-up passenger and some very delicate tapes aboard, but I couldn't know exactly how badly off Quest was. And if he died, so did the case against Willie.

The Malibu Emergency Room was still located just off PCH on Webb Way, a stone's throw from the exclusive Malibu Colony. It was housed in two mobile home units standing side by side in a parking lot next to a market, but that's where the sheriff's deputies took urgent cases. I hoped they wouldn't be around tonight.

I rolled into the parking lot, pulled up in front of the Emergency Room, and ran up a ramp designed for ambulances. A young nurse in E.R. scrubs looked up from a counter with tired, incurious eyes.

"I've got a man in my car who's been shot," I told her, eliciting a little more response.

She padded away across the plastic tiles on rubber soles and reappeared with two men in identical scrubs pushing a gurney. We all ran back down the ramp and over to the Chrysler. The medics looked like beach boys, but they got Quest onto the gurney efficiently enough. He moaned in pain, opened his eyes wide, and looked right at me. "Told you . . ." I think he said. Or maybe it was, "Sold you."

The men rushed the gurney back up the ramp and the nurse turned to me. "There are some forms you'll have to fill out." Smart girl. I knew that at my mention of a gunshot victim she would have phoned the cops.

I showed her the palms of my hands. "Hey, I just found him alongside the road. I'm a good Samaritan, but I don't want to get involved."

Her lips thinned. "It's required. We need the information for a police report in cases of gunshot wound."

I shook my head and went around the Chrysler to the driver's side. "I got a wife and kids that come first, honey," I said, getting behind the wheel. "Like I said, I don't get involved."

The contempt in her narrow eyes was the last thing I saw as I started up. If she had a brain in her head she'd try to memorize my license plate, so I backed up and let the headlights hit her straight on as I reversed out of the parking lot.

• • •

233

Across the highway from Pepperdine University, large estates hide in the lush greenery of the palisades above the coastline. I followed a little tar road that meandered along the heights above the beach until I came to an empty lot at the lip of a cliff with a view of the world. The Malibu Colony nestled below, and beyond that a necklace of lights stretched around the bay to the Palos Verde peninsula. I could see coastal Santa Monica and the bluffs above Highway 1, where developers had begun to build high-rises before the city stopped them. Lights from the ships plying to and from L.A. Harbor winked offshore.

I reached into the glove compartment for the tequila bottle and saw Gil's .45. It would make sense to get rid of it, but I could imagine his indignant protest. "Throw away a piece that's been smoothed out like that?! Do you remember what I could do with that beauty?"

"It shoots high," I said. "I was aiming for the asshole's chest."

"Your hands always shook. I could've taken out his left eye."

"Someone could conceivably match it up with the round, you know." Small chance of that, though. Hollow-points splatter.

"Are you kidding? It either spread out or went through him. Anyway, he'll probably float to Catalina if the sharks don't get him."

"Okay, okay." I wanted to keep the gun anyway.

After a moment he asked, "Have we got him, Jonny?"

I took a long pull at the tequila. "It's going to be close."

"Close only counts with horseshoes and hand grenades, old friend."

"If Quest dies, Willie will get dirty by association, but that's about all." Even that depended on Iris's testimony and the cops coming to the right conclusions about Murdoch's death.

"He still has to get past your old man," Gil said softly.

I sat up. Jesus Christ! I'd forgotten about Pop in the turbulence of the last hour. He was still a loose cannon out there, drunker than I was and determined not to be done out of being a hero twice. I pitched the tequila bottle out the car window and started the engine.

234

• • •

The Mirador Hotel was on Ocean Avenue in Santa Monica, overlooking Palisades Park and the sea beyond. Built in the twenties, when construction expanded outward instead of upward, it occupied an entire city block. Originally, the hotel had consisted of a handful of bungalows surrounding a generous pool. Then two brick annexes were added and finally a sixteen-story "tower" with a large banquet room under a skylight spreading out from its base. The tower was Art Deco, with beveled edges and recessed balconies, a daring, even controversial piece of architecture in its time, but it had long since been dwarfed and demeaned by taller, glassier buildings put up before the city council declared a hiatus on high-rises.

I remember when the Mirador was a haven for airline stewardesses and a happy hunting ground for Gil and me. The bar was dark and intimate; the rooms high-ceilinged and airy. The last I heard it was running in the red and the Japanese were going to buy it, upgrade it, and add it to a chain.

When I got there I had to drive on and park a block away because the parking lot was full. I wasn't surprised that Willie had chosen it for his election-night party headquarters, because it was in the heart of his constituency and unassuming enough to fit his plebeian image. As I walked back along Ocean Avenue I noticed two groups of demonstrators in the park, being kept apart by police. Willie's supporters shouted, "We care!" and waved posters of him. The opposition paraded a long banner suggesting Willie and Monica return permanently to Hanoi.

I cut through the parking lot toward the main entrance and stopped dead, having spotted exactly what I dreaded to see. Gleaming black under a street light was Pop's 1939 Packard convertible, top down, exposing the rich leather seats, huge whitewall tires recalling a more elegant era.

Walking fast, I shoved through the revolving doors into the lobby. The desk was on the right, and well beyond it the bar and the banquet room faced each other across a carpeted passageway. A few people loitered around the lobby, tourists by the look of

235

them, curious about the hoopla. I went down the corridor where the crowd was spilling out of the banquet room and worked my way in. A muscular black man in a short-sleeved shirt looked me over carefully, but no one tried to stop me, and I didn't notice any extraordinary security precautions. Pop could be mingling with the mob down here, waiting to get a shot at Willie.

The big room was set up for the occasion. I saw a raised platform at the far end, with flags of the United States and California framing an enormous poster of Willie. Four huge TV monitors angled downward, giving the latest state and national election returns. Tables and chairs had been shoved against the walls to make room for impromptu dancing, and a makeshift bar served beer and wine. The crowd, smelling victory, was loud and very restless.

I pushed my way through, searching for Pop with or without a hat, but he wasn't around unless he was hiding behind the drapes. For good measure, I checked there too. A clutch of people under one of the monitors gave a ragged cheer and I looked up at a printout that made Clewes the clear winner in his contest with Rydell. Another set featured Dan Rather as Big Brother, trying not to gloat as he reported that the Senate seemed to be going to the Democrats. Willie was nowhere in sight, probably waiting to be summoned by the faithful. I practically had to fight my way out.

By contrast, the dim bar across the way was nearly empty. Half a dozen male customers sat staring at the TV through the smoky haze, and only one booth was occupied. Captain Norman Kling sat in it facing me, across from a girl with long blond hair who had to be Iris. I turned away, hoping he hadn't seen me, and went into the men's room. No one stood at the urinals, so I squatted to peer under the stall doors for the telltale elevators that would identify my father.

Kling came in while I was splashing water on my face, trying to clear my head. "What are you doing here, Storm?" he asked. "I thought you went to Mexico."

I dried off with a paper towel. "I came back."

"I don't like it. Monica Loring nearly filed a complaint about you harassing them, and you come here."

"Just as a spectator."

He shook his head. "I've got enough problems. Don't make any more."

"Santa Monica's out of your jurisdiction, isn't it?" But I knew why he was here. I'd practically sent him.

"I came to make an identification." He sighed and brought out a pack of cigarettes. "I'm waiting for Clewes's campaign manager, Jim Quest. His people say they're expecting him. All kinds of crap is breaking loose. When I went to his house, I found a homicide team there investigating another matter. His wife's hysterical, and no one knows where he is."

He offered his pack and lit my cigarette as we walked out of the men's room. "Look, Storm, you came to me and asked what happened to Gil Buckler and I gave you what we had. Then you went to Clewes's place and made a scene, even hit Quest. Monica Loring told me that. Now I have evidence that may involve him in Gil's murder. And here you are. I don't believe in coincidence, so here's your chance to contribute to an investigation."

At the bar, I turned so that Iris wouldn't recognize me if she looked around. I couldn't tell Kling where Quest was without involving myself, but he'd soon find out. Hospitals report bullet wounds. In the meanwhile, my father was wandering around the hotel somewhere with a gun and a grudge. I had to get away from Kling. "I can't help you, Captain. I'm sorry."

"Bullshit. You going to pretend you're not even curious about what I said? I don't have to read you the law about concealing evidence—"

A cry arose from the banquet room. "We want Bill! We want Bill!"

That would be the summons Willie was waiting for. I had to get between him and my father. I said to Kling. "Try the Malibu Emergency Room." Hell with it, he was going to get it out of Quest anyway. Or Iris would bring me into it.

He gave me a bitter look. "What happened to him?"

"You'd better call. Look, I've got to go." I walked out of the bar and then ran back to the lobby, where a bank of house phones stood by the registration desk.

"Suite sixteen-oh-one," the operator told me, adding, "Sorry, it's busy."

"I'll hold." The phone grew slick in my hand as I waited. I could hear them roaring for Willie in the banquet room.

"Clewes's headquarters!" a jubilant voice finally shouted over the line.

"Let me talk to Bill," I snapped. "This is Jim Quest."

"Sure. I didn't recognize your voice, Mr. Quest."

Willie came on the line almost immediately. "Where the hell are you, Jim?"

"This is Jon Storm, Willie. I want to come up right away."

"Don't be ridiculous."

"Listen, Willie, Jim isn't coming. In fact, the cops are looking for him. As you might have been told by now. Well, I know where he is. Do you really want me to create a media event down here?"

He didn't answer as the seconds crawled by. "Willie?"

Finally he said, "All right . . ."

I went back past the bar and the banquet room to the tower elevators. What I was going to say to Willie might give him an edge, a chance to prepare, if it didn't hit him hard enough. I hadn't planned it that way, but I couldn't let him go down there and make a murderer out of my father.

As I walked down the corridor of the sixteenth floor with its elegant but worn carpeting, past the lamps bracketed in wrought iron along the walls, I saw an exodus from the suite I was looking for. Understandably enough, Willie wouldn't want any witnesses to our conversation.

I stood aside politely as they came piling out, looking perplexed and irritated at their eviction. Several of them had been at the beach house picnic, members of Willie's inner circle.

The former governor of California was trying to grow a beard, making him look more than ever like a demented monk. The dapper black named Prime, who Quest had told me was a pal of the mayor, was complaining to the scowling ex-president of the Screen Actors' Guild, who stomped out in shirt sleeves, matted black hair sprouting out of his open collar, sweat stains under his arms. There was a lanky singer-actress who should be heard but never seen and an actor who performed mostly in protest marches outside military bases. They looked at me with curiosity and resentment as they left.

Willie's bodyguards stayed behind with me. The young, impudent one shook his head as he frisked me carefully. "I just can't figure what the assemblyman sees in you," he remarked.

I walked into Willie's suite, closing the door behind me. The TV was on and bottles of champagne stuck out of ice buckets on the bar. Glasses and smoldering ashtrays stood around. I'd interrupted a celebration.

Monica sat on a sofa wearing an elegant white sweater dress with a turtleneck collar and a wide lizard belt. She watched me cross the room with loathing. Willie was as pale as his shirt, but that didn't mean much in his case. The tiny knot in his tie was snugged into place and I saw a jacket slung over an easy chair near where he stood. Neither of them said anything to me at all.

"If you're wondering about Jim Quest, he'll be okay," I told Willie. "Your friend from Mexico put a couple of holes in him but when I dropped him off to get patched up, he was already trying to make a statement." I shook my head. "He's really sore at you, Willie."

"Where is Jim?" Monica asked evenly.

"Malibu Emergency Room." I hoped to God he hadn't died, but I had to take the chance.

Willie picked up the phone and asked the operator to connect him. After a while he said, "Malibu Emergency Room? This is Assemblyman Bill Clewes. I'm inquiring after a colleague of mine who is reported to be in your care. A Mr. Jim Quest."

**239**

He listened for a moment and then asked, "What is his condition?"

Finally he said, "Thank you," and hung up.

"Well?" Monica turned toward him calmly.

"They just took him to St. Johns. They won't discuss his condition."

That figured. An emergency facility would stabilize him and pass him on to a regular hospital. "He's all right, Willie. Talking up a storm as I drove him to emergency."

"I suggest you shot him yourself," Willie tried. "You're playing out some insane vendetta against us."

I ignored him and looked at Monica, surprised that Willie was letting her listen to this. But then, he couldn't just hustle her out with the rest of them. She wouldn't stand for that. "You're the one I can't figure, Monkey. Were you looking over his shoulder when he typed the notes? Did you watch him poison your dog?"

"You have a sick mind."

"Maybe I do. Because I got a kick out of these." I took one of the cassettes out of my pocket. "Of course you didn't know Quest had you and Gil bugged. He played the tapes for Willie. And that's when they came up with the bright idea of how to win the election by having Gil murdered and pinning the whole thing on Rydell's kid." I tossed the tape into her lap. "It also got rid of some of that hatred Willie's been storing up since we were kids."

Willie's thin lips had disappeared. He was staring at the tape in Monica's lap. "If Jim did something like that, I didn't know anything about it. He was on his own."

I turned back to him. "He'll testify it was your idea. He knows you tried to have him killed tonight along with me. He knows a witness heard him contract murder on your behalf. What has he got to lose?"

Willie sneered. "The famous witness."

"Just for openers." I walked over to the bar, but there was nothing but champagne, which isn't my drink. "Did you know

240

he had a wife in Mexico, Monkey? Hell, he just had her killed last week. But not before she gave me the letters he wrote her from Russia. Signed, 'Your loving Comrade,' but not very sexy stuff. Just some more hate mail, really. Directed against his country this time."

Monica was looking at her husband with an expression I couldn't read at all. Her face was a mask. Willie's was white stone with black pebbles for eyes.

"He's Moscow-trained, Monkey. Disciplined. Came back from Mexico and snapped himself up a rich little radical with all the money and connections he needed. Didn't let her father stand in his way, either. When that gentleman objected to the relationship, Willie tried to blackmail him into changing his mind. Only the poor man snapped and shot himself instead."

Monica's eyes came back to me. "I don't believe you," she whispered. Tension made the tendons stand out in her throat.

"Did you talk to your mother before she died?"

"She was in a coma."

"I'm not sure she would have told you anyway. The material Willie used was a legacy from his father. Extortion was kind of a family tradition, in fact. Clewes senior kept track of your mother's indiscretions in a journal and blackmailed her for years." Telling her this made me feel more than a little sick of myself, but I couldn't think of another way. Forgive me, Aunt Kitty. "My father saw a copy of the journal. He was involved, you see."

Willie made a strangled sound and took a step toward me.

The phone rang. For a long moment no one moved or said anything as the insistent trilling went on and Willie stared at me, contemplating his next murder. Finally he reached for the instrument like an automaton. "Yes?"

After a moment he forced his eyes away from me to the TV set, still holding on to the phone. Monica and I followed his gaze. On the screen, Buck Rydell had come down from his suite in the Bonaventure Hotel, the camera tracking him as he passed through a group of glum-looking supporters in the ballroom,

241

shaking hands solemnly, working his way toward a podium. An excited off-screen voice predicted that this would be a concession speech. Slowly Willie put the phone down, his eyes fixed on the screen.

I pulled an open bottle of champagne from an ice bucket, grabbed a glass, and went out to the small terrace. Beyond the park, the Santa Monica pier thrust a finger of light into the dark waters of the bay. Directly below me the giant skylight over the banquet room glowed softly. I could hear the cadenced shout, "We want Bill! We want Bill!" I poured some champagne and drank it down with a grimace, deciding I'd never get to like the stuff, but hell, this was an occasion.

" . . . people have made their choice, and I accept their verdict." Behind me, Buck Rydell droned the ritual words of defeat. I went back inside with my bottle and half-empty glass. They looked up at me reluctantly, pulled back from the edge of a sweet dream. If I disappeared the dream could go on. That's supposed to give you a feeling of power, and it did.

"This deserves a toast." I held up the champagne bottle. "What'll we drink to? Murder and treason? The first United States senator ever to be executed?" I drained my glass and grinned at them.

Monica gave a small cry and stood up. The tape slid off her lap to the floor. Willie lunged for it, going down on his knees. I got over there fast and stepped on his hand as he reached out. He yelled as I picked up the tape and dropped it back in my pocket.

"Congratulations, Willie," I said softly, looking down at him. I shifted my weight so all of it was on his hand, grinding down until I could hear bones crackle. He screamed like a ten-year-old being tormented in a schoolyard.

The door to the suite burst open as I stepped back and the two bodyguards rushed in, the younger one already in an eager crouch, a hand under his jacket. "Easy, Ralph," the other man cautioned.

I stood there holding the champagne bottle in one hand and

my glass in the other. Absolutely still, because I've known a lot of guys like Ralph. Willie still knelt on the floor, hunched over his hand.

"Are you all right in here?" The older man looked from Willie to Monica.

"We're fine," she said. "He just took a fall, Mr. Kennedy."

He sure did.

Kennedy asked, "Want me to get a doctor?"

"No . . ." Willie managed. "I just twisted my wrist." He caught the edge of the coffee table and pulled himself to his feet. His right hand hung limp and raw. The phone began to ring, but no one answered it. We all just stared at each other.

Monica broke the silence. "I'll see he gets some ice on it." She added pointedly, "That will be all, thanks."

I'd half expected someone to try and get the cassette back from me, but then I remembered Ralph and Kennedy were probably off-duty cops. Willie and Monica couldn't risk using them for the purpose. Not while I could tell them what everyone would be missing if the tapes disappeared.

Kennedy turned to go, but Ralph stood watching us suspiciously. Willie was breathing hard, his face as mottled as his injured hand. He turned away and lurched toward the terrace. I kept looking at Monica, trying to decide if she wanted to get out of there. All I needed was some sign, a flicker.

Her eyes were cold mirrors. "Mr. Storm will be leaving, too."

Ralph inclined his head in a curt, tough-guy motion. I put the bottle and glass on an end table next to the sofa and walked out, Ralph crowding me from behind. Kennedy closed the door once we were in the hall.

"I know something was going on in there," Ralph snarled at me.

I looked at him with undisguised admiration and said, "Keep this up, you could be a cop someday, Ralph."

The phone was still ringing inside the suite as I walked down the hall.

•　　•　　•

Someone had released balloons in the banquet room. Red, white, and blue, they floated through the air and bounced gently against the skylight, like moths nudging a light bulb. A conga line snaked through the crowd, shouting out its rhythms, picking up new adherents like lint. TV news teams maneuvered for the best footage and little knots of viewers under the TV monitors howled derision during the pauses in Buck Rydell's concession speech. But a flavor of expectancy hung over the celebration. Several of the honchos I'd seen in Willie's suite were in a huddle near the door. One of them, the actor, broke away and went out, perhaps delegated to go fetch the candidate.

Then I saw Pop. He was over by the door too, scanning everyone who came in or went out. Waiting. He was leaning against the wall with his arms crossed, wearing a beige linen jacket and an open-necked sport shirt, a light felt hat tipped over his forehead. I didn't need to see his features because I know how he stands and moves. He always plays himself, anyway.

He hadn't been there when I came in and there wasn't time to wonder where he'd kept himself while I'd been searching for him. There was a fair chance Willie would come down in spite of the working over I'd given him, with or without Monica. Then Pop could haul out eight inches of horse pistol and go into his act for Kitty Mars and country, grab a week of headlines, and spend his golden years in jail.

I launched myself toward him, breaking through the conga line by slapping the hands of a bearded, chanting participant away from the waist of the woman in front of him. I was in the center of the room, more or less in the clear and moving forward, when a splintering crash imploded almost directly overhead.

I crouched instinctively, clasping my hands above my neck as an object thudded onto the terrazzo next to me. Behind it came a shower of glass and splintered moldings. I felt the shards dance off my back and shatter on the mosaic around me. The shrieks and cries began a full second later, after the debris had settled.

244

I uncovered and looked around. The body of Willie Clewes lay face down a yard away. I recognized it because I knew what he was wearing and the color and cut of his hair. Otherwise it was just a corpse, oddly flattened and shapeless after a sixteen-story plunge through a skylight onto an unyielding surface. Blood leaked from the ear I could see, and I had no burning desire to turn him over. In spite of everything. It passed through my mind, The son of a bitch nearly got me after all.

People converged around us hesitantly at first, shocked into temporary silence. Then the circle tightened as some bold spirit nudged Willie onto his side and made a tentative identification. Hotel personnel appeared and shoved through the crowd, which raised a chorus of shouts and wails as the identity of the body was passed along. The TV monitors beamed down, reflecting the scene as camera crews got into the act and we went to the nation, live.

A strong hand caught me above the elbow and helped me rise shakily, shrugging fragments of glass onto the floor. I looked down at Pop's compact figure, the fedora tilted rakishly on his head. No one was paying any attention to us.

"You okay, kid?" He glanced down at my hand, which was bleeding profusely. "Christ, that looks bad."

It did at that; the veins were probably lacerated. We pushed our way to the bar, where I found a reasonably clean towel I could fold into a compress. A bartender was standing there staring at the gaping hole in the skylight, mesmerized, so I jerked the skinny black tie from under his collar and Pop used it to bind the compress into place.

The turmoil eddied around us. A TV news team trying to work in closer paused to focus its camera on a woman who was kneeling on the floor, literally tearing her hair. Celebration had turned to pandemonium. Then I saw Norman Kling bearing down on me, angry eyes glaring out of his crumpled baby face. At least Iris wasn't with him, but that might not matter much anymore.

I fished the three tape cassettes out of my jacket pocket with

245

my good hand and slipped them to my father, standing with my back to Kling. "Take these and get out of here. Go home, all right? I'll see you back there."

"But—"

"It's important, Pop."

He stuck out his chin. "Got it," he said, barely moving his lips, and ducked away through the crowd, using his shoulders when he had to. I turned back as Kling came up and planted himself in front of me in a way that was pretty easy to read.

"What about Jim Quest?" I asked him, not expecting much good news.

"Shot. But you knew that."

"How is he?" I held my breath.

"D.O.A. at St. Johns."

I exhaled. If I'd kept my mouth shut about Quest, maybe I could have walked away clean. Maybe. If Iris didn't bring me into it. So much for twenty-twenty hindsight. I glanced up at the hole in the skylight and started to grin. Just couldn't help it.

Kling's scowl deepened. "You think it's *funny* he's dead?"

Oh yes, I wanted to say. He's dead and Willie took a plunge for nothing. What could be funnier than that? "I just can't explain it," I told him.

"Well, you're sure as hell going to get a chance."

Together we listened to the keening approach of a siren.

After my hand was rewrapped by the ambulance crew that removed Willie, I was taken to the West L.A. Police Station and booked. They read you your rights while you empty your pockets on the counter in a little room with one wall of wire mesh. Then you are fingerprinted and asked some surpassingly stupid questions by way of establishing identity. You are strip-searched, which includes a thorough probing of your body cavities, and your clothes are returned minus belt, shoelaces, cigarettes, and matches. I'd booked a lot of people into jail myself and realized it could be a bit degrading, but then they were suspects, usually pretty funky types, and they could use a little degrading. That's what I always told myself.

With the formalities over, I was entitled to a phone call before being locked up, if I had two dimes. I called Jim Constantine at the Federal Building, but all I could do was leave a message, so they took me to a tiny holding cell and I spent a sorry night sporadically dozing and bumming cigarettes from the turnkey.

Even so, I couldn't help grinning from time to time, even laughing out loud. I was high as a Zeppelin on the events of the evening. "We did it, Gil! He took the long fall!" No one else could appreciate it.

"You brought him tumbling down, old friend." Gil would have taken a night in jail in his stride. I could see him sitting there on the narrow bunk, as if the whole affair were mildly amusing, one eyebrow cocked in affable contempt when they came to grill him.

"It's not over, either," I said. "Tip of the iceberg."

"I'm not so sure. I think it is."

"You willing to settle for it?"

"The black hats are dead."

"Willie was just an outrider. The worm's still in the apple."

"Leave it to the pros."

"Like Constantine."

"Like Constantine. A man's got to know his limitations." I recognized Eastwood's line from *Dirty Harry*, Gil's favorite picture.

"Suppose I'd done that when I found out about you?"

Gil made an imaginary chalk mark in the air. "Score one for you. I apologize. A dead man should be a silent partner." He gave me the grin he used when the joke was on him and stood up. "Well, either way, you can tidy up without me."

The way he said it sounded ominously final, and I got up too. I wanted to put the moment off. "Wait a minute, Gil . . ."

"Good-bye, old friend."

The duty officer came over and said, "This is a holding facility, not the giggle ward. I'm trying to read."

I started to tell him to fuck off, and then realized he had a point. And maybe when I admitted that to myself, I tore something.

Because I never saw Gil again.

# NINETEEN

onstantine didn't let me down. By ten the next morning, I was back in the tacky conference room of the FBI offices in the Federal Building. He had come for me personally, arranged for my transfer to his custody, and we were out in minutes. My car was still back in the police impound lot. I hadn't been allowed to shower or shave, so I was rumpled and unsavory, conscious of my own jailhouse stink, but I suppose that was intentional.

At least he had some coffee brought in. I raised my cup. "To the power of the federal government."

He didn't respond to the gesture. "You'd better hope it's enough."

I changed the subject. "No one gave me time to buy a paper. What's the dope on Willie?"

"They're calling it a tragic accident. He drank a little champagne to celebrate his victory. He wasn't used to alcohol. Went out on the balcony and lost his balance. According to Monica Loring. We still have to hear from the coroner."

"Everybody going to buy that?"

"Why not? She was alone in the suite with him. Everyone knows she was devoted to the man and his career."

"And Willie will live on in the memory of his followers as a hero," I predicted bitterly. "Maybe even a martyr. You're not going to open up the case at all. That's why I'm here, right?"

He gave me a very steely look. "That's exactly right. One wrong move and you go back to Kling. I'll throw in the tape of our interview with you in Mexico, and he can sort it out any way he wants to."

"You're forgetting he can prove Quest killed Murdoch. He doesn't need me anymore."

"You also stated you ran down two motorcycle freaks and contributed one of the bullets that found their way into C. H. Herlinger. Think of what he can do with that."

I conceded the point in silence.

He went on bitingly, "Maybe you could return to your former candor long enough to explain what happened to Quest. If that won't wash, you may have to go back to Kling anyway. I can only do so much."

Briefly I told him about my meeting with Quest at the beach house and described the shoot-out that followed. I didn't mention the tapes of Gil and Monica.

Constantine stood up and jammed his hands in his pockets, where they balled into fists. "Another body? Jesus Christ, I wish I didn't have to deal with you!"

I said flatly, "You don't. Throw me to the dogs and then I can get the whole goddamn story off my chest. I'll sleep better, even in the slammer. You're lucky I don't just do that anyway, but then I'm a self-interested son of a bitch just like everyone else. And I think I once promised you if Willie and Quest got theirs, I'd settle for that, to hell with politics. So you decide."

He took his fists out of his pockets and put them on the table, leaning over at me. "What you are is a self-*righteous* son of a bitch! You seem to think the federal government and this bureau are in league with traitors, or at least trying to avoid taking responsibility for allowing them to infiltrate government to some degree." He straightened up and put his hands away. "Down in Mexico, we made a mistake and told you things you didn't need to know. Since you were a former law enforcement officer, we thought you might understand the limitations imposed by the law and the delicacy of our position,

249

but you were too involved emotionally. Now I'm going to spell out the situation as it stands after Mr. Clewes's timely demise."

He sat down and leaned back in his plastic chair. "You know Clewes was identified as a mole by a defector named Yurchenko, who later elected to return to Russia, either according to plan or because he had a change of heart, or whatever. We couldn't determine the validity of his information about Clewes until you came along and confirmed it. Then State made the decision to watch and wait, which you did everything you could to sabotage, even after we warned you. Now Mr. Clewes is dead under circumstances I predict will be judged accidental. And you come farting along on your white steed with the idea of exposing him as an enemy agent, using as evidence letters he wrote his wife and recruiter from Russia and maybe a defector's accusation." He looked a question at me.

"Something like that."

"Which would telegraph to the Russians the fact that we received invaluable information from Yurchenko and are acting on it. Let's assume the man was, at least temporarily, a genuine defector. Do you think Bill Clewes was the only name he gave us? What do you think the others will do when they realize we knew about Clewes? Why, head for the hills, Storm! Just like Howard, remember?"

He had a point. "Why not just use the letters and forget about Yurchenko?"

"Because they'll just figure we went looking for evidence after Clewes was fingered. The biggest kid in the fifth grade could figure that out."

I fumbled around for cigarettes and realized I didn't have any. Constantine drank some of his cooling coffee and made a face. We shared a moment of hostile silence.

"I guess there's a dimension to this that escaped me." It's not easy to admit you're wrong when you've been insulted.

He just gave me a look.

"Well." I rubbed my hands together briskly. "What do we do now?"

He didn't answer right away, still disgusted with me. Finally he said, "Your friend Captain Kling will be the hero of an investigation proving that Jim Quest, on his own initiative, arranged the murder of Gil Buckler. Because you made some kind of gypsy switch with the gun, he'll be the prime suspect in the Murdoch shooting, too. I'm going to suggest the idea that Quest was found shot on the highway, victim of an assault, and delivered to the emergency clinic by an unidentified man."

"If you could find that pistol I heaved into the surf and plant it by the road, he'd be a natural for suicide," I suggested.

Constantine glared. "Don't push me, Storm."

I nodded. "I understand. Limitations imposed by the law, and all that."

His rich, Mediterranean complexion darkened and I shifted gears quickly. "Will Kling go along with it?" I asked.

"If I'm any judge of character. He's smarter than you are. I've already explained the priorities in this case. He's gone along so far, and I don't see why he should balk at the idea of Quest being shot by an unknown assailant. Happens all the time out here. If he handles it right, the whole thing's going to make him shine."

I guessed Norman would see sense in that. Which left only one question. "How about me? No hard feelings?"

He leaned back again and thought about it. "If I were you, I'd say a bunch of Hail Marys and get my ass back to Mexico."

I stood up, slapping at the knees of my wrinkled slacks. "Well then . . ."

He just kept looking at me, so I walked over and opened the door. Before I went out I said, "Ask yourself this, Jim. Aren't you better off than you were before?"

It sounded vaguely like a quote, but I couldn't remember where I'd heard it.

# TWENTY

**B**efore going back to Mexico, I decided to buy the Chrysler an overhaul—valve and ring job, new hoses, brakes, tires, the works. I drove over to my old mechanic in Venice and told him to make her a going machine, but skip the cosmetics. In Puerto Vallarta, a junker changes ownership less often. Even so, by his estimate it was going to cost me over three thousand dollars, nearly all the cash I'd brought up with me. But hell, it really wasn't mine anyway.

Meanwhile I borrowed one of Pop's cars, an old Porsche Cabriolet in mint condition. He'd been pretty subdued since that night at the Mirador, not anxious to talk about it, but I finally pried the story out of him.

After he got to the hotel, he obtained the number of Willie's suite, which was not exactly a state secret. Then he decided to ride the freight elevator up to the sixteenth floor, evidently because that's how they'd do it in the movies. There he got stuck, probably because he was drunk and pushed the wrong button, which never happens in the movies. Maybe he took a little nap, he wasn't sure. Next thing he knew he was up on the sixteenth floor all right, but there were a couple of guys parked in front of Willie's suite so he went back downstairs (on the guest elevator) and decided to make his move when Clewes appeared below.

"Why didn't you just blast your way in?" I asked him sarcastically.

He gave me the hard eye, "I wasn't out to shoot innocent bystanders."

I couldn't picture Ralph as an innocent bystander, but in a sense I suppose he was. I wonder how he would have reacted if he'd found himself staring down the barrel of Pop's old cannon. "Well, it's over now, so you can hang up your gun, okay?"

"Somebody had to do something," is actually what he said.

The call from Monica didn't surprise me at all. She was at the beach house, and would I come by? There was nothing in her voice beyond cool invitation. Neither eagerness nor hostility.

I'd been watching TV and reading the papers with fascination, for the first time in years. The dramatic death of a U.S. senator on the night of his election dominated the news. The coroner confirmed that Willie had imbibed some champagne, not much, before his dive from the tower suite and officially listed his death as accidental. However, as Quest's role in the deaths of both Gil and Murdoch surfaced under investigation, there was speculation that Willie might have committed suicide over the felonious conduct of his top aide. Iris gave clear, damning testimony linking Quest to Gil's murder; Murdoch's fingerprints were found in his Oldsmobile and, of course, the murder weapon in that case was traced to him. The weight of fresh evidence popped Charlie Rydell out of jail like a cork, but his father didn't get much out of it because under California law, given the circumstances, the governor appoints a replacement to fill a Senate vacancy and Buck didn't seem to be on his list.

Monica went into seclusion. She added nothing to her original statement. Her husband, exuberant over his election to the United States Senate, had enjoyed an unaccustomed glass or two of champagne and stepped onto the balcony. From the living room, she had watched in horror as he lost his balance and toppled over the low rail. She dismissed disdainfully any conjecture that he had taken his own life; he had known nothing about Quest's murderous intrigues. According to what I read and saw, the public was buying it. Skeptics were lying low, content to use innuendo.

Nowhere did my name appear as the last visitor to 1601 before Willie became airborne. I'd half expected Ralph or Kennedy to supply that information and maybe more, but they simply confirmed that the assemblyman and his wife had been alone in

253

the suite at the time of the tragedy. I wondered if their testimony had been edited courtesy of pressure brought by Constantine or the Clewes camp, but it didn't matter. I was in the clear.

The stitches were out of my head and the bandage was off my hand. I felt good, better than I had in a long time, and I was ready to go home.

There was just this one last thing.

The weather had turned cool, but I put on a turtleneck and a tweed jacket and left the top down on the nimble little Porsche. As I turned off the Coast Highway on Zumirez, tendrils of fog reached out to welcome me, a chill, ghostly escort to the beach house on the bluff.

Monica met me at the door, dressed in a soft velour jumpsuit. I thought she was wearing no makeup at all until I noticed the subtle work she'd done around her eyes. She led me to the living room, where logs crackled in the fireplace.

"We're alone," she said, reading my mind. "I make a pretty good fire." Then she went to stand with her back to the flames as if she were cold.

I didn't give her any help, just sat on the comfortably cracked leather sofa and lit a cigarette.

"I suppose you're going back to Mexico." It was an assumption, not a question.

"Yes. In a couple of days."

"Well." She left the fire to stand in front of me. "Can I get you anything? Tea? Something stronger?"

"Something stronger. It's whiskey weather."

She went out and came back with a glass of Scotch from the same bottle I'd raided the night of the shoot-out. She handed it to me and said, "Who would have imagined this would happen when we were kids? Nothing ever turns out as planned."

"On the contrary. I planned it carefully. The last part, anyway."

Something flickered behind her eyes, but she managed to suppress it. "What you said about Bill. About a wife in Mexico and those letters. Was it true?"

I nodded, drinking some Scotch and setting down the glass. "And the tapes. They made tapes of Gil and me?"

"Yes."

"You took the tape back."

"Willie tried to grab it."

She went over and stood by the fire again. "The hardest part is about my father. You couldn't have made that up."

"I didn't."

But that wasn't what was on her mind. "Did you listen to the tapes?"

"Oh yes." Indeed I had. Again the little twinge of envy. The visceral throb of excitement looking at this woman and remembering what I'd heard.

She came over and sat on the sofa next to me. "I loved Gil."

"Not just scratching an itch?"

"I had to tell you something, didn't I?"

"Well, I guess Willie just didn't understand."

"Our marriage was more like a partnership. I was pursuing an ideal I believed he shared. If what you say is true, I was blinded by it. Can you understand how that could happen?"

"Sure."

She moved closer to me, seeming just to shift position. "You're so much like him, you know."

"Willie?" I exclaimed in mock horror.

She frowned. "Of course not. Gil." She didn't really have a sense of humor, I remembered. "When we were kids, I think I loved you both. He was so much bolder, though . . ."

I lifted an eyebrow at her, much as Gil would have done. "Are you contemplating a transfer of your affections to me?" Jesus, I even sounded like him.

If she detected any irony she decided to ignore it. She laughed instead, twisting gracefully on the sofa to end up with her head in my lap, looking up at me. "I'm not going to live in the past. I'm not like that."

"I'm forgiven for derailing your train?"

Again the flicker, quickly hidden. "That's over."

255

"What do you want, Monkey?"

She reached up to the trace the line of my jaw. "Someone."

"That's pretty inclusive."

"Remember when we were kids? You guys, well, Gil mostly, were always trying to touch my breasts. He used to claim if he could feel my heartbeat, he could prove I was just as worked up as he was."

"And you'd slap his hand away."

She took my hand in both of hers and placed it on her left breast. Her flesh was firmly molded below the soft material, the nipple already taut under my fingers. "What do you think?" And she laughed again because from where she lay she could feel the answer.

"What do you really want, Monkey?" I asked again.

"The same thing you do." She squirmed her head around in my lap, chuckling at the reaction I couldn't control.

"Afterward, I mean. Is there anything else you're going to want before I go back to Mexico?"

Now her hand was in my lap too, and the time I had to exert any control over the situation was growing short. I took her by the shoulders and set her aside, standing up, my condition no less evident that way. "Answer me, Monkey. We're not teenagers anymore. There's all afternoon."

She looked up at me. "You're right. We're not children anymore. But you've always wanted me, I know that. Now we can be together whenever we please. I wanted to make it clear, whether you leave or not."

"That's not an answer."

"Why haven't you offered to give me those damn tapes? It's only decent. I don't want you listening to them anymore."

I kept a straight face. "Well then, why don't we listen to them together?"

I think she really misunderstood for a moment. She gave the suggestion of a smile, accepting my kinky nature. "If that's what you want."

"Not that part," I told her, taking one of the cassettes out

256

of my pocket. "Come on." I walked away from her, out of the living room and into the study where the tape deck stood on the library shelf.

I waited until she was in the room, standing there, watching me with dawning suspicion. Then I shoved the cartridge in the machine. "I'm picking it up after the slap and tickle's over. Right around the postcoital cigarette. Or joint."

"You've got to get out of this, Monkey-face," Gil said, and I turned up the volume. "You've got to get away from him." You could tell by his tone he was saying it for the first time, as if he'd just made up his mind.

"What?" Surprise. "Don't be silly, Gil. You know that's not what we're about. We're about what you like to call R and R. Please don't go and spoil it. You'd be hard to replace."

"I don't think you heard me right."

"I heard you suggest I leave Bill. Let me guess what happens next. Our relationship ripens, as they say in that kind of novel. Your wife is about to divorce you anyway, so why not a whole new kind of life?"

"You heard me but you didn't understand me. You can set up housekeeping with an ape in a tree, but get rid of Willie."

Silence. We could hear some more smoke being ingested. "Are you going to give me a reason outside of the fact you don't like him and never have?"

Now it was Gil's turn to hesitate. Maybe he had an idea what a goddamn fool he was being, but finally he said, "Willie's got problems."

Monica's voice changed; the levity was gone. Funny how you can read more into a voice when you can't see the speaker. The blind learn to do it instinctively. "Everyone has problems."

"Not like his."

"Enlighten me."

"They think he's a mole, baby."

"They?" Very soft and neutral.

"Government types."

"And what about me? Do they think I'm one, too?"

"No, you're just a garden-variety radical with too much money."

"Is that what you think?"

"You don't think I'd be telling you all this if I thought you were a spy?" Some agent, old Gil. Thinking with his dick.

"For God's sake, Gil, those bastards think everyone who opposed their Fascist war is a spy!"

"They've got a reason in Willie's case."

"What reason?"

"I don't know." Maybe he did; maybe he didn't. It depended on what Constantine told him.

"And how would you know all this?"

"Let's drop it. I told you because . . . Well, we go back a long way, Monkey-face. I don't want you to take a fall with him."

For a while we couldn't hear anything. Then there was a shifting, perhaps snuggling, it was hard to tell. "They're wrong, but I love you for telling me," she said softly. "You care, way down under that cynical shell."

Talk about the cat and the canary. Well, she could get under the toughest hide if she could con Gil.

"I don't think they're wrong," said Gil, opening it back up as he was intended to do.

"Gil." She was exasperated now. "You won't tell me how you come by all this nonsense, so why should I believe it?"

And then he jumped in with both feet. "Because I'm part of it," he said, locking in his fatal error. The first time I heard that, I cringed for him.

"Oh, come on! I suppose you're some kind of plant?"

"They approached me later. What difference does it make? They might just have something, baby."

"What in God's name makes you believe that?"

"They told me to find out if he has any contacts in Mexico. If so, with whom. And what do you know? He calls Mexico from phone booths when I'm driving him around. Talking Spanish. At least he did once, because I heard him as I went by the booth. And I saw him look up a number in a little book he carries. Later on he took off his coat because it was hot, and the book was inside. He wanted to stop by the office, and while he was up there I took down numbers. One of them, with a five in front of it, is a Mexico City number, according to the international operator. That was the day before yesterday.''

"What a lot of crap, Gil." Scornfully now. "And I suppose you told them about it?''

"No. We meet on Fridays, when I'm not busy.''

She took about a five-count. "Really, I should be furious. You spying on us. But it's so damn silly." Here was the underreaction that should have warned him.

I killed the tape because nothing more they said was going to be relevant, just repetitious. "You don't seem surprised. Maybe you've heard it before?''

"You bastard!" She'd been listening to the tape in silence but now she moved past me and popped the cassette out of the machine, clawing at it until the ribbon was a tangle hanging down to the floor.

I said, "Gil died on a Thursday night. I'll bet it was the same week this stuff was recorded, before he could meet his contact. That number down in Mexico must have been important. What was it, the Russian embassy? Some Soviet agent like his other wife, who was running him?'' This would have hurt Willie even without Quest's testimony. At first, I'd wondered why Quest hadn't played this particular tape for me, but then I remembered it wouldn't matter. I wasn't supposed to survive our meeting.

"How would I know? Are you crazy?''

"Well, Willie knew, and he could have blown it under pressure. Look, nobody believes he just went out and fell off a balcony. Nobody. After all the dirt that's come out about Quest, everyone out there thinks he jumped because of the scandal shaping up. Being an individual of such high principle. But you and I know better. I know he didn't jump because I know Willie. You know because you pushed him.''

"Do you think there's anything on this silly tape or any-where else to prove that?" She was calm now, under control. She threw the tape aside in disgust.

"Of course not. As I told Willie the other day, it's just a matter of knowing the people involved. He'd never commit suicide; he'd run first. They'd treat him right in Moscow. In fact, I took a big chance of losing him when I came up and made that speech, but I had a reason." I looked around for my drink, but I'd left it in the other room. "You know, Monkey, I'd be the first to applaud heaving Willie over the side if you'd done it for the right reason. Because of what he did to your mother and father, for example. But I don't believe that entered your mind. You'd have learned to rationalize years ago."

"How the hell would you know?" The vertical lines deep-ened around her mouth, stealing her beauty.

"I'm guessing Willie passed on the benefits of his training to you, making you capable of just about anything. When I left your suite at the Mirador, for instance, he was pretty rocky, heading for some fresh air on the terrace. You probably followed him out and asked him what the hell he was going to do. Maybe he didn't have an answer and you could see yourself going down the tubes with him. Not to mention the bigger plan. It wouldn't be hard for a strong, resourceful woman like yourself to reach down, pick up his ankles, and tip him over the rail. *Ciao*, partner. I wonder what he thought on the way down. Did he at least keep his feet together?"

I didn't get a rise out of her. She slipped back behind her second line of defense, ridicule. "What a fantasy world you live in!"

I took the two remaining tapes out of my pocket and tossed them on the oak desk I'd hidden behind that night. The bullet holes were still there to remind me. "Copies. Play them when you get lonely."

"So you'll keep the originals. What can you possibly do with them now?"

"Oh, I don't know. Maybe sell them to one of those bandit

radio outfits, like the ones operating off the coast of England. They'll authenticate them from a voice print. Your fans should get a hell of a kick out of them. All that moaning and groaning . . ."

Her face was slipping into ugliness now, her breasts heaving under the sleek velour. "I can pay you more than they would."

I laughed at her. "Or maybe I'll send them to the feds along with Willie's letters from Russia." I wasn't going to tell her they already had them because, just maybe, word could get to the Russian consulate before the end of the day, and that would ruin Constantine's play. I'd made a deal, after all, and I couldn't really do anything. But Monica would never know it.

"Why? Why would you do something like that now?" Genuine curiosity peered around the edge of despair. "He's dead, isn't that what you wanted?"

"Sure it is, but what about you? Suppose you all listened to the tapes together and then sat around and decided how to handle the problem of Gil? I just heard you at work, remember? You squeezed him like a tube."

"I didn't know!" Her control slipped another notch. "I didn't know anything about the damn tapes or what happened to Gil!"

"Maybe not, Monkey. As you say, I can't prove you did." I walked out of the study, heading for the front door.

She followed me, clutching the back of my jacket. "You can't just leave it like this! What are you going to do?"

I had to pry her fingers loose. "Think about it while I'm down there in the sun." I stepped out of her house and closed the door.

Half a mile from the coast, the fog released me to a cloudy sky. There was a bite in the air, as if California had suddenly remembered it was almost Thanksgiving. I'd be back in the tropics by then, and I wondered if I could talk Chispa into roasting a turkey. She'd probably stuff it with *frijoles*.

I couldn't wait.

# ABOUT THE AUTHOR

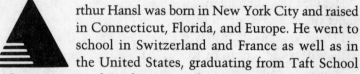rthur Hansl was born in New York City and raised in Connecticut, Florida, and Europe. He went to school in Switzerland and France as well as in the United States, graduating from Taft School in Connecticut and Washington and Lee University in Virginia. After three years in the U.S. Marine Corps, he went to Mexico for two weeks and stayed for four years, becoming, he says, an accomplished beach bum. He moved from there to California and then to Europe, arriving in time to enjoy the last years of the *dolce vita* in Rome, where he became an actor starring in some forgettable films and doing supporting parts in somewhat better ones. He returned to Mexico in the late sixties for another dozen pictures over half a dozen years. *A Call from L.A.* is his third novel. The author now lives in Pacific Palisades, California, with his French wife, Nicole, and two dogs and a cat, in a house overlooking the sea.